DEATH PANELS

DEATH PANELS

A NOVEL OF LIFE, LIBERTY, AND FAITH

MICHELLE BUCKMAN

Saint Benedict Press
Charlotte, North Carolina

ISBN: 978-1-935302-47-6

Cover art and design by Tony Pro

Printed and bound in the United States of America

SAINT
BENEDICT
PRESS

Saint Benedict Press
Charlotte, North Carolina
2010

CONTENTS

ACKNOWLEDGMENTS

First and foremost, I must extend my gratitude to my family for enduring this long creative journey. Their support has been vital in walking this road.

Huge thanks to Don Griffin, Sylvia Roller, and Jill McCall for early reads, and to Nahomy Crespo, Regina Smeltzer, and Jane Blum for their expertise. Special thanks to my editor, Todd Aglialoro, for his dedication and commitment to this story, and to Conor Gallagher for taking my words to heart.

All glory be to the Father, and to the Son, and to the Holy Spirit.

DAY ONE

JULY 2, 2042

David Rudder stood over the hospital bed, his weary eyes drawn for a moment to the busy streets outside the Northern Virginia Public Medical Services Center before settling back on the patient. He heaved her ample body to one side to release the IV tube that had worked its way under her shoulder, then pulled the covers into place.

The woman, Gretta, had been admitted that morning, but nothing had been done for her yet. He rubbed the brown bristles on his face and watched her suck in shallow, laborious breaths as he considered what he could realistically do about her case. If he protested, they might check his credentials and discover his false identity, maybe even figure out that he was from the Dome. He couldn't risk that.

She had everything going against her. Repeat visits. Poor diet. Failure to comply with mandated weight reduction since her previous visit. No *productivity*. She was over 65 and her heart was failing. The bottom line was a Healthcare Score of a measly twenty-five out of a thousand.

1

"Are you coming?" came a deep voice in the hall; Charlie, the doctor taking over the next shift. There was no avoiding it. He patted Gretta's plump arm, then joined Charlie in the Life Office, where he found a blank space on the wall to support his tired body. He glanced at the clock. If he could keep his cool through this meeting, he'd make it through another day undetected. With any luck, the Healthcare Overseer wouldn't even show.

Unfortunately, the man strode into the room right on time like a soldier and went directly to his data screen. With a touch, Gretta's record scrolled up. "Where's Doctor Brown?" he asked.

"Right here," she answered as she slipped in the doorway, sank into a spare chair, and smiled across the room at David with a look that said a lot more than merely *hello*. Elizabeth used to tell him he looked like a picture of a guy from the 1970s, with his jawline scruff and tousled hair that hung almost to his collar—a raw, masculine look that modern women found appealing, almost exotic. But it panged David to see the look he once loved to get from Elizabeth spring into the eyes of these women he didn't even know.

The moment passed. Doctor Brown sighed and turned to the official with a scowl that summed up her exasperation over having to attend Health Continuity Council meetings. The official didn't notice. "Any challenges to the data I'm seeing?" he asked.

Charlie played with his cuticles.

Doctor Brown swept a lock of hair out of her eyes and pushed up her sleeves. "We could give her the IV and renew her prescriptions."

"With that score? She's been back three times this month. And she repeatedly makes the wrong dietary choices."

"You think?" Doctor Brown said. "What's the actual cost of that new diuretic, anyway?"

The Overseer cast a demeaning glare at the junior med. "Does she have family?"

None of them responded.

"I take that as a no," the Overseer said. He looked pointedly at each of them. "So, no objections?"

A dozen replies rose in David's head. *She's breathing, for one.* But insubordination would only draw attention, and it wouldn't save this woman. He steeled himself against everything his conscience was urging him to do, mumbled, "No," and turned away.

The Overseer nodded and clicked a button. "Okay, she's a write-off." He turned a haughty gaze on Dr. Brown. "That's how we've earned the state HCC award three years running. Strictly by the book, right, doctor?"

"Sure," she replied as she strutted toward the door, waving David ahead of her and then gliding up beside him so that she brushed against him in the hallway as she winked. "You win some, you lose some."

David wondered when it was possible to win.

He clocked out at the main station and headed toward the employee exit. *Another day with nothing gained.*

But he also hadn't been arrested, and there was much to be said for that.

It was only midafternoon. He could investigate records, though that had become tedious. Or he could wander the streets, browse through stores, or sit in restaurants to mingle with people, hoping to overhear a conversation that would provide a lead, but he felt too drained to make small talk with strangers.

He stopped short as an overwhelming sudden urge crept over him. He changed direction to take the side exit and slip into the next building over.

He worked his way back past the nurses' station and down a long hall that carried him through the main lobby area where he noticed an old woman, another skeleton in baggy flesh dressed in a nondescript pale blue dress stained with dribble. There was nothing to set the woman apart from the fifty other patients seated in the waiting area except that she was probably the oldest person he'd seen. Her fingers, twisted with arthritis, lay still in her lap until his shadow fell over her. She jerked involuntarily and pain leapt to her face in narrowed eyes and furrowed brow. As the pain eased off, her eyes opened: empty gray eyes revealing a stagnant mind. He imagined sights and sounds imprisoned inside: dreams, achievements, disappointment, loss, happiness, and anger. A whole life full of images and memories. Did she still have memories like he had, of playing with a childhood best friend? Axyl Houston, now a senator, a political celebrity, had been his constant companion in his youth, and the possibility of seeing him again was one of the things that had intrigued him about this mission. But he couldn't just walk into Axyl's office. He hadn't seen him since the Unified Order of the World—the UO—was established, not since Axyl's mother and sister were killed by an anti-Christian mob and he was remanded to a UO Institute for reprogramming. David didn't know what that might have done to his friend's mind. It could be that he had no recollection of their friendship, or anything about childhood at all.

David refocused on the old lady. He liked to imagine she'd had a good life, perhaps been married, with memories of her husband clear in her mind. That's what he wanted for himself. He feared that his memories of Elizabeth were becoming only what pictures kept alive; the real smiles and laughter and tears he'd shared with her were starting to fade. He tried hard to recall things they had both loved, like the night sky, which had always carried them back to their teen years and their first fumbling kisses.

The old lady's face didn't show any signs of happiness, though. Maybe all her good memories had faded away, too.

He wasn't her doctor, but he still had a tongue in his head that could serve her. He thought to tell her, "God loves you," but he couldn't use Exclusionary Speech here. Hospital surveillance was tight. Instead he laid one hand gently upon her arm and leaned close. He pressed a sample pain killer into her palm, whispered, "Go home," and walked on without looking back.

He emerged into the quad and paused as the sunlight struck him full force, so bright that the distinction of details was lost, like the fuzzy screen of an old television set. After a moment, his eyes adjusted, and he continued down the sidewalk. He didn't know the exact location of the maternity ward but trusted bits gleaned from overheard conversations as he moved across the quad toward the east entrance. It would be a relief to examine things in another ward, to see life at its beginning rather than making excuses and watching people die. He wanted to wipe away the memory of patients thrashing or even just whimpering at the end and to erase the faces of the ones turned away.

Through a door, down a hall and up an elevator. A sensor picked up his presence and a soft female voice whispered into the air from hidden speakers, first in English, then in Spanish:

The Good Life Maternity Center is here to serve your community.
For the Good of the Nation, for the Good of the World.

He'd heard the voice echoing in the halls of the medical center so often that it barely even registered.

The maternity center didn't have a formal lobby, but double glass doors led to a counter where three nurses sat snickering over a date gone awry. One looked his way, but he turned, hurried down the hallway that veered to the right, and ducked into the next doorway.

Inside the dingy room lay a woman on a birthing bed. Dark hair, coffee-colored skin. *Spanish? Indian, maybe.*

He glanced at the light switch, aching to turn it on. The constant dimness depressed him, but lights were not permitted in rooms with windows until after nightfall, and then only for emergencies.

At least the medical panel lit up. Her record said her name was Sola.

He checked the readings then sat on a stool and stared at her swollen lump of belly.

Sola groaned out two words. "*Me duele.*"

He nodded. "I know it hurts."

He couldn't do anything for her. Delivery drugs were kept under lock and key. Even emergencies required special coding for release.

As Sola groaned and arched her back against another contraction, he chided himself. Only a fool would believe he was there to wash from his mind the deaths in the other building. He could have done that by walking through the park where children played, except youngsters brought him no solace. Today his daughter would have been two.

Heavy footsteps came down the hall and stopped outside the door. He picked up the computerized medical chart and held his breath. It beeped and made him jump.

He hadn't thought this venture through. Of course someone would come to attend the girl. A med would have to deliver the baby. He should have gone to the nursery and pretended to be the father of one of the infants.

Too late. Now he was trapped.

The door opened with a thud, admitting a huge doctor whose narrow eyes were lost above cheeks that pudged and sagged in proportion to his belly as he looked from David to the patient.

David flinched. The small, blue birthing room closed in around him like a cage. He forced the nervous tension away. This guy wasn't likely to suspect anything; David had been passing as an Outer State med all week. He wasn't an obstetrician, and he had delivered very few babies, but his general medical skills exceeded anything he'd seen in the other ward. Chances were this guy wasn't an obstetrician either. He sucked in a calming breath. His false ID hung nonchalantly from his pocket. He could pull this off. *Lord*, David silently prayed, *be with me*.

Aloud, his voice was deep and even. "Her contractions are three minutes apart. She's hurting pretty badly." He pointed to the reading on the machine behind him.

As if to affirm his statement, Sola screamed then droned on in agonized whimpers as she pounded the bed with her fists and tossed around frantically.

The doctor, holding the door open, leaned his head back into the hall. "Hey Mersrisha, five milligrams of Q2. Pronto."

"I've clocked out."

He cursed under his breath. "Well, send someone down here with it."

"Under what code?"

He cussed. "Get it! I'll take care of it on this end."

He stared at David's back until a nurse scurried in around him, checked vitals, administered the pain-killer, and left again. The drug dropped the girl into oblivion almost instantly, and the cramped room became a monotonous blend of hospital sounds: the rhythmic beeping of the monitor and the occasional clicking of the intravenous drip machine mingled with her quiet whimpers.

Only then did the med completely enter and let the door close. With authority, he took the chart from David, punched a few keys and passed his palm over the chart scanner, then watched as it beeped recognition and displayed *1:05 p.m. July 2, 2042, Markus Holmes.* His eyes remained locked on it in a moment of indecision, and then he turned, his gaze moving over David's lanky frame, taking in every detail. "Why didn't Lui administer anything?"

David played it cool and reached over to a side table to pick up a hospital pamphlet with big black letters stating, *Know Your Rights! The Unified Order grants all women the right to two live children.* In smaller print below that, *Government surrogates may conceive and bear beyond that number under proper supervision with Unified Order authorization of approved birth-count parents.* Surrogates were an issue he knew nothing about; he didn't deal with them at home. He shifted uncomfortably, trying to contrive words that might make sense. "Surrogates weren't provided for or had to sign acceptance for billing or something." That's what was listed on the chart: Surrogate—no billing provided. He tensed on the edge of his seat ready for flight.

The med's steely expression didn't soften. "Yeah. Right. Always by the book." He turned to the bed. Without comment, he pushed the woman onto her back, pulled her knees up, and proceeded to check her cervical dilation. "Wow. Didn't you check her? We shouldn't have given her anything so late. Screwed up my delivery." He glared at David, then buzzed the nurses' station and spoke into the air. "I need a setup, stat."

"Shift ended ten minutes ago, you know," the med said.

David's angled features became tauter as he looked at the girl and swept the hair back from her homely face. Should he go? Escape while he could? Or would that raise more suspicion?

He shrugged.

Markus arched one brow. "It's your life. Don't expect me to stay, though. When the clock hits eight, I'm outta here."

David couldn't sit still under such scrutiny. He moved to the girl's bedside, stared at her a moment, then glanced around the room. Everything was scrubbed clean yet had a worn, secondhand look about it. An intolerable disinfectant odor was making him light-headed and dulling his concentration.

After a moment of silence, the med held his hand out. "Name's Markus Holmes. Med III." David shook it. "Rex Montane." He had practiced saying the alias until it rolled off his tongue with ease.

As their eyes met, Markus was momentarily transfixed. *Jesus eyes,* Markus found himself thinking: like in the picture of the Messiah that had hung in his parents' den a lifetime ago. Those same deep brown eyes, full of compassion, that devoured all there was in a person yet revealed nothing. He wondered where that picture went. Confiscated and burned, probably.

The monitor whirred. Both men turned back to the patient as another contraction registered. She only moaned.

"So you're new here?" Markus asked.

David breathed slowly, desperately trying to exude a calm exterior as he gave his canned response. "Been at a country infirmary for two years. Not much action."

Markus harrumphed, shifted his bulky frame, and went back to the electronic chart. The guy was no Messiah. *Joanne's messing with my mind. Last night she gets me to say one desperate prayer to God, for the first time in twenty years, and I expect Christ to land right here in a hospital room with me.* He watched puzzled as David examined a tray of instruments. First-day jitters? Not that Markus cared; he only pulled his hours and left. Five more years and they would force him to retire. Nothing but a bunch of political crap; Kim Lui making all the money and him being passed over again, no doubt because she was in bed with the Administrator. He would be glad when his five years were up. The whole hospital could fall apart for all he cared.

He pushed his straight black hair off his forehead—a habit he repeated constantly without realizing it—and continued to watch the stranger. Something about him piqued his interest. For one thing, nobody stayed past shift end, ever. "You may as well go back to the country. You won't last long here. You'll see. Too much work for too little pay. Research is the only place to make money anymore." He sighed. Times sure had changed. He pulled out a handkerchief and wiped his brow. "I wish they would run the air conditioning."

David nodded. Some of the wards were stifling hot. There was no reason for him to get upset about it, though, because this med was right: he would be gone in another day or two. He couldn't risk staying much longer. Someone or something was bound to catch him if he didn't move on. If the ubiquitous scanners and cameras identified him as a Dominian—a resident of the Cloistered Dominion, the federal reservation for Christians—he'd be hauled in and probably imprisoned, achieving nothing for the cause.

As the med stared at him, he realized how careless he'd been in crossing into another ward. He needed to extricate himself without complicating things further.

As he took a step toward the exit, the door swung open again, this time for a nurse who entered humming something like the tune of a child's ABCs. She checked pulse and temperature readings. "Shakita's on her way," she said as she left, and resumed her tune, words floating in the air as the door slowly pulled itself closed behind her. "*And praise your liberty every day; UO deliverance is here to stay. The Unified Order is your friend; we take care of you to the end . . .*"

The last of the tune was almost inaudible, but Markus bobbed his head back and forth to the beat with a frown that creased his whole face. "Right to the end all right. Bah."

The contempt in the man's voice set David's heart pounding. The med had to know that the walls had eyes and ears, yet he didn't seem to care. Could God have blessed David with just the sort of man he needed to meet?

David had illegally ventured out of the Cloistered Dominion—the "Dome"—to infiltrate medical centers in search of medical supplies and life-saving advancements, but even more importantly, to investigate rumors of a Christian underground gathering secretly to pray and worship and read the Bible, of priests preaching and baptizing and saying Mass in defiance of the state-run church. Some said there were hundreds of such groups across the country, all disconnected yet aware of one another. Silenced by fear. Waiting, maybe, for a leader. He was supposed to find out if it was true.

Could this man, with his attitude, possibly know something? David looked from the woman to the door to the med. If this guy was the link they needed . . . *Be not afraid,* he whispered.

The patient groaned and arched.

"Here it comes," Markus said. He buzzed again for a nurse and cursed into the intercom.

The room suddenly came alive with activity. Three nurses jostled around to get trays in place. The bed was shifted to delivery position. Masks were pulled up and birthing lights were focused. The sudden brightness reflected off the shiny chrome tables and faded into the blue hue of the walls.

"Okay, lady—push," Markus said.

David moved to the background and watched the woman's efforts.

He wanted to love once more.

In his mind, the baby was his daughter Bethany, delivered all wet and wailing, placed in his arms. He ached for that quiet time in the dimness of the room after her birth when he had held her and stared transfixed by her beauty. He wanted to see a baby and feel joy again. To look at an infant, think of Bethany, and not coil inside with guilt and anger.

The girl cried as a fuzzy round head crowned. Markus continued to bully the girl. "Again. Push. Now! Push."

The head finally emerged. With the next contraction and one deft motion, the infant slid in to Markus's huge hands. Markus's smile puffed his full cheeks up into his brown eyes. "Baby boy born at . . . 13:23."

A nurse filled in the record, then reached for the baby. He didn't cry, but mewed like a kitten as if he knew he'd better state his case immediately. "Hi, sweetie," she trilled. "Aren't you beautiful? Wait till your mama sees you."

David swallowed the glob of tears in his throat and turned away.

Markus pressed on the surrogate's stomach, delivering the placenta. "Is the mother in the waiting room?"

"No." The nurse's shrill baby-talk voice dropped to normal. "But she's been called."

A stern-faced male nurse entered with an empty blood sample vial and a syringe. After making the baby squall with a poke from the sharp needle, he left without a word to anyone.

The baby's whimpers languished, and silence fell over the staff, all absorbed in their duties. David watched, made some notes, pretended to be busy.

Markus made fast work of the stitches, glancing intermittently at the stranger. He didn't seem to actually be taking part in any of it. Something was up.

With a nod from Markus, two techs transferred the drugged woman to a gurney.

"What'd she get?" asked the taller of the two.

"It's on the chart. Q2. She was endangering the kid."

"The Administrator won't like this, wasting funds on a surrogate."

"I'll take care of the Alligator. Get this girl out to recovery."

The nurse ran a tub of warm water, her eyes on David as she smiled and shook her kinky curls at him. David shooed her away and gently cleansed the tiny infant himself. He marveled at the newborn nickel-sized ears and pursed lips. He touched the little fist, uncurled the fingers, and stroked the tiny palm. Bethany had been premature; so much smaller than this fellow and yet perfect. He had felt so immediately protective of her. He had loved Bethany more in that first instant than he had ever loved before. Oh, how he wanted to be a father!

Markus looked over his shoulder and groaned. "Isn't that a shame. It's a Down's kid."

Tears welled in David's eyes and spilled over. He brushed them away. "I've never seen a case except in text books."

Markus looked at him suspiciously.

David shrugged. "With gene corrections and terminations . . ."

Markus pointed. "Look here, the single heavy wrinkle across his palm and the space between the first and second toe. See? And the slanting of the palpebral fissures making the eyes look Oriental. And the ears are set low and fold over just slightly. Really a textbook case. Of course, we'll check the blood work to be sure . . ."

The intercom phone buzzed. "Dr. Holmes?"

"Yeah."

"Surrogate 2090, Infant 2090-5?"

"Yeah."

"The test shows Down's."

Markus frowned and sighed. "Yeah. I figured. Send the data up."

"On its way."

The machine buzzed out a page of medical jargon.

Then Kim Lui, Head Med, slipped into the room. To David she looked like a kindergarten teacher, maybe, with her short stature and soft, brown features. But Markus grew tense, even as she smiled a dimpled smile at him. "Did you get my memo about that sonogram machine?"

David could see him physically pulling his animosity into check as he turned to face her. "Yes. I did."

She leaned around him and glanced at the newborn. "What a waste. Luckily, I just saw the Overseer in his office. Got the documentation?"

Markus handed her the report. She examined it and made a call. "Code four, irreversible genetic mutation on infant 2090-5. Need the go-ahead." After a moment she hung up. "Authorization 9654376. Go ahead and euthanize it."

David clasped the baby tighter, exerting every ounce of will to stand still, to not react.

Kim looked David over with a raised eyebrow, then glanced at Markus's expressionless face, and turned abruptly, her generous hips swaying slightly as she walked back out.

Markus clenched his fists. "Death Panels." He growled it as if it were a curse but shook off the anger almost as fast. He turned to the newborn, his fingers almost touching the dark fluff of hair, but he resisted and busied himself with removing his protective wear. "As long as you're sticking around, you can dispose of it. I had to do two last week." He smiled weakly. "So much for them not reaching this far."

"Two?"

"Cerebral Palsy." He looked at his watch to emphasize his next words. "Fetal distress during shift change. Oxygen loss."

David ignored the implication. He wasn't worried about shift change being long over. "And the other one?"

Markus sighed, the weight of the admission hanging on his shoulders. "They expected a boy and got a girl. Someone screwed up the prenatal."

"They killed their daughter because they wanted a son?"

"Well, they don't look at it that way."

David stared at him.

He shrugged. "They already had a girl."

Distress bled through the poker face David tried hard to maintain.

Markus couldn't figure this guy out. He looked ordinary enough, except for those eyes, but he acted like he was from Mars. "They only get two kids. They wanted a boy."

Markus couldn't understand David's naiveté, but he could understand his disgust. Unfortunately, the practice was so commonplace that no one seemed to care anymore. Or if they did, they were forced to keep silent. Speaking against the right to choose euthanasia was an Intolerance Crime. "I'd like to choke those idiots in the Nab Lab. We shouldn't have to deal with this so late in the game, but so much funding for prenatal care has been cut. Well, you know. Let's get on with it. I assume you'd rather let the machine do it."

David looked at the little boy with his wide gray eyes staring trustingly up at him. Suddenly the fists of miniature fingers struck out as he wailed.

He wanted to run out the door with this little baby boy, but instead he stood shaking with uncertainty. As he closed his eyes to gather his wits, the image of Elizabeth, her calming smile, flooded through him. She had always had such faith in him. The memory of her filled him with courage he could never possess on his own. She would tell him to look for another way. *Another way? This med already suspects something.*

The tiny hand clasped one of David's fingers. He had to stall. "I've never, uh, done this before."

"Come on, I'll show you where to go."

David swaddled the baby clumsily but tenderly and held him close, quieting him with a whispered prayer.

This mission was going to test the very core of his faith.

* * *

Anne Shelton, tall, blond, and fine-boned, hurried down Restaurant Boulevard wishing she could skip her luncheon and head straight to the hospital. It was an odd thought for her, considering how much she loved attention. Nothing empowered her and filled her with a sense of well-being like the rush she got from a crowd of photographers snapping her picture or a throng of onlookers staring enviously as she exited a limo at some gala event with Axyl.

Today was different. For starters, the heat was unbearable, and she imagined the back of her suit marred by sweat. She couldn't stand to be seen in less than flawless attire. But it was more than that. Her mind was on the impending birth of her son. How could anything be more important than that?

Nevertheless, Axyl had insisted she attend this meeting, and there was no ignoring her darling Axyl's orders. Not if she expected to remain *his* darling.

She pushed her way between two white-shirted business executives standing midsidewalk in deep conversation, skirted around the homeless people, waved off the ragged, kerchiefed lady selling flowers from a pushcart, and ignored the kids begging for food on the corner as she dashed across the road while the light turned from caution to red. A dozen cars raced toward her.

She didn't notice. She couldn't focus on anything but Axyl and the baby. She knew if she pushed Axyl, she could have just about anything she wanted, but he hadn't been too thrilled about the whole baby idea, and now that the baby was due, he'd become almost hostile over everything to do with it. Her best course of action was to keep him happy by doing what he asked and hope he'd fall in love with the baby when she got it home.

She was out of breath by the time she reached her destination: Clover Restaurant. Twenty ladies waited to hear her discourse on Population Put to Rest, with a side line of Water for the World, which they would carry back to their school districts to implement. She'd given the speech so often lately, she could recite it from memory. It was right in keeping with her other speech on Saving the World through Sterilization. They both had the same theme and the same conclusion: *Our goal of zero ungoverned pregnancies is within reach! Zero growth!* She could see herself saying the final salute, *For the Good of the Nation, for the Good of the World!* It made her blood rush with patriotism.

Two hours later, she shook the hand of the last attendee and was headed toward the exit when a very pregnant woman stepped into her path. "Anne!"

She had to do a double-take. "Debra Sykes?" She and Debra had been friends in high school. She leaned forward and gave her a social hug. "Forgive me; I must look a mess from the heat outside."

"You look wonderful," Debra said.

Anne touched her hair in agreement. "What are you doing here?"

"I saw the meeting listed under Town Happenings and decided it was a good excuse to have lunch on this side of the city. Have time for a bite?"

Anne nodded and the two of them settled into seats.

"You're having a baby," Anne said.

"Any minute now."

"Really? Me too."

Debra laughed. "Well, you're doing a much better job of hiding it than me."

"A surrogate, of course."

The baby chat continued until the food arrived. Debra pulled her chair as close to the restaurant table as she could manage and plunged her fork into a bite of steak. Anne nibbled at a salad. Debra shook her head. "How can that little salad possibly fill you up? I'm famished." Eating meat was uncivilized and priced high enough to restrain the most carnivorous, but she was venting anger at Harve, her co-hab. He was really getting on her nerves. So she was going to savor every bite of this meal and dare him to complain about how much she'd spent. In her heart, she knew their Civil Partnership was coming to an end; thankfully, the process was easy and would make closure expedient.

Anne paused over her salad to watch in disgust as Debra chewed a mouthful of beef. "So . . . anyway . . . Frank may be born today. Sola—that's my surrogate—was admitted a couple hours ago."

"I've dilated three centimeters, so I'm hopeful," Debra said with her mouth full. "I hope I go into labor tonight. I'm tired of lugging this belly around." She chewed, swallowed, and pierced another hunk.

Anne grimaced. "You know that was a harmless cow standing in a field last week?"

Debra smirked at Anne's vegetarian platitude and let *au jus* drip from the hunk of meat on the tip of her fork, just for effect. "So you're really into the whole political thing?"

"Huh?" Anne narrowed her eyes at Debra. "Of course. After all, Axyl is a senator . . ."

"Yeah, yeah, I know," Debra said. Anne actually believed the animal rights stuff, as well as all the lies she'd just spewed to the room full of ladies. In Debra's opinion, the real objective behind the zero population movement wasn't to eliminate pregnancies but to produce a calculated failure rate and more clients for the abortion clinics. Not that she cared one way or the other, but it amused her that Anne was still preaching all that garbage and believing it.

* * *

From a discrete table in the corner, where she sat slumped over a bowl of broccoli and cheese soup, Jessica Main watched the two women, her thoughts hidden behind the pleasantness of her round face. She remembered Anne and Debra from high school and could have joined them at their table if she'd had a mind to, but she had nothing in common with them anymore. The two of them with their airs and fancy hairdos wouldn't know what to say to her in her present state. She still looked the same—still had the same fleshy figure, the same short, curly hair—but she no longer shared their worldview.

She had to admit, though, that the real reason she wouldn't approach them was because they would look at her and remember . . . remember the one thing she tried desperately to forget every day of her life. Nowadays, she blended into the walls whenever possible.

Anne obviously hadn't changed. She had always loved being in the limelight, and now she had reached a lifetime goal by landing in Senator Axyl Houston's bed. And Debra, from what she'd overheard, was as in-your-face as ever.

Jessica sipped at her broccoli and cheese soup—a thank you gift from a friend in the kitchen for pet-sitting—which was fantastic and much appreciated, but that steak was making her mouth water. She only had five food credits left, though, and that had to last through the next week. However, even if she'd had a hundred, she wouldn't have ordered beef. It might place another flag by her name in that all-knowing UO computer.

The UO global database had been online since social security numbers were translated into sixteen-digit codes. The new codes were implemented for Universal Medical Charts, which enabled every physician, every medical center, every emergency room to view comprehensive health records at the click of a button. When cash went defunct and all transactions became strictly electronic, financial data was tied to the same ID. No one could earn money; get medical treatment; or buy food, clothing, or shelter without the new government code— initially kept on magnetic-strip cards but quickly converted to chips imbedded under the skin for convenience and security. When they worked, that is. The early-generation chips were notoriously unreliable—failing, blinking out, causing infections—forcing many people back to cards.

Jessica sighed. She felt like the only paranoid person alive, constantly worrying about the ID chip and her cell phone, both of which allowed the government to track her. The paranoia kept her from even trying an iThot system; plug into one and control every motion and word with your mind. Sounded great, but what might the government learn about her in the process?

She slurped up the last of her soup, waved at her waitress friend across the room, and escaped to the sunshine outside.

* * *

The Public Medical Services hall appeared dim after the glare of the birthing lights, but the same scent of cleaning fumes permeated every corner.

As the nursery-care nurse approached, Markus scowled. He wished he could hand her the baby. "Never mind, Judy," he said with a wave of his hand, "it's a dump."

The young woman shrugged and headed back to the nursery.

David peered at the little boy: the spit-bubble on his lips, the newness of him rising up like an aura of purity. He pulled the blanket protectively around him.

Markus led him into a small room and motioned to a metal drawer. "Over there. It pulls out. Strap him in and push the button."

David took a step forward, his stomach heaving.

"Not yet," said Markus. "Wait until I'm down the hall. I can't stand to hear them cry when you strap them in; they hate the cold metal. You'll have to fill out the tag and drop the body into that bin over there. Don't forget to scan the tag over at the terminal."

They hate the cold metal. Does that matter when you're killing them?

Markus took in David's thin frame and shadowed eyes. He didn't look like a novice med. He looked too old and undernourished, like an overworked executive, not a shift-work doctor. And he was too emotional. His face was turning green.

"They don't feel it," said Markus. "Just gases them. It's over in a few minutes. Really."

Markus had only been in deliveries a year. His first months had been wonderful, a dream come true. He had always wanted to be an obstetrician like his father, but by the time he graduated, specialists were already being frowned upon. Family medical doctors—meds—were given tax credits; they were good all-purpose doctors that the government could place in any location across the country.

Obstetrics had been a nightmare. Kim Lui had made sure Markus's very first dump was a severe deformity. She had dropped the baby girl into the drawer like a grungy rag doll and left him to fill out the tag. After that, dumps had arrived more frequently. He had thought of asking for another transfer, but he knew where he would end up: in general obstetrics, doing government-induced abortions on a daily basis. Or on the geriatric floor. There was less chance of running into the bad stuff at this end of it. And sometimes he could intervene.

Again Markus glimpsed the Jesus look in David—his lean body shaking with emotion, fighting to keep tears back as he stared at the drawer.

The device was simple, just a drawer with a smooth metal lining that slid into a miniature gas chamber at the push of a lever. It hadn't taken much innovation, but it had taken a lot of red tape to get it installed. Doctor Brewster had been considered squeamish for complaining about the obviously easy methods: He refused to perform brain suctions, claiming the infant wiggled too much and that fetal brain tissue was no longer a scarce commodity. Nor would he hold a rubber pad over the neonate's face or hold down its kicking body to give it a lethal injection. The no-life-support method took up too much room and time and caused tension among the staff. After constant reprimands for making the support staff perform the duty, and finally threatened with losing his position, Brewster designed the lethal gas chamber, now universally called the Brewster Box. He had patented it and retired.

A chemical smell drifted up to David as he stared at a puddle of secretions not wiped away from the previous termination. Little metal belts lay open for use. Above it, in bold letters, a sign read, *For the Good of the Nation, for the Good of the World. Por el bien de la nacion, para el bien del mundo.*

He looked back to the door, his heart pounding in his ears.

He wanted to ask all kinds of stupid questions, but that might show him as a fraud. Bethany had died because of his negligence.

He wouldn't fail twice. With his thin lips mashed together and his pale eyes determinedly dry, he stared at Markus.

The soft white blanket kicked with life.

Markus turned away. He refused to look at him. "All right. We'll go to Rod and see if he will take him. He took the Cerebral Palsy kid last week for me. At least we won't have to be involved."

"Thanks, Markus." He didn't want to ask what this Rod person would do with him, as long as it meant life instead of death. He closed the drawer and hugged the bundle a bit tighter.

"Right. If the Alligator finds out, I'll be chewed up and spit out."

Down the hall, he motioned David to sneak around the corner while he stopped at the assistants' station and mumbled something to a perky brunette who visibly dulled during her exchange with him, then rejoined David.

Sunlight blinded them as they crossed the concrete quad, which joined the various divisions of Public Medical Services. Several employees seated in the shady picnic area to the left turned to look as they passed. David's skin pricked with tension. *Please God, protect me*, he prayed in silence.

Markus ignored them. "So she was a friend of yours or something?"

It took David a moment to figure out he was talking about the surrogate. "Well . . ."

"That's what I thought." He held his hand up. "Don't tell me the real story. I don't want to know. When we're done with him, go ahead and leave. I'll take care of the paperwork."

A row of garbage containers—solar-powered recycling compactors—were noisily grinding their contents at the edge of the sidewalk, making further conversation impossible.

The Children's Hospital stood at one end of the quad, huge from the front street entrance, with a reception area large enough to seat a hundred and halls running off at all angles. Nevertheless, the quad entrance opened into a long hall of offices with a set of double doors to the left labeled "Laboratory Transfer."

Markus led the way to the third office and entered after a cursory knock.

The wiry old man behind the desk peered over his reading glasses. "Oh, Markus. Come in."

"Hi, Rod. This is Rex Montane."

David smiled warmly, not showing any surprise at his alias.

The man glanced at David standing in the doorway with the baby and slammed down his pen. "Not again, Markus. I told you. . . ."

Markus pushed David back into the hall, out of sight but not out of earshot of the conversation. "There's not a thing wrong with the kid's organs. He's just a Down's."

"The devil! You know there are some abnormalities, and anyway, I can't just take every deviant you don't have the guts to dump. I've got a case load so full now I can't keep up with it."

Markus stared unwaveringly.

Rod met his eyes. "You're a gutless jerk, Markus. You can't bear to dump them, so you let me do your dirty work."

"At least they're alive."

"No. What you mean is, you don't have to dispose of them. Unless it has some rare tissue type making a transfer to

National a possibility, I'm not interested. And knowing you, Markus, this was a spur of the moment escape route without any blood work."

Markus waved some papers. "I've got the blood work printouts."

Rod nodded. "And we don't need him."

Markus clenched his teeth. "What do you suggest?"

"Go back and dump the deviant. Or take it to the research lab. Or sell it to a Fun House."

"I would dump him before resorting to that." Markus cussed and slammed the door behind him.

* * *

Anne Shelton moved down the grocery store aisle with a regal air befitting her status as a high-society senator's co-hab, trying to decide which baby formula to buy. Other shoppers pushed by her and reached around her, buying by rote. She realized she should have researched baby formulas and couldn't think why she hadn't.

As she passed the first shelf, an automated display called out to her. "*Preferred Infant Formula* is the best possible start for your new baby. Produced by the government Good For You manufacturing plant, it qualifies your child for Healthcare Points that you can put toward your child's Healthcare Score. What could be more important than giving your baby the best possible score? So choose *Preferred Infant Formula*. Good for the Nation, Good for the World!"

She nodded and reached for the purple can as the display repeated the message in Spanish. It was wonderful how the government thought out everything. It made life so easy.

She glanced at the Preferred Baby face staring down at her in triplicate from the row of cereal boxes. It would be months before her Frank would eat solid food, but she smiled to herself at the reality of his impending arrival. Soon she would be pushing this cart with him settled into a baby seat, and he would look up at her with that same cereal-box "I Love You" expression.

She grabbed a rattle from a hanging display, noting happily that it was made from recycled material and was fully biodegradable, then hurried to the check out area. Minutes were ticking by, and her baby was being born! She had to get to the Med Center right away.

* * *

David followed Markus through an unmarked door, down another hall of various executive offices, to a parking lot exit with UVPA APPAREL RECOMMENDED emblazoned on the door. In small letters underneath, it stated, *Neglecting to wear Ultraviolet Protection Approved apparel may reduce your Healthcare Score—the care you want when you need it. For the Good of the Nation, for the Good of the World! Se recomienda usar ropa adecuada para protegerse de los rayos ultra violeta. Por el bien de la nacion, para el bien del mundo.*

"Bunch of crap." Markus pushed the door open.

Instinctively, David knew Markus was talking about the baby and not the UVPA message but suspected the warning would elicit the same outburst.

Lord, David prayed through silent lips, *give me courage to expose myself as your servant.* "So what is the Fun House?"

Squinting in the harsh sunlight, looking for his vehicle, Markus jerked at the remark. "What hole have you been living in?" David's serious expression sufficed as an answer. Markus resumed searching the rows of solar-powered and electric short-distance cars. Exhaust-driven vehicles meant permits, daily passes, and city pollution fines, so few people owned them anymore. Markus wanted a hydrogen car like Kim Lui had, but for him, just renting one for vacations was a luxury. At least he had an old solar model and wasn't stuck carpooling from the depot. Unfortunately, his wife Betty had needed the car.

"I forgot I rode with Hal." He yanked his handkerchief from his back pocket and mopped his brow.

David pulled the blanket over the baby's face, hiding the tiny puckered mouth sucking at the clenched fist.

"You don't have a car, do you?"

David shook his head.

Markus wiped his whole face and stuffed the damp cloth back in his pocket. "Let's walk," he said. "This whole day has been a nightmare, and when I wake up tomorrow, I'm going to pretend that you and the boy never existed."

He glanced at the bundle in David's arms, glad the blanket hid the baby's face, and squeezed his eyes to narrow slits against the sun as he focused back on the path, determined not to look again. "The Fun House is public slang for the fine establishment of public erotica. You don't have one, wherever you come from?"

David swallowed. Sweat ran down between his shoulder blades as they crossed the parking lot, avoiding three women who approached them with their palms out, and continued to the winding blacktop path. "No. I've heard of them, of course, just not called Fun Houses." *He'd heard of them, but hadn't believed it was true.*

Markus nodded. "They were established under some nice sounding little amendment to a bill because . . ." He eyed the stoplight and bit back the rest of his sentence. He was going to say because no one was expected to control any type of sexual urges anymore, that the fulfillment of those urges was considered a basic human right, but the cameras at every intersection recorded audio and visual, and you never knew who might hear you or who might slam you with an Intolerance Crime when funds were running low, which of course they always were.

David followed his gaze, realized there was a camera watching them, and turned his face away.

When they reached the cool shade of a pine grove where the path turned to gravel, the temperature eased off at least five degrees. Markus stopped to catch his breath, then pulled out his cell and turned it off. He wasn't taking any chance of having this conversation overheard in case his hunch about this guy was right. Along this path, without any compupanels or cameras in sight, he was fairly sure they could talk freely.

David did the same, and relaxed slightly. "I thought they were government-run prostitution rings, to control infectious diseases."

Markus nodded. "Yup."

"But a baby?"

"Rod is perverted. But so are a lot of other people. No telling."

Markus wondered about this guy. A Dominian maybe? It wasn't often you heard of one being found in the Outer States. Prisoners of outmoded Christian morals, incapable of grasping the freedom of the United Order of the World. But why would a Dominian risk his life posing as a med in a hospital? In some ways, Markus sympathized with this guy's distress. He'd had nightmares about the babies he had terminated. Maybe this fellow was searching for more than visitor propaganda. Markus could provide the dirt. And maybe soothe his own aching conscience.

As David's Jesus eyes locked on him, he cringed. When the Unified Order began closing churches, shipping off children to UO Institutes, and arresting outspoken Christians, Markus had renounced his Christian upbringing. He had denied his parents any help in sustaining their church, and mourned them as fools for losing their lives over a building and a tradition that he felt could just as easily be honored quietly in one's heart. Now he wondered about that stance. He lived as a good person, never judging others or infringing on their rights, yet his soul felt rotted. Why? He had nothing but scorn for the banal, self-adulating World Church that had supplanted Christianity, and though his dear friend Joanne had been urging him to join the underground . . . well, he wasn't that radical.

She did get him to pray, but only one time. And he had never expected an answer, almost hoped for no answer. No answer, no God, guilt would fade, life could go on. Then this man appeared out of nowhere. Wasn't that as near a miracle as he could expect in response to one lone prayer? He wanted to ask this guy outright. He wanted assurance of God's existence. But he couldn't ask; if this guy wasn't from the Dome, even broaching the subject could cause trouble. You never knew if you were being set up. Like right now—this guy could pull a badge and arrest him for removing this baby. That would be major. He would lose everything.

Markus halted, pulled out his handkerchief, swabbed his forehead again, then jammed it back into his pocket and swept his hair back.

David stopped a pace ahead, patiently waiting.

Markus took in what he saw—a lean, bearded man, an outsider, unsure, too emotional, too trusting—and his own distrust eased away. Something told him this guy was okay, and that they needed each other. He waved David onward. "Then there's the NFCCs, the National Family Counseling Centers, which are supposed to offer parenting solutions, but I think they do more harm than good. They claim custody for the smallest offenses. The name, Counseling Centers, confuses people. Makes them think they're doing the right thing."

"The Counseling Centers send them to UO Institutes," David added. He didn't mention that had been the fate of his best friend.

"Yes. And some—the brilliant ones—are trained for specialized jobs. Most are indoctrinated and trained as city-state patrollers, or soldiers, though the armed forces have been reduced to almost nil since the UO took command. But then there are the unlucky ones who end up with a fate worse than death. Not many people know that, and those that do have their reasons for keeping their mouths shut, if you catch my drift."

David couldn't fathom how such a thing could be allowed. "But how did they convince people . . . ?"

Markus knew what he was asking. "Through the courts, of course. Dumping started first. They found a case of a severely deformed child who was a burden on his family and got court permission to withhold treatment and sustenance."

"They starved him to death?"

"Pretty much. It was argued that if abortions were permitted because fetuses were totally dependent, and if full-term fetuses who survived botched abortions were legally left to die in a bin at an abortion center, couldn't the same be allowed for a day-old infant? What was the difference other than the way in which it entered the world? And how was that different than an infant five days old who couldn't survive without sustenance provided by a mother or guardian? After a few cases were pushed through, the courts ruled that children aren't independent until age four, when they can feed and dress themselves. And there you have it. Kids who don't develop mental and physical independence are never considered fully human; they never have rights. They are a *burden*." He sighed, and then continued. "I don't even want to tell you what happens. You're better off not knowing."

David stopped walking. In his mind, he pictured every possibility and turned the images aside before they could manifest themselves in his head. Every muscle in his face flexed into gritting his teeth so that for a moment he couldn't speak. The Dome really wasn't well informed. What he'd learned in the Life Continuity Center was bad enough, but this? "No one says anything? Nothing about dumps? Nothing about the counseling centers?"

"And get charged with an Intolerance Crime?" Markus picked up a twig and kept walking.

David wanted to be back home again, ignorant of this perverted society. At times he had resented the poverty and restrictive lifestyle of the Dome, but not now, not knowing what the outer states were like.

The Dome had been established in the ruins of Detroit. Much of the city had already been bulldozed, scavenged, and left to rot long before the United Central Bank foreclosed on the city during the economic collapse of 2019, after which the government invoked eminent domain over the remaining impoverished neighborhoods. The following year, after Christian groups were tenuously implicated in a day of bombings and gas attacks that killed thousands at twelve National Institutes of Health research facilities—which the news media quickly dubbed the "Judgment Day Massacre" and "the worst terrorist attack in American history"—Congress passed the Christian Homestead Act. For their "own safety," and in the interests of national security, all professed Christians would be relocated to a federal reservation; two years later, old Detroit's ravaged homes, collapsing buildings, and deteriorating factories became the Cloistered Dominion. The nickname of "Dome" was both an abridgement of "Dominion" and an apt description for its forced isolation from the outer states: High walls and military checkpoints would keep its occupants at bay.

At that time, other countries around the world were suffering the same economic collapses, riots, and national crises. The reigning powers' solution: global restructuring. The Unified Order of the World was established, its secular biases dimming any hopes the Christians had of reversing their fortunes. As a last resort some resisted with arms—in the Southern and Mountain states especially—but after much loss of life they were finally overcome, and the Christian relocation began in earnest. Throughout the 2020s the Dome filled with new arrivals, at first living off government aid but eventually building from the ruins a basic economy and society. Life there was hard, but the Dominians endured.

On an afternoon like this, David would normally be in the Dominion medical center. Not the big one by the river, but the smaller one on the outskirts of the Dome, located in what had actually been a medical complex housing a variety of specialists.

They were lucky that the city also had a hospital, and by default, they gained all the hospital equipment left behind—the little that hadn't been looted—but most of it was old and inadequate. And they lacked ambulances. *Elizabeth! Bethany!* The lack of emergency equipment had cost them their lives.

He couldn't think of them now or he wouldn't be able to function.

He pulled the blanket back and gazed at the baby sleeping peacefully in his arms, his chest rising and falling. With a pang, he realized the corruptness of the outer states was no longer an absurd illusion. "How could they not do everything possible to help you?" he whispered to the sleeping boy.

Something crackled in the leaves ahead.

Markus grabbed David's arm. "Watch."

The baby started crying. A dark furry thing scurried across the shady path to undergrowth beyond.

"A rat," said Markus.

David placed the baby on his shoulder and patted his back. "Baby's getting hungry."

"Those mutant lab rats are everywhere. You know they've just about reached California?" He frowned. "Save the rats, run tests on babies and kids. No one protects them."

Thoughts of home vanished as David wondered how far he could push Markus. "Isn't there a chance the mother would want him the way he is? I mean, dumping hasn't really become mandatory, has it?"

There was no pretending between them now. No one in the medical field could be this ignorant. Markus figured he may as well explain it with the exact legal lingo. He stared at the clouds as if the sky was a giant textbook opened before him. "Any abnormalities in a fetus are permissible if the carrier, meaning mother, is a free citizen, meaning not government supported. The carrier has the option to keep the child if she can care for it independently." He looked at David. "Which means she'd have to be rich, because everyone else is at the government's mercy when it comes to healthcare."

"But I remember when the push was to help all the handicapped. All those regulations for parking and elevators and education and accessibility and equal opportunity."

Markus blinked a few times. "Well, sure, there are still regulations for parking and stuff, but you're right. Absurd, isn't it? And there's a bill being pitched right now that won't allow any deformities to survive, for any reason. There'll be no parental say left at all. Who'd have thought it would flip so dramatically? Remember when the 'extremists' warned about that? No one believed them."

"I was just a kid when we left for . . ." he stopped himself from finishing the sentence.

Markus sighed. He'd been right. This guy was a Dominian. For a brief moment, his naiveté made Markus wonder what kind of wonderland the Dome was. "Look, the government has taught the lesson well—self-preservation. Keep your mouth shut and be happy with the portion they give you. Don't rebel. Don't make waves. Close your eyes to the crap that seems crooked."

"Or?"

Markus looked both ways, then stared at the baby. "Use your imagination." He picked up his pace again, as if anxious to get away from his words. "In the case of surrogates, the entire pregnancy is government controlled. They follow stringent rules on acceptable levels of normalcy for births."

As they walked in silence, both mulling things over, David concentrated on the infant in his arms. The baby suckled David's fingers, all warm and moist around his knuckles, pulling at them like a nipple. Names were running through his head: Matthew? John? Andrew? Francis? None of them seemed to fit. The little fellow, red and puckered, clenched his pale eyes so tight they wrinkled in the corners. He smelled poignant, like salty sausage.

Markus, twisting off pieces of his stick, remembered how simple life had seemed when he was a kid, when his dad had a small private practice. He could remember working in the office, filling drawers with gauzes and jars with tongue depressors, sweeping floors, and filing papers. The patients revered his father. That's the kind of doctor he'd wanted to be. He wished he had at least left the city. He would have if Betty hadn't whined and moaned so much.

Dropping the last of his twig, Markus picked up a smooth gray stone and rubbed the coolness of it between his fingers. He could remember when the graveled path had been a jogging trail through the state park, before the turn of the century. He had lived with his parents in the best neighborhood, and they had all attended church together. He had always hated going to church, choked by a necktie and stewing in a suit. Now he missed it. He missed the soaring harmony of the choir's Alleluia and the pretty girls prissied up for Sunday school.

That was before the Unified Order established the World Church as a "peaceful unification of all faiths." Christian doctrine and morality were dissolved in favor of the singular virtue of tolerance. Liberal Jews and Reformed Muslims, both groups by then a majority within their religions, eagerly joined in. Worship services became social gatherings, and sermons couched UO propaganda in terms of ambiguous spirituality. Most citizens were thoroughly secularized and had no use for the World Church—Unified Worship Spaces were rarely more than a quarter full—but it gave the government a safe, controllable outlet for those who still had religious impulses.

The remaining Jews and Muslims, their beliefs also odious to the new tolerant order, retreated into watchful silence, waiting—the Jews for their Messiah and the Muslims for *jihad*. The few diehard Christian groups that dared to continue to worship at first relocated into buildings stripped bare of crosses and bell towers and limited their services to quiet devotions without public evangelization. Their membership floundered under the persecution of Intolerance Laws, holding only the most devout to regular attendance until UO prosecutions drove them to the edge, and they went underground, like his friend Joanne.

Or retreated to the Dome.

He looked at David.

* * *

Axyl Houston clicked through his electronic calendar while he waited for Senator Jack Friday to get off the phone. Axyl ran his life on two premises: Time Wasted Is Time Lost and Power to the Elite. Each success and power play created even higher expectations. Becoming the most powerful member of the Senate was an achievement but hardly a stopping point. He had another position in mind: right-hand man to the Unified Order's Minister of World Peace, the visionary behind the Hundred-Year Plan.

That's what separated him from the crowd. He understood the vision. The nation wasn't a mountain with the world at its feet, but rather one small piece in the vast, unified world. It had taken monumental efforts to make people understand true equality, but the task had finally been achieved, and now the final forces were in place to bring the citizenry totally into compliance with World Unity.

Other would-be world leaders had tried in the past to force the country into assuming a humble slot in the scheme of things, but those efforts had met with rebellion: populist backlashes, grassroots media movements, even armed uprisings. The Minister, a quiet man far wiser than his predecessors, had identified the secret to success: take it slowly. Big changes created suspicion, but small ones could be accomplished with little resistance.

Apathetic citizens, obsessed with little pleasures, don't pay attention to what's happening around them. That was the other great lesson Axyl had learned. They rely on the government to tell them what's happening in the world, to teach their kids right from wrong, to solve their problems for them. Legislators, dependent on an endless stream of promises to keep themselves in power, passed bill after bill, each just a little more coercive than the last. Finance, major industry, healthcare, education, the media—without firing a shot, the state eventually gained control of most every aspect of public life. When a consortium of international billionaires founded the Unified Order of the World, out of the ashes of the old United Nations, it was then but a small step, a very well-planned step, for America to cede national sovereignty in the interests of global peace and economic stability, with jurisdiction handed over in the signing of a few pertinent treaties.

In fact, they clamored for it. Axyl smiled.

World domination stood within the Minister's grasp. And Axyl Houston intended to become his right-hand man. First he had to prove his worth to the cause, and his current project was sure to please: the final victorious enactment of *A Better World*, an American bill. The states still had laws and passed new bills, but only within the boundaries of UO authority. If the UO denied the passage of a bill, it was invalid, much like a presidential veto. In the case of *A Better World*, the idea originated with the UO, but Axyl had been chosen to present it to the States as being American ingenuity, to keep citizens from rebelling against it.

He swelled with pride. *A Better World.* The elimination of deformity and disease. A nation of perfect productivity, with citizens powerless to stop it.

Of course there was still the problem of eradicating the last of the Christians to complete the UO ideal of perfect unity, but Jack Friday would know how to get rid of them.

Axyl glared at Jack with eyes so dark that his pupils were indistinguishable from his black irises. He knew the look would put an end to Jack's phone call. Even the lionhearted stopped midspeech and dismissed themselves from his presence when he cast his eyes upon them. He prided himself on his stern look. It expressed his authority, which got him elected; anyone would trust him above the mouthy Danita Bridges with her lengthy dialogues on Getting Back to the Basics. Members of the Senate like her didn't grasp the need to maintain air-tight control. They didn't understand the ultimate goal. They didn't share the vision of a perfect submissive society wiped clean of disease and judgment.

One of the office girls stepped in and deposited a file on Jack's desk just as he concluded his phone call. As she left, closing the door behind her, Jack salivated. "Perfect, don't you think? I just hired her. A body with a mind to match."

Axyl stared at the door a moment as if the girl's image still lingered, wondering if Jack was right. Most women were so bossy he couldn't tolerate being around them. His preference leaned toward brainless robots that could dress right for occasions, were ready at his convenience, and otherwise left him to his work. Like Anne. And even she was wearing on him.

His early fascination with Anne had been sparked by her pale blond beauty and public charisma. Together, they were labeled the most striking couple on the Hill. Reporters stepped over each other to catch flashes of them together at black-tie functions. She was a political asset. And surprisingly imaginative in ways he appreciated.

Unfortunately, she had suddenly become maternally preoccupied. She had actually interrupted a meeting to tell him her baby was being delivered, as if he would rush home to see some wrinkled kid in a hospital cart. He had considered cutting her loose; except now, with the baby, he had to tolerate her for a while longer to create a public perception of family values, of wholesomeness. For some strange reason, citizens were more apt to trust a man with a family, and right now he needed their trust.

Returning his attention to business, Axyl pounded the document in front of him. "I want a plan initiated by the end of the month."

"Axyl, my boy, you worry too much. We're at the end, and ahead of schedule. This is the last step. Haven't I kept us on target for years?"

Jack settled his stooped figure back in his chair, propped his bony hands behind his bald head and continued. "We have the citizens where we want them: receptive and pliable. They have no hope except through us. They are totally dependent. The bills have been enacted, the laws are in place, our bases are covered, and the Unified Order is firmly established, rooted in everyday life. By the end of next year, we'll denounce the Dome's separation and enforce the laws. The Minister will be in total control."

Axyl frowned. Jack understood the goal of Universal Unity but didn't really care about the ideology. He only went along with it for his own cut of the pie. "But they pollute the perfection we're so close to achieving." He spoke with venom. "How can we turn Jesus Freaks to Universal Unity?"

"A cage. We hand them to you in a cage with lions guarding the gate. How can that be a problem? After all the years they've been stuck on that reservation, they'll jump at whatever we offer them."

Axyl remained silent for a moment, staring at the pen in his hand, thinking, then wrote on a pad: *I think we should just eliminate them. That would be the easiest way. We could poison the water. They'd be dead in weeks.*

Jack laughed. "Not only are you a sadist, you're an idiot. Don't you think that might raise public alarm?"

Axyl stared hard at Jack. True, Jack had seniority, but *no one* called him an idiot, and if Jack considered him a sadist, he didn't fully appreciate the worldwide vision of perfection. Nevertheless, he let the statement pass. He needed the situation resolved. "Something more subtle." This time he wrote, *Poison one food product that only goes to the Dome.*

Jack rolled his eyes.

Disease?

"Huh?"

Axyl dropped his voice to a hiss. "Mandate inoculations that actually cause a disease."

Jack didn't bother to whisper. "If we said that there was a disease that the Dome needed to be inoculated against, don't you think the entire country would insist on being inoculated?"

"So we give them placebos."

Jack shrugged. "I guess that would do it. If it does create panic, we can twist it to say that it's something unique to the Dominians, like leprosy in the Dome." He laughed. "If I know our citizens, they'd be glad to see Dominians die off if it saved them from catching something."

Axyl nodded, thinking it through, envisioning the panic, the hatred people would develop toward the Dominians and their disease. "I can't have any doubts. I have my career staked on this."

Jack handed him a black-market cigarette and laughed. "We wouldn't want to jeopardize that, would we?"

Axyl narrowed his eyes at Jack before lighting up.

Jack blew a few smoke rings. "What's in it for me?"

* * *

Even standing alone in her kitchen, Betty Holmes posed like she had on the runway years before, one hip out, her long limbs held gracefully, artfully, in front of her as if waiting for a camera flash. Her hair styled to the last strand. Her makeup painted on with precision. As she'd hoped, good looking, rich Robert—the knight who would help her escape from the bondage of marriage to Markus—was there on the visual looking at her, asking her if she was free that afternoon.

She checked the schedule Markus had taped to the refrigerator, looked back into the camera, and licked her lips. "Yes, come! Please come. He works until five today. We have plenty of time. I'll be waiting for you, my darling."

She hung up and leaned against the wall.

She was going to divorce Markus no matter what it cost; it just wasn't worth the headache anymore, now that she had Robert waiting in the wings.

She wished—not for the first time—that she and Markus had dissolved their marriage vows and accepted a Civil Partnership when they had the chance. Fortunately, she had finally found an attorney who knew a few loopholes in the divorce tax law. She could legally sell everything she had, gift the money to a relative, divorce Markus on some grounds or other, and then get everything back. It was all timing, the attorney had promised—timing and not getting caught.

If she could just continue the marriage charade long enough for her investigator and attorney to dredge up some trumped-up illegal activities on Markus, she would be home free.

* * *

Anne's compusystem greeted her as she opened the door of her condo. "Hello, Anne."

Anne pictured the male voice as forties, thick hair, gray at the temples—the kind of man who would prepare candlelight dinners. Nothing like Axyl.

She pushed one grocery bag in the door with her foot and dropped the other two from her arms to the floor with a sigh, then pulled the broad-brimmed hat off and released the pins from her hair as she hollered out to the system, "Start coffee."

The computer-controlled coffee machine, preloaded with a week's supply of coffee grains, coughed and spurted to life. The bitter aroma filled the purified air of the eight-room aqua-green prefabricated recycled-plastic waterfront space. An executive's home, decorated in Luster White with black metal furniture and ecru accents. Axyl had a penthouse in D.C. and a beach condo in the Caribbean that far surpassed this home base. This condo was considered Anne's domain, and Axyl had decided less grandeur would be best.

Two Persian cats strutted into the foyer and wove around Anne's ankles. She ran a hand down their backs then pulled them to her lap to caress. "Hello, sweeties. Ah, Natasha, have you missed me? Come, come, Sasha. That's my pretty."

She set the cats down and muttered annoyance as she locked the door and picked up her packages. Vicky should have been here to unload the bags, but she'd begged a day off.

Anne stored her purchases in the nursery closet, then paused to touch the slick white laminate of the crib and the soft, freshly laundered blanket showered with ducklings, puddles, and umbrellas. Sunlight from the triple crank-out window sparkled over it all and lit upon the row of yellow wooden ducks posed in step in front of the toy box.

With a sigh of satisfaction, she closed the door and continued down the hall to the master suite. She loved being a senator's co-hab. No income restrictions. All the luxuries of life at her fingertips.

Her voice boomed out in crisp pronunciation as she changed out of her beige suit. "Temperature?"

"The current interior temperature is the required 75 degrees."

She groaned. She wished it were 65. It would be if she'd had a good black-market thermostat that didn't track every adjustment. Axyl was such a stickler about the temperature.

"Outdoor forecast," the voice continued, "clear skies dropping to a low of sixty degrees tonight."

She selected a pair of slacks from one end of her closet, found her favorite blue blouse and hurried to pull on both. She glanced at the time, spent five minutes fixing her hair, applied some lipstick, and ran out the door, coffee forgotten.

* * *

Trudy Bullock shifted uncomfortably in the hard chair of the Public Medical Services conference room, losing patience with the nurse sitting across from her. She had been at the PMS Center for four hours and knew Norman, her assistant, would be having a nervous fit back at Senator Houston's office. Her eight-week maternity appointment last month had been remarkably fast—only three hours including her wait in line, but today they insisted on blood tests and then this ridiculous tirade of questions.

"Your records show that your pregnancy was an insemination. Is that correct?"

Trudy would have growled with impatience if she hadn't spent years training herself in social etiquette. Her Latina heritage had given her certain advantages, but she wanted to be taken seriously in the world of politics for her talents and professionalism, not for her race, and she had worked hard to evoke the elitist image and attitude necessary to run with the top dogs. "Yes, I used a sperm donor."

"Was there a medical reason for that choice?"

As much as she thrived on her career, and on the danger that came with her secret involvement with the Liberty League, life had still been lacking. She needed more. She needed a connection to another person, which she hadn't found with a partner. She'd decided she wanted a child, even if it complicated everything else. She raised her chin slightly, her high cheekbones and wide, dark eyes giving an impression of confidence. "It was better than risking a disease or a relationship."

"Were you told by anyone that you classified for," she consulted the paper in front of her, "an XRO-5 insemination?"

"I have no idea what that is." *But I will find out!* She pushed back her chair and stood up, her lanky frame towering over the bulky nurse. "How much longer is this going to take?"

The nurse scribbled something on the paper and left without responding.

Trudy stared at the black plastic clock on the wall, clicking away the passing minutes while she willed the nurse to return. It was already 2:10. All the tests had been done, the examination complete. What more could be needed?

Below the clock hung a propaganda poster like the one in the senator's office: *Government tends to perfection.* Trudy sighed. That was Senator Houston's slogan. Her boss saw himself as the great creator of national mottoes.

A solemn nurse entered. She didn't speak until she was seated across from Trudy with a file settled beneath her clasped hands. She had a bright red Trust Authority button pinned to her white uniform. "I'm afraid I have bad news, Trudy. The tests revealed that the fetus has a DNA anomaly."

"What kind of defect?"

The nurse read from her paper. "A DNA configuration inconsistent with normal fetal development."

"But what? What exactly is wrong?"

The nurse ran her finger down the rest of the page. "I'm not sure."

"You're not sure?"

"As you can see on this information sheet I printed for you, this condition is irreversible."

The woman's eyes watched her, expecting fear and submission, Trudy knew. But she was looking at the wrong woman for that. Trudy saw more power in one day in the senator's office than this lady could hope to wield in a year.

The nurse continued her monotone speech. "I've already checked the schedule and found a slot open at three o'clock. I have the file all in order right here." A paper and pen glided across the laminated table. "If you just sign the termination permission, we'll be done, and you can make yourself comfortable in the waiting room."

Trudy sat motionless. Termination permission? They couldn't even tell her what was wrong. She hadn't scrimped and saved for an entire year for one successful artificial insemination just to have her baby sucked out of her.

And she hadn't become regional assistant to Senator Axyl Houston by being rushed or pushed around. "Really. Do you think the government runs by itself? I've already been here for hours. I'm sorry; you'll have to remove me from your schedule for today. I'll reschedule next week, after I review Senator Houston's agenda." A promise she had no intention of keeping. She knew what happened in the clinics. She made a point of knowing. What she did with her body would be her decision. She pushed the paper back at the nurse and stood up. "Good day."

The nurse's chair screeched against the floor in her haste to follow. For some reason the lab tech and med were both in a tizzy over this report; she had assured them it would be no problem to terminate. She was a pro at these procedures. "Ms. Bullock, it's much tidier to take care of it at once and not disrupt another day of your schedule."

The nurse continued to follow her out the door and into the hall. "I'll have to keep your file pending. Please reconsider."

Two more steps and into the waiting room, into the public eye. "You don't want a deformed child. The citizens don't want a deformed child."

A dozen women stared at Trudy.

"It's really not up to you, you know," the nurse continued.

Trudy quickened her pace to the glaring sunlight of the glassed exit.

* * *

Markus guided David down a narrow, building-lined street of pavement, cement, and bricks from one end to the other without a blade of grass in sight. Toward the far end, he tapped David's arm and led him up wide granite steps and through a heavily pillared entrance into an old three-story brick building that had once been a courthouse. The imposing grandeur of the exterior dissipated inside, where harried foster-care caseworkers babbled into phones or sat grimly typing at computer stations.

No one did more than glance up at Markus. He'd been visiting Joanne Korany's office for the last five of her twenty-year tenure, and they accepted him as part of the scenery.

Always hungry, he stopped at the lobby vending machines, passed his palm over the scanner, and chose corn chips. It bleeped, then spoke. "Markus Holmes, please select the dried banana chips to ensure your recommended daily allowance of Vitamin A and potassium, or your Healthcare Score will be reduced by one-tenth of a point." Markus groaned, ignored the voice, and pushed the corn chips selection again. The machine responded, "Credits being debited from account." For just a blink, TRUST AUTHORITY flashed across the tiny display.

Markus pulled the pack open as they rounded a corner and entered Joanne's office without knocking. Her head lay pillowed on her arms atop a disorganized pile of folders. Her dull brown hair was in disarray, and her bifocals were tossed to the distant corner of the ancient oak desk, almost out of her range of vision. The blinds had been pulled up, but the glaring sunlight only accentuated the gloom of the room.

Markus smiled at Joanne with wonder. In her, he always saw goodness, solid morals, old-fashioned values. Nothing like his vain and catty wife, Betty.

David stood just inside the door watching as Markus turned off her notebook computer, which sat bleeping a recurring error across its screen.

Markus touched her arm with a tender stroke. "Joanne?"

She woke with a start. "Yes, ma'am." She brushed her hair back with a swoop of her hand, and a smile immediately lit up her full face. "Markus!"

As their eyes met, the tired wrinkles of Markus's face disappeared into laugh lines around his eyes and mouth. Their hands entwined, expressing words that were never spoken aloud and never acted upon.

As David studied them, he ached over the memory of Elizabeth. He rocked the baby in his arms, soothing the baby, soothing himself, thinking of how Elizabeth would have crooned over him. Elizabeth would have known what to call him. She'd pored over baby-name books and practiced names over and over, walking around the house saying the names, reciting their meanings, again and again to see if she really liked them. Her favorites were easy to recall. *Michael*, who is like God. *Patrick*, noble. *Gabriel*, strength. *Frank*, free and truthful.

Frank. That was it. Free. Seeking freedom. There was something about accepting him despite his disadvantages as being the very core of truthfulness, true to the belief in the equality of all men. Frank. Frankie.

David kissed his head and whispered it to him. "Frankie."

Frankie startled in his sleep and mouthed air until he found David's knuckle again, slurped loudly, and settled back to sleep.

Joanne nodded toward the suckling noise. "Who's your friend?"

"Rex." Markus waved him to the vacant seat opposite Joanne. "Come in and close the door."

Joanne had learned to trust her gut feelings and first impressions. David was good. She could sense a warmth, almost an aura around him. With his long face and muscular frame he in no way resembled the large-boned, fleshy Markus, but they shared a certain something in their expressions, maybe the earnestness in their eyes. "Nice to meet you," she said as she waved him toward the chair in front of her desk. "I take it you're here about the baby?"

"Yes," David replied. He was hopeful; she had called Frankie a baby.

Markus didn't have to explain. "Can you help?"

She hesitated a second, but succumbed and reached for the child, taking him gently into her arms. Frankie howled at being removed from David's finger, but his cries didn't faze Joanne. "He's beautiful."

"I think he's hungry."

She rummaged through a deep bottom drawer, shoving notes, napkins, and other junk aside until she found a sample bottle of formula, which she held up triumphantly. "Got it in the mail two weeks ago," she said. "I couldn't just throw it away!"

A suckling, gulping brought smiles to everyone's faces.

"What's wrong with him?"

"Down syndrome. Mental deficiency, some health issues."

"I remember," said Joanne. "I've never seen a newborn case."

"So can you take him?"

"It will take time. I'll have to create a case study, a history. You know the drill. The little girl wasn't a problem—she was perfect and I knew a couple already. Friends. But for a Down's child?" The unspoken message hung in the air: How impossible it would be to blend him in, and what would happen if they were caught?

She looked at the baby's pale gray eyes fluttering as he sucked on the bottle. "Give me a week to create the case and I can get him into a children's home. He'll probably be there for life."

David spoke up. "For life instead of death."

Markus shattered their hopes. "We don't have a week. We don't even have a good hour. I've got to get back to the unit before they raise alarm."

Joanne chewed her lip in the heavy silence, then turned and made sure her computer and phone were both turned off before she continued. Her voice wavered. "If there was a way to set up a safe house." Her eyes pleaded. "I know we've talked it around in circles for ages, but there must be a way to do it." Tears welled up. "I hate this. Knowing what they do to these poor children and being helpless to do anything about it. Nobody cares. Why can't they see what they're doing?" Her voice rose an octave. "I would quit if I could, but it wouldn't stop the deaths, and I might miss the chance to save one."

Markus took Joanne's hand gently in his. "We have helped a few, you and I."

She smiled weakly. "Yes. But that doesn't help this little fellow." She kissed the soft infant cheek, still red and wrinkled from birth, and then with a quick glance at her computer to make sure it was off, settled her intent gaze on David. "Can't you help?"

Markus looked from her to David. Of anyone in the world, he could trust Joanne. "He's not . . . from here."

Joanne gazed at David, her eyes widening as a thought dawned on her. "He sent you to help us, didn't he?"

David blanched. "Who?"

Joanne kept her eyes locked on David, and, cradling Frankie in one arm, she fished a fine gold chain from beneath her blouse, letting the links slip through her fingers until an ornate crucifix rested in her palm.

David's eyes widened. "It's true. There is an underground?"

"There aren't a lot of us, but there are pockets of us around the country, highly secretive. We've been praying you'd come."

"I'm not a savior." *I wasn't even a good husband or father. I am no one, Lord. Don't rely on me.*

She didn't relinquish her intense gaze. "You are the answer to our prayers."

"No, I'm not. I don't even understand what's going on out here."

"You can take him. You can take the children and give them homes."

"If you knew where I was from, you'd know that's not possible. The restrictions, the poverty . . ."

She finally broke her gaze and looked away to the ceiling as she swallowed the tears in her throat. "Anything, *anything*, would be better."

David closed his eyes. *What are you asking of me, Lord?* He rubbed his temples and searched for an answer. "I just don't know . . ."

Markus moved to crouch at Joanne's side. "I didn't mean to upset you. I shouldn't have brought the baby here. He pulled the infant from her arms. "Go fix your make-up. I'll be back in a few minutes. We'll talk."

She let him take Frankie, then eased the necklace over her head, draped it around David's neck and tucked the crucifix under his shirt. "Let Him guide you," she said and patted the crucifix through the material before turning to talk to Frankie in Markus's arms. "God bless you, sweet darling. The Lord has a plan for you, I know it. You're going to live."

David stuck his hands in his pockets as he followed Markus and the baby back to the exit. He felt helpless. He had no business meddling in the outer states' practices. Taking this baby back with him could bring wrath against the entire Dome. He didn't have the right to do that. The Dome Council hadn't given permission to take action.

As they left the building, Markus gazed at the baby, so alive in his arms, and then at David, knowing he had a sympathizer. He still found it hard to believe that God was involved in all this, that God would in any way involve him—a man who had abandoned his faith and his parents, a man who had put newborns in a box to be killed. But Joanne believed it. She had been telling him for ages that God had a plan.

Markus thought of the safe house he and Joanne had envisioned, and he thought of the Dome. Maybe Joanne was right. If this guy was from the Dome . . . If the Dome could take the babies . . .

The sun blazed down on them. Their eyes squinted to tense slits, pulling their faces into unreadable masks. To speak the words aloud would be to set it all in motion. No turning back. He wasn't sure he had the courage to do it. And yet, he realized with a sudden feeling of buoyancy, he'd been doing it all along. The only difference would be having a definite plan in mind for every child he snuck out. He might get caught, but there had always been that possibility. It gave purpose to his life. A chance to atone for his sins. He had to follow through. "Joanne is right. We need help. Someone who can keep the babies until we find homes. In secret, of course. Someone willing to risk the consequences."

David knew he should wait; the plan had only been to make contact with the underground Christians if he could, and to find a source for medical supplies—not to initiate some Save the Children crusade. There was a long-term plan: the Redemption. But that was still in the planning stage of outlines and theories. Any trouble at the outset could end the effort before it began. Nevertheless, everything he had been raised to believe meant he had to save this life, this person, this child. Frankie. Without a word, he took the baby back into his arms and held him close.

Markus steered him away from the park path and down a curving sidewalk running in front of a string of brick buildings. Electric cars passed, their tires whirling on the blistering pavement. At the corner, perched on the top of an elevating lift truck, a technician was repairing a traffic signal connection; the camera was temporarily inoperable.

Markus pointed down the road. "Across the intersection and down the road about half a mile and you'll be back to the carpooling depot, the one across from the PMS main entrance."

Neither of them said anything for a moment. Thoughts sparked between them like electricity.

David broke the trance by looking down at Frankie and stroking his hand a moment before he finally spoke. "I don't have permission."

Markus laughed. "Neither do I."

David scanned the distant depot, weighing his odds as he calculated the number of people mingling around the entrance and the number of shops along the road. "Are there any other options? Some sympathizers willing to take them?"

"It's illegal."

"Illegal to save a life."

"A problem that's easier to ignore."

"Ignorance and tolerance. That should be changed." David wondered if he could possibly manage it. He could go straight to the Dome and give the baby to—whom? Someone. He would think of that later. His cover was blown by now anyhow. And he never left anything in his hotel room that couldn't be abandoned. "Where can I find you?"

"At Happy Zack's, two blocks over from here. I go there most evenings. Always on Fridays." He turned and took two steps away, then stopped. "Do you like living . . . on the moon?"

Compared to this mad world? "Definitely."

Markus couldn't bring himself to ask anything else. He wasn't sure he wanted to know what he had just involved himself in; he just wanted to save the babies and rid his heart of the blackness he felt growing inside. "If I had a rocket I would come visit."

"You would do well there—you are a good man. Your heart is sincere."

Markus thought about the Dome for a moment. He could go there. Anyone could approach the Dome Council and

request asylum. They just had to be willing to live by the Cloistered Dominion's biblical moral system, profess faith in Christ,
and understand the consequences if they broke Dome laws. If
it weren't for Betty . . .

Markus gazed at the baby, really looking him in the face
for the first time. He absorbed his features into a photo in his
mind, then turned and walked away.

Neither of them said good-bye. The parting was understood as a brief interlude in their conversation.

* * *

Axyl Houston straightened his tie and strode across the platform
to take center stage behind the podium. He took a sip of water,
then waited, stone-faced serious as usual, until the clapping subsided, and then launched into his speech, knowing he must hit
his message fast and hard to squeeze it into a news clip. "The
invalid crisis in our country must be met with swift action." He
paused for effect. "The ideals we brought to fruition through
the Healthy Selections Bill relieved much of our nation's stress
by taking the burden of difficult decisions off the shoulders of
emotionally challenged parents. We cannot expect parents to
choose the wisest course of action when facing a medical crisis.
We must act on their behalf in order to save them, and in truth
save all of us, from facing the strain of hardships created by pro-
longing the inevitable." He paused again, giving a nod to the
clapping that rose on cue, then scanned the crowd for effect,
to make them think he was connecting with each one of them.

"I want to tell you the story of a woman I know named
Cindy. Cindy is one of the most loving people you'll ever meet,

but she had an insurmountable problem: a man-sized child strapped in a wheelchair. He couldn't care for himself in any way. He had to be fed through a feeding tube. He had to wear diapers, and she had to change those diapers three, four, sometimes five times a day. All 180 pounds of him had to be hauled out of that wheelchair and onto a bed, stripped of his clothes, cleaned up, and heaved back to the wheelchair. He had to have around-the-clock care. Poor Cindy couldn't do anything other than care for this man-child. She had no money and no life. She needed relief, but there was none."

Another pause, and then he continued in a louder voice. "We are here to help women like Cindy!" *Clapping.* "By removing the burden from her life with the Better World Bill, we will free her from the overwhelming stress that no woman ought to face today. We will bring balance and prosperity not only to her life, and to others like her, but to the nation as a whole. We will relieve this country of infirmity and disability. We want a disease-free world, and we will be the first country to reach the disease-free goal we so courageously set forth two decades ago!" He stretched his arm above his head, filled with righteousness, filled with the glory and power of his words, and cried out, "For the Good of the Nation, for the Good of the World," and glowed in exhilaration as the chant came roaring back at him.

* * *

Outside Public Medical Services, David pulled his cell from his pocket and stared at it. Workers approached from the crosswalk, ignoring him in their haste to reserve seats on carpool vans. He wanted to call Don, his brother-in-law and council-man, to tell him what was going on, but knew he couldn't, not even with his alias and phone tied to a phony local address, because any phone call to the Dome would be traced, would jeopardize his identity. And the mission. He wouldn't risk it unless things became so dire that he had no choice.

He gazed at Frankie cuddled sleepily in the crook of his left arm and shoved the phone back in his pocket. "It's you and me against the world, buddy."

He was sweating from nerves and heat. The stagnant air inside the depot didn't help. As in most public spaces, there was no air conditioning—not without mandatory carbon-offsetting measures, which were expensive—so the numerous people added to the rising temperature and the unpleasant smell.

The place was crowded. Many people headed to the airport to access the car rentals based there and preferred to ride in a depot van rather than the slow busing system with its numerous stops.

He would fly to the Detroit Metro airport and then, if he couldn't find some means of traveling the last twenty miles, he'd get there on foot, sleeping wherever he could. As he stepped up to a ticket server, he whispered, "Please God, let there be a seat left on the airport van."

The prayer had barely left his lips when an elderly gentleman poked his wife. "I'm hungry. Let's eat before we go." The old guy tottered over to a ticket-server and changed their reservations to a later van just as David entered his airport van selection.

* * *

Harve Johnson, six foot four, two hundred and fifty pounds, was usually fully aware of the eyes that followed him wherever he went. A bodybuilder. The guy every girl wanted back in high school. Most Likely to Succeed. The life of every party. A take-charge type. But as he strode from a ticket server to the vending machines at the back of the room, he was too aggravated to care what anyone thought of him. His co-hab, Debra, had taken their car because she had a luncheon. A luncheon! And he was stuck catching a bus home.

He had suspicions about Debra. An affair. He'd been through it before with his last co-hab. The difference was that Debra didn't go out all the time like that girl. Or at least not until today. Lunch with an old high school friend, she'd said. With Debra, it was as likely to be a girl as a guy. He couldn't say for sure which would make him madder.

He attacked life with the same vigor he used in his daily workouts, and it was time to deal with this problem.

* * *

At a ticket server, Trudy composed herself. She was mentally shaken from her appointment at the Public Medical Services Center, and out of breath from having run straight from there to the depot. She had decided to skip work for the rest of the afternoon and make arrangements to rent a hydrogen car to travel to her mother's country home for the weekend. She would still have to work tomorrow, but she would leave right after work. She needed the break. She needed time to think about what the nurse had said, about her baby having a genetic deformity, though she wouldn't tell her mother about her pregnancy situation. She stood a moment, staring at the ticket server, wishing an old wish that she'd had the type of mother that could discuss problems with her and help her make decisions. Her mother had been caring and attentive enough, but there was little depth to their relationship. Her father had been the glue of the family, the backbone and driving force. He had taught her and her brother Jimmy how to catch fish with a stick and a string, how to kill and pluck a chicken, how to hunt wild game. He had molded them with old philosophy and out-of-print history books, with an ethic of individual freedom and responsibility.

He'd taught her to be resourceful, too, and after Jimmy's death, he had given her a secret weapon. She touched her left palm. A second life.

As a mole for the Liberty League working undercover in Axyl Houston's office, there was a good chance she'd need that second identity someday.

She thought through her schedule. She could wait until tomorrow to rent the car, but then she'd be caught in the rush of Friday rentals. Better to pay the extra and avoid the crowds. After all, as a federal employee she had a hefty enough salary to splurge.

She passed her right palm over the scanner twice before it picked up her UIC, the Universal Identity Code, then waited. The server was slow today. She drummed her fingers impatiently on the side of the booth, perusing the room: first stopping on the muscle-bound guy striding to the vending machines and then closer at hand to the good-looking man with a lean physique, skin-hugging beard, and longish hair. He had something in his arm. A blanket? No, a baby. She watched perplexed as he entered a user verification code on his screen. She had a thing for numbers. Her mind worked that way—picking up numbers and cataloging them, not just IDs, but phone numbers, zip codes, addresses, whatever. She had a photographic memory that just stored such info without any effort on her part. And this guy was entering a Dominian code, she was sure.

As if alerted by her thoughts, he caught what he was doing, cleared it, and entered a local one.

A real Dominian? A transplant? An escapee?

Curiosity overwhelmed her. Top-secret information was her life's blood. She had infiltrated Senator Houston's office, at the risk of her life, for the cause of freedom. But the thrill, the rush, was discovering what was really playing out behind the scenes, the reality behind what the government media fed to the public.

Gut instinct told her this guy was from the Dome. There had to be a story there. The question wasn't whether or not she should approach him, but rather how she should go about it. And what she could gain from the encounter.

When the ticket server beeped, she responded, her fingers flying across the keys rhythmically tapping out her request. With a final pop of the entry key, she stared back at the Dominian while the machine printed her ticket.

* * *

David sighed with relief. "Two seats available," he said aloud to no one. "Due in twelve minutes."

He took his printout and turned to inspect the lobby. Two plate glass windows flooded the large waiting area with natural light. Activity thronged around the restrooms and vending machines, but the majority of the clock watchers sat in the secured plastic chairs staring at their hand-held devices, reading, watching videos, or Web surfing.

He settled in his seat, laid Frankie across his lap, pulled out his cell, and linked to his favorite news site, scanning the article subjects for something interesting, some quirky story that he could ignore but look busy with while he contemplated what to tell the council. He found what he wanted: a story about a boy growing a huge cucumber. He switched back to verbal display so that he wouldn't have to page through the prose, then settled back with Frankie resting peacefully in his arms.

As the video started, he realized that he must have pressed the wrong link. On the screen, a sleek newswoman sat behind a business desk, her husky voice exuding confidence. "UO officials stated today that records show the nation is still exceeding population limits. However, officials feel confident that the administration is dedicated to producing a balance between the productivity tax base and expenditure needs." Her voice dropped a chord at the end of the sentence, issuing an end-of-topic delineation.

He turned the system off and shook away thoughts of Gretta and what he'd been a part of in his short time there, and turned his thoughts to the Dome. No Death Panels there.

"What will you think of our home?" he asked Frankie. As he stroked the baby's arm, he thought of his daughter Bethany's unused nursery: pale peach walls and giant stuffed animals, a collection of worn out storybooks sent to the Dome general store from libraries' discard piles, and a tiny crib from generations ago made to hold a precious newborn for the first few months of life . . . months long past. Eventually, Elizabeth would have rearranged it all for the large walnut crib that was stored in the attic.

The room was probably empty now. His mother had taken his house keys when he left the Dome. She had said the time had come to take it all down, before it became a permanent shrine dedicated to their memory.

For an insane moment, he imagined returning with Frankie and putting him in Bethany's crib, staying there and carrying on with life. No rules, no regulations, no council, no government. A dream.

* * *

Anne arrived at the carpool depot in a fluster, already half an hour late for retrieving her baby. Lateness was an unforgivable sin for which Axyl continually reprimanded her. She paused inside the back parking lot door to cast a vacant glance around the crowd in the reception area and panicked with the thought of having arrived after Public Med shift change. The nurse who had called her would no longer be on duty. Her eyes rested momentarily on the lean man gazing at the tiny, bundled infant. Like him, she would soon be holding her own baby! Her adrenaline pumped, spurring her into a brisk walk out the front entrance to the Public Med crosswalk.

* * *

Jessica felt faint.

She leaned her weight into the mop in her hands and closed her eyes as she regained her equilibrium and debated what to do.

When she opened her eyes again, she focused on the food court between airport terminals B and C and lost heart. She still had those restrooms to clean. In fact, the only thing she'd really accomplished was mopping the main hallway, which admittedly was no small endeavor. A huge grid of windows, running floor to ceiling the entire length of it, provided views of airplanes arriving and departing. Gift shops and classy clothiers vied for business up and down the corridor, while a fancy bar welcomed weary travelers at the front lobby. Several elegant restaurants provided comforts for the luxury customer. A giant screen tuned to the government network held some viewers' attention in the food courts, but the ten new virtual reality graphic booths in Graphics Mania claimed more money than the vendors.

All this food and activity eventually resulted in travelers searching for restrooms. They weren't hard to find. There were twenty-two of them. And Jessica Main was the unfortunate soul designated to clean them. Every day. And today was worse than usual.

She rubbed her forehead. The dizziness was most likely mental, a side effect of having overheard Debra and Anne's conversation at lunch, but the throbbing felt real nonetheless. She really couldn't stand either woman, and wished . . . no sense wishing. The past couldn't be changed.

She thought of the fortune-cookie prophecy she had taped to her cell phone: *You will do something brave and wonderful, and that will change your life and lead to something profound.* She didn't believe in fortunes, but she kept it anyway, always a glimmer of hope that something would change but thought perhaps she'd jinxed herself because she'd done something cowardly instead. She'd chosen the wrong door, taken the wrong path, and would forever be bound to this disgusting job with nothing and no one in her future.

She just wanted to go home, crawl into bed, and have a good cry.

She decided to finish the airport's main-gate bathrooms, then find her supervisor and beg to leave early. She hoped Clara at the International counter would page the boss lady and save her a thirty-minute search.

Erecting the "Temporarily Closed" sign, she propped the men's door open and heaved the heavy bucket and mop ahead of her.

What could she possibly do that was brave?

* * *

Axyl spoke abruptly into his cell phone. "Norman? Where's Trudy? Oh. Yes, she did mention a PMS appointment today. Fine. Leave her a message. I need info on that local ad campaign for the bill. Tell her to have it ready and on my desk. I want it plugged by midweek. And tell her to cancel my Monday meetings. I have a meeting with Bonita Gonzales I can't miss."

He ended the call and dialed the secretary to the Minister of World Peace. "Houston here. I have a plan. I need to present it at the next meeting. Schedule a slot for me."

* * *

Anne stood rather meekly at the information desk in the PMS Good Life Maternity ward, waiting for the heavy-set receptionist to complete a call. The PMS unit was busier than ever. Or at least all the help seemed busy. A big-boned woman in a dark suit walked past with an air of authority, accompanied by a dour, overweight med. Two nurses chatted nonstop as they passed an assistant pushing a gurney, and an inspector in a bright yellow pullover suit reached past her to retrieve a scanner from the receptionist's desk. The waiting area buzzed with conversation over the drone of compupanels. All the noise was somewhat hushed, but irritating, like the awful semi-partitioned offices she used to work in after college.

A huge blond receptionist with a bulldog face and a voice to match finally turned to Anne. "May I help you?"

Anne made every attempt to keep disgust from showing on her face. She resented fat people. She couldn't understand why they couldn't follow the Healthcare Fitness for Life recommendations. They were an embarrassment to the nation. "Senator Houston and I have a baby being delivered here by surrogate today," she proclaimed with her chin jutted out, knowing while she said it that Axyl would have her head for flaunting it here in the hospital over a kid he didn't want, but she deserved special treatment—like a personal escort or something—not to be left standing here like some ordinary citizen. "I'm here to pick him up."

The bulldog's voice was bland, almost yawning. "Surrogate birth? Left wing, main nurses' station. You'll need your ID and contract." She dismissed Anne by picking up the ringing phone.

Anne drew herself up and turned away. Following the designated hall, she approached a skinny little redhead with a face full of freckles who greeted her with a smile of small perfect teeth. "Hello. Can I help you, ma'am?"

The hall was quiet. Anne felt much more in control. "I received a call saying my surrogate was delivering today."

"Wonderful!"

The nurse's happy mood was contagious. Anne relaxed and smiled.

"First I'll pull up your record, get the paperwork done, and then I'll introduce you to your baby and we'll have a little feeding and bathing lesson, just to make sure you're comfortable before you head home together." Everything in her voice said *I'm so lucky to have this fun job.* "What is your name, ma'am?"

"Anne Shelton."

"Oh! You're listed right here. The senator's partner. Nice to meet you. Your surrogate arrived at 9:15, Dr. Kim Lui on duty. I don't seem to have any birth details down here, though. I suppose there is a chance she hasn't delivered yet, but Dr. Lui left an hour ago. Let me see if I can locate the replacement med."

She made four calls, each one sending her to another extension.

"It seems that Dr. Markus Holmes took over, but he can't be reached at the moment. Hmm."

A blond walked up, searching the lower counter for a pen.

"Judy, do you know when Dr. Holmes will be back?"

"No, why?"

"This is Anne Shelton. She is supposed to be picking up her baby, a surrogate delivery today, and I have no doctor available for the contract."

"Who was the surrogate?"

"Sola Myers," interjected Anne. She was leaning across the upper counter as if she could find the answer at the nurse's fingertips. She hated disorganization.

Judy paged through a screen of names.

"No. Back up," Dolly said. "I already found her on there, Judy. There's no data about the baby."

"Oh." Judy smirked. "I bet I know which case it is. Come with me, Ms. Shelton."

Anne was ushered into a conference room and offered a plush chair at a heavy wood-laminate table. Left alone, growing more anxious with each passing moment, she couldn't sit still. She got up and paced, trying to think what Axyl would tell her to do. She had no patience for waiting around when action needed to be taken. The nursery. She had filled out the birth certificate as Frank Shelton. If he had been delivered, he would be in the nursery.

She set off through the maze of halls in search of the nursery but came instead upon another nurses' station, smaller than the first, with the same blond nurse propped on a desk talking earnestly to an older woman with a badge that stated "Head Nurse."

Anne stepped back around the corner, out of sight.

"I'm sure that's the one she's looking for, but the file hasn't processed."

"Dr. Lui doesn't usually leave loose ends."

"She was off duty by then. Dr. Holmes was handling it. He saw me in the hall and said it was a dump, but he never sent the data up."

A perky brunette arrived, tapping the top of her datascanner in a rhythmic beat until she reached the desk and parked it back in the charging cradle. "What's up?"

The head nurse frowned in annoyance. "Rita, did Dr. Holmes give you some data on a dump earlier today?"

"No. He said he had a meeting with Rod McIntyre in the Gift Center, but that he'd be back in a few minutes. That was around 1:30 or so."

"Let me go get this straightened out."

Rita scowled behind her departing figure. "She thinks she's so tough."

"She's just tired. So am I. I didn't need this hassle," said Judy. "This day's gotten too real. I need a Liberty pill to calm my nerves."

Anne was still standing in the shadows, listening, trying to piece it together.

Rita reached into her pocket, snapped open a small case, and passed a small pink tablet to Judy. "What's happened?"

"We've lost a baby. Dr. Holmes was supposed to have delivered it and dumped it," Judy explained, talking around the tablet melting in her mouth.

Anne shuddered. What was dumping? It couldn't be good. She wanted to scream but held herself in check, tensing at every word.

"I bet Markus didn't dump it."

"Why do you say that?" asked Judy.

"He never does unless you force him. He's such a sop. One of those mild, sensitive types from the twentieth century. I don't know how women found that attractive."

Judy could guess Rita had tried to seduce Markus. "Well, someone did. He's married. Real old-time married in a church and everything."

"Yeah," Rita said. "But his wife doesn't like him any more than I do. I see her at the gym all the time. The truth is, Markus won't agree to a divorce. He said they vowed marriage and he planned to stand by it. Like the vows were really for life. Can you believe it? His wife said the problem is they waited too long."

Judy nodded, mellowed by the pill. She knew people who had lost everything they owned to the divorce tax. The Freedom of Legalized Living Act had initiated legal tax breaks for couples living together without marital ties. It required a contract for disposition of possessions and finances upon termination of the co-habitation arrangements, like prenuptial agreements, except they were required by law and untouchable. Fines were imposed on couples who chose traditional marriage and later divorced, based on the theory that family courts were a drain on public funds. But a last-minute amendment had allowed two years' leeway from the date of the bill to transfer traditional marriage vows to co-habitation without penalty. After that time, divorce would mean the government took practically all possessions, and also control of minor children. In effect, it had abolished marriage. Who in their right mind would enter a "forever-binding" contract with the possibility of losing everything to the Divorce Tax? Co-habitation, a kind of open-ended civil union, was the only sensible solution.

She enjoyed her partner, but nothing was forever. "I think Markus might be Christian, you know? I can't imagine any other reason to actually marry someone and be tied to them permanently."

Rita shook her head. "I don't think so. Just a romantic. I told you—a sop." She chuckled. "And she's cheating on him, but he doesn't know it."

"Really?"

"Older guy, rich I hear."

Judy slumped, her tension eased now. "Well it doesn't matter; it doesn't help me with this baby mess. Are you sure you didn't see him dump it?"

"No. Like I said, he told me he had some records to take care of in the Gift Center, and that was the last I saw of him. Besides, I told you, he always gets someone else to do it."

Judy perked up. "Come to think of it, I did see someone else with him. A thin guy with kind of long hair and a beard. A new med." She slumped again. "But I don't know who he was."

"I didn't know we had a new med. I haven't met him. Hey, I know. You could go look through the bin. They're tagged."

"Are you crazy?"

Rita took a nail file from the drawer. "That bin isn't so bad. Most of them were cleaned up first and they're whole, not pieces like the in-vitros."

Judy shook her head. Even sedated, the idea of deformed infant bodies made her skin crawl.

"Maybe Travis will do it. He'll have to ship them out this evening anyway. Write down the surrogate and the parents' names."

Judy grabbed a notepad and wrote down the info off her device.

"Okay. Go back to your nursery of screaming babies, and I'll call if he finds it."

"I left Ms. Shelton in the conference room. Tell Ms. Burke when she comes back."

Anne slouched against the wall out of sight, limp, near to fainting.

* * *

The airport van was crowded three to a bench, which would normally bother Trudy, but not this time; she'd ended up on the same airport van as the man who'd entered the Dominion code into the ticket server. After making introductions, she decided she had to find out what he was up to, but that meant choosing her words carefully to get him to reveal something of importance. "That's a different accent you have there. You must be from out of town."

David didn't think he had an accent. He smiled at the young professional woman, even though inside he quivered with paranoia. "I am."

"Whereabouts?"

"Michigan." He turned to look out the window, hoping to stymie further conversation. He could lose her once they got to the airport.

"Really?" That fit. "Have you ever been to the Cloistered Dominion? I've always been curious about it."

David was prepared. "Actually, yes. I lived there when I was a kid."

Trudy thought a moment, then decided he was being honest. He had a face that couldn't lie. Still, something about him didn't click. She clutched at the small purse concealing a snub-nosed .38 caliber revolver—very illegal but comforting to possess. "Did you like it? Living there?"

He shrugged. "Sure."

She hoped he would elaborate, but he didn't, so she pushed a bit more. "You must have been there quite a while, since you started to use a Dominion code."

He didn't even blink. "Old habit. You in government?"

She laughed. "Who isn't?"

He nodded agreement, noticing she was elusive as well. He kept a calm smile plastered to his face, hoping that was the end of it, but she didn't give up.

"Is it similar there to things out here? Or really different?"

"Different. No real connection to things outside. There's a wall around it, you know. Media restricted. Nothing gets updated, really. But you get a good education there. And there's very little crime." He thought about what else he could say. "Families are large. Goods are scarce."

"Why did you leave?" She knew that leaving the Dome meant renouncing Christianity and accepting a probationary citizenship in the outer states, but she'd never met anyone who'd done it.

He hadn't anticipated that question, though he realized he should have. He took a deep breath. "My family died." He ended it there, turning back to the window so she wouldn't ask him anything else.

* * *

Packing her restroom cleaning supplies back into the storage room, Jessica stood hesitating over whether to keep her airport overalls on until after speaking with her boss or to drop them in the laundry chute. With an inexplicable sense of urgency, she kept them on, slammed the door of the storage room, and hurried toward the airline reservation counter where she could page her boss.

She practically jogged down the hallway only to find she had to wait while five people were registered. A calm descended on her as suddenly as the urgency to get there had.

She leaned on the counter and watched Clara work through the customers.

In the distance, something caught her eye. A lean man pausing just inside the entrance with a bundle of blankets in his arms.

A baby?

That wasn't so unusual. They saw plenty of babies. But it was the man who drew her attention. The way he walked. The way he carried himself. And the way he carried the baby with such attentiveness, peeking at him, talking to him. So sweet.

* * *

David stood still and scanned the airport crowd, trying to decide what to do.

He spotted three cameras and lifted little Frankie up to his shoulder. A kiss on the newborn cheek. Soft pat, pat, pat on the tiny back. Easy steps. Not too fast. Move through the crowd, down the busy corridor to the reservation desk.

A short, plumpish girl in an airport uniform leaned wearily against the counter. Her face, resting on her arms on the counter, was round and soft with more true color in her cheeks than was fashionable. Her half-closed eyes were rimmed with thick brown lashes. She looked nothing like his dear departed Elizabeth, who had been a willow, a ballet dancer dancing through his life, and yet there was the same immediate warmth about this woman. But sadness, too. She needed comforting more than him.

Feeling his eyes on her, Jessica lifted her head to return the stare. She didn't trust men, as a rule. Not after her heartache in high school, followed by the guy who stole her savings, and another guy failing to comply with the co-hab laws by taking most of their belongings because he knew she had no resources to fight him. But mostly it was about her father. It always went back to her father and the rejection from him when she needed him most. No, she didn't want anything to do with men.

Nevertheless, this fellow was smiling, not smirking or calculating or devouring. Just smiling and bouncing his tiny bundle. She glanced at the group still waiting for Clara, and decided to ask if she could take a peek. For sure, he wouldn't interpret that as a come-on.

She produced a wan smile. "May I see your baby?"

He hesitated, wondering if she would know about Down syndrome. "Sure."

"Oh, he's beautiful. It is a boy, isn't it?"

"Yes. Frankie."

"He's oriental, isn't he? How adorable."

David was relieved. The Down's features would look slightly oriental to an uneducated onlooker. "Yes. From a donor, you know."

She bristled. "Right. Hmm. There's a way for anyone with money."

"Do you have any kids?"

She had practiced admitting it. "Yes. Mine was a little boy, too. But he died."

"I'm sorry."

"Me too."

Clara, her face set in a serious knot of concentration, cut in. "Can I help you, sir?"

He handed her his form.

"Boarding is scheduled for 3:20."

He glanced at his vintage Rolex, not only an antique but by modern standards obsolete. No one wore watches anymore. But he had inherited it from his grandfather and refused to give it up. It was his lucky charm. "Exactly thirty minutes."

"Yes, sir. Have a pleasant flight."

"Thank you. Could you tell me how to get to a store that might sell baby supplies?"

Jessica spoke up. "Oh, I'll show you." She turned to the reservation clerk. "I'll be back in a bit, Clara. I'll need you to page Ms. Jones for me."

Clara nodded and turned to the next customer.

"Come on, sir. I'll show you where it is."

David tensed as she led him down the airport corridor. On an ordinary day, it might be a pleasant walk, seeing fancy shops and restaurants, but his nerves stood on edge expecting to be stopped any minute. For sure an alarm had been raised by now. That woman in the van . . .

They arrived at the airport pharmacy.

"What do you need?"

"Everything." *Think fast.* "They wouldn't let me bring his bag through."

"Figures. You'll need what . . . three or four bottles of formula? And a bag of these disposable diapers. Don't get caught dropping them into a regular crushing bin or they'll fine you. Most restrooms have the diaper bins. And you'll need a pacifier, too. *Umph,* we're getting quite a load here. How about a baby tote bag or a knapsack or something?"

David, grinning at her enthusiasm, picked up a navy duffle bag, and added a cherry red shirt with the Unified Order emblem woven into the airport symbol.

He smiled at Jessica. "A souvenir."

The round-bellied cashier reluctantly put down his car magazine and scanned the purchases.

David shoved the items into the new duffle bag Jessica held open and handed the man his magnetic strip card. The cashier looked at David's raised palm and ran the card through. "Pain using a card, huh?"

David nodded, tense, waiting to see if this time there would be a problem, if this time they would catch him. So far, what his brother-in-law predicted had been correct—so many chips failed that no one would question it.

The cashier looked at the card and selected Verification of Substitute Cards on the system and stood there tapping the card on the counter, waiting.

The computer added his transaction to the required 90-day memory file: a false name and false address attached to the items purchased.

David heaved the bag to his shoulder and turned to go.

"*Amigo,*" the man said.

David stopped. His spine tingled as he turned back to face him.

"You get a free UV hat. You know, for spending so much." He shrugged toward a sign and tucked a blue and red airport hat into the bag.

Relief splashed over him. "Thanks."

Jessica pulled at the bag. "I'll help you carry it back to the terminal, if you like. I have to go back anyway, to page my boss."

"Why don't you carry Frankie, and I'll take the bag."

Jessica was thrilled. She carried Frankie like a crystal ornament.

As they were approaching the waiting area, Trudy spotted him.

David whispered, "Follow my lead."

"Hello, Rex. We meet again."

"Hello, Trudy. This is . . ." he hesitated an imperceptible moment, "my wife, Jessica." He hoped she would go along with him on the ploy.

In answer, she grinned and laid a hand on his arm.

Trudy didn't question the possibility but wondered if he meant it literally. "As in actually married?"

David hadn't considered the outer states' civil unions, but he had an easy comeback. "As I explained . . ."

He was interrupted by the sound of ringing, coming from Jessica's front pocket.

"Sorry." Jessica blushed, thrust her hand into her pocket, and silenced the ring. "Whoever it is, they can wait."

"Like I said," David continued, "I was brought up in the Dome. Some old teachings are hard to shake."

Trudy nodded. "I understand." She gave Jessica the once-over. Then she calmly slipped her own cell from her purse as if she'd felt it vibrate, looked at it as if she were checking a call, and selected *BumpScan*, an old hacker's application for retrieving data from other phones. Illegal, of course, but Senator Houston thought it useful for her to have it. "Well, best of luck to you both. That's my flight they're announcing," she lied, and handed him a business card. "If you ever need a connection with the senator, give me a call." She had never offered that line before, ever. The thought of him being a Dominian intrigued her. The Dome went against everything Axyl stood for; the Christians and the Liberty League didn't see eye to eye on religion, but they both wanted freedom. She definitely wanted this Dominian to remember her name.

As she moved past them, she pretended to stumble slightly, brushing her phone against Jessica's pocket.

David stuck the card into the bag without looking at it, without seeing *The Office of Senator Axyl Houston* in bold italics under Trudy's name. All he wanted was to get on a flight, to get Frankie to safety.

Jessica settled into a chair, not bothering to mention that she was an old high school friend of the senator's co-hab. Name-dropping meant nothing to her. What she wanted to tell this man was how much she wished that she really was his wife. She didn't even wonder why he had lied to that tall, pretty woman. All men lied. But the thought of being someone's wife was still wonderful. She could imagine marriage without actually attaching a man to it, as if marriage could be like one of the old videos she constantly replayed: having a family, cooking suppers with fancy cakes for dessert, and kids hollering over the graphic booth as it buzzed with weird 3-D programs. Of course, most women had that without a husband, but the thought of being called a wife added a warm glow to it all.

She nuzzled the softness of Frankie's cheek. "I wish he was mine."

For a split second, David thought of just telling her to take him. What an easy fix that would be. But he didn't *really* know this woman. Would Frankie be safe with her? Would she call an alarm against both of them?

David couldn't risk it. He scooped the sleeping boy into his big hands. "Maybe you'll have another one someday."

"No." She said it quietly, all color draining from her face as she forced the words from the dark abyss of her mind. "I can't have any more."

They let the awkward pause pass. "Look," he said somberly, "I'm sorry about lying to that woman back there, but I lost my wife and daughter and I just don't like explaining it to people."

Jessica absorbed this statement: his honesty, his integrity, his emotional distress. And his availability. "Oh, I didn't mind. I mean, I'm sorry about your wife and daughter and all. Really."

"Thank you for helping me, Jessica."

"You're welcome. Thanks for letting me hold him."

She stepped up, kissed Frankie, then ambled away.

David felt very alone.

* * *

Anne held on to the hospital wall for support, her whole body shaking with anxiety. Should she go back to the conference room? Or should she find the nursery? She took three deep breaths. She was an independent woman, wasn't she? She could handle this situation.

A muscular man in blue scrubs stepped up to the nurse's station. "Hey there, Rita. What you be doin' me for?"

"You didn't have to come up here. I just wanted you to call me."

"That's okay. I be over this way anyhow. What you need?"

"I've got a dump we can't find any paperwork for. Could you go ahead and empty the dumping bin now and see if it's there for me?"

"Sure, Rita." His eyes gleamed. "I always did think of you. You want to talk with me later?"

Rita knew precisely what he meant. "I don't know. I got me a co-hab last week. But maybe. I'll have to see how I feel at quitting time."

"Okay." He took the paper. "I come back at ya."

Anne, hidden from view, let him amble half way down the hall before straightening her shoulders to walk purposefully behind him. Around the corner, out of sight of the nurses' station, she slowed as the man entered the dumping room. The door didn't quite shut tight behind him. She leaned back against the wall, giving herself a few minutes to summon the courage to enter. Having made up her mind, she noiselessly pushed open the door and stepped into the room.

A tiny body hung upside down, unnaturally stiff and pale, its right leg totally engulfed in the clasp of the man's fingers. Wisps of red hair dangled and lifeless blue eyes stared out at the upside down room. The lips were black with death. *Her* lips. *Her* hair. Nothing disguised the sex of the rejected infant girl. The man was reading the tag tied to the left foot.

Anne screamed.

The miniature corpse was thrust into the waiting bag as the man spun around.

"What you doing here?"

"Oh no. No. No!" She was in the bin before she could think about it, peering at the pile of discarded bodies, the cold stench of the refrigerated remains enveloping her. She touched one, a boy without arms, wanting to move him to see the one beneath, hoping to find Frank alive.

"You can't be getting in there. Now you go on out afore you get your clothes nasty."

"My baby. My baby can't be here." She backed out of the bin, sobbing, until she was looking him straight in the face, panicking. "What are you doing here? What is this—these babies? You've killed them."

"They was already dead." He took her by the arm. "You got to go. Go talk to Rita."

Her feet were cemented in place.

He dropped the half-full plastic bag and propelled her out the door and back down the hall to the nurses' station.

"This lady followed me into the bin. Think she never seen nobody dead afore."

Anne was coming to her senses. "Stuffing babies into bags like garbage. Just wait until I tell the senator what that man was doing. Do you know who I am? I'm Axyl Houston's co-hab. I will tell him. I'm going to call him right now! The Feds will be in here by morning."

"Calm down, ma'am." Rita eased her into a chair and shooed the technician away. "It's just the dumping bin. Everybody knows about it. The BMR, uh . . . Bio-Med Recyclers, come every week to pick up."

"You can't get away with this! Someone is going to be told you're killing babies."

Rita shrugged. "They already know. There was something wrong with them."

Anne sat, dazed. The vision of the lifeless pinched face and wisps of red hair immobilized her. So unreal. Of course she knew that deformed infants, if they somehow weren't successfully terminated before birth, must be eliminated for the good of the nation. It only made sense to eradicate a health problem immediately if it couldn't be fixed—some things still couldn't be fixed. No one would want to be abnormal. And more importantly, who would want to raise an abnormal child? She knew it was the right thing to do.

She'd just never envisioned what it meant. To actually see the cold naked bodies . . .

She shook her head, and forced relief to drive away the horror: *Frank could not be in there.* She knew he was perfect. The tests said so.

Her chest heaved. "Where is *my* baby? You incompetent people. Find him. Now!"

"Ma'am, I think you better talk to the head nurse. Let me find her."

"I've done enough waiting. You tell me where my baby could possibly be. Where's the nursery?"

The man, hovering a few yards away, waved at Rita. "I tell you if I see it."

Anne stiffened. "He won't be there. He is healthy. Normal. Check his records. Don't you have them? Where's the surrogate?"

Rita groaned as she poked at her keyboard. "The surrogate is in recovery. It's definitely the right surrogate, see? Guardian: Shelton, Anne. Co-hab: Houston, Axyl. Restrictive rights."

Confidence and authority rose in Anne at the mention of Axyl's name. Demanding action and getting a response empowered her like a drug. She heard herself imitate Axyl's tone: "Okay. So he's been delivered. Where could he be?"

Judy reappeared, catching her breath at the sight of Anne.

Rita tried to sound helpful. "Maybe the donor . . . I mean, the *Gift* Center? Really, though, you need to wait for the head nurse."

"How do I get to there?"

Judy pointed. "It's beside the children's hospital. Down that hall, to the right, through the quad. But it won't do you much good. They'll deny he's in there."

Rita scowled at Judy.

"Why would they deny it?" Anne asked.

Judy stepped back. "Oh, I don't know. Maybe they'll find him." She picked up a scanner and left.

"Print out his record. I'm taking a copy with me."

* * *

David shoved the diapers and formula into the new carry-on bag and prepared a bottle. Frankie was having a hard time sucking on it and had only swallowed a few mouthfuls. Time to worry about that later. *Three twelve.* He had to get to the boarding gate. He tucked the baby bottle into the corner of the bag and headed down the airport corridor.

* * *

At Public Medical Services, the Administrator shook her head at the Head Nurse, grabbed the phone, and punched zero. "Give me security." She had a gruff voice and body to match, much more of an Al than an Allison.

Markus stood hunched in the corner of her office. The Administrator had ripped into him the moment he returned from Social Services. Pieces had already been linked together by Rita, Judy, and the Head Nurse, pointing Allison Gatryl's finger directly at him. "Gatryl here," she barked into the phone like a tough cop. "We have a code 207. Male, newborn. Last seen with a civilian posing as a med. Roughly six foot, 170 pounds, brown hair, moustache, close beard. He's probably left the premises. Send two guards out to the depot and two out to the parking deck." The voice on the other end uttered a mumbled statement that Markus couldn't make out, but he heard the Administrator's response clear enough. "No! You better find him before the public hears about it. Report to me in my office at four o'clock."

She slammed the phone down.

"Okay. That takes care of finding the perpetrator and the dump. Now, where did Ms. Shelton go?"

Judy half hid behind the wide white expanse of the head nurse. "To look for the baby."

"Where?"

"The Gift of Life Center," replied Rita.

"Who sent her there? You idiots! What does she look like?"

Rita held out a paper. "I have her record."

"Markus, I expect a full report on your part in this. Ms. Topler, check with Travis when he's done with the bin write-up. Okay, Rita, let's go."

Markus gazed after them, cuss words streaming from his lips before he turned heel and headed to his office. Somehow he had to warn his friend.

* * *

David paused at the reservation desk and looked up at the listings. Flight 443 delayed. Departure time: 3:45. The big wall clock said 3:14. He decided to take a chance and change Frankie's diaper before boarding. The restrooms were just across the hall.

* * *

When Markus reached his cubicle, he dropped the man-handled file onto the shiny gray plastic desktop. A mug of pens and a neat stack of folders filled one corner. He frowned, thinking of his father, wishing he had the nerve to take the picture out of the bottom drawer, to look into his father's long-dead eyes, and admit that he again lacked the courage to do the right thing, to take responsibility himself for saving the baby. But he could at least warn the guy that the officials were on his trail. Things could go bad for the guy if he was caught. Unfortunately, they hadn't exchanged numbers. He had no way to reach him.

His keyboard and monitor stood in the opposite corner. He flicked the screen on.

Terminal update . . . please wait.

Terminal! That was it! He was headed to the airport ter-minal. Markus glanced at the clock. Three sixteen. He grabbed the phone with one hand and tapped at the selections. No one knew he was headed for the Dome. They were only looking as far as the depot. And they didn't know his name was Rex, only that an outsider had snatched the baby. "Ah, there it is." He tapped the listing and worked his way through several menus before reaching a real person. "Airport information? This is an emergency. I need to page someone . . . Rex Montane."

"I'm sorry sir, but I can't page an individual."

"It's an emergency."

"Perhaps you can reach him on his cell."

"*Perhaps* I don't *know* his cell."

"I'm sorry, sir."

"Look, I'm from Public Medical Services and I'm telling you this is an emergency . . ."

The tone became suddenly obsequious. "Oh, I'm sorry, sir. Give me the name again . . ."

"Rex Montane."

"Please hold."

Markus plucked a pen from the Grouchy Morning mug and doodled nervously on a notepad.

* * *

David half-peeked under the stalls before pulling down the change table and carefully unwrapping the sleeping infant. Frankie's arms shook as he woke and wailed. "It's okay, my little Frankie. We're going on a trip. You need a diaper. Hush now, little guy. It's okay."

The intercom in the corridor crackled. "Rex Montane, please call the information desk. Rex Montane please call the information desk."

David strained to hear over the crying but glanced at his watch and relaxed. "Three twenty-one. Can't be our flight yet."

He swaddled Frankie again, then looked wistfully at the urinals but couldn't decide how to manage it. Hefting the bag over his shoulder, he scooped Frankie up and headed back out to his gate.

"Flight 443 boarding at gate 16."

"Just in time, Frankie. Just in time."

The intercom drawled on, "Flight 502, arriving at gate 28 . . ."

* * *

Markus stared at the clock. Three twenty-two. "Where is he?" His computer monitor cleared. He tossed his pen across the desk and tapped in Anne Shelton's name. The server was bogged down. It took a good sixty seconds for her record to load.

The airport information clerk came back on the line. "Sir, there is no answer to the page."

"Can you try again? It's urgent."

"Well, they're announcing flight data right now, but I'll try once more when they're done."

"Thanks. I'll hold."

* * *

David stepped through the gate to the boarding ramp. A man and woman caught the door, then let it shut behind them with a muffled thud.

"Will Mr. Rex Montane please call the information desk."

The door opened again, admitting two giggling girls with a grandmother. The intercom voice entered with them. "Mr. Rex Montane. Your party is still holding. Thank you."

David faltered, half-hearing the name. The couple squeezed by him single file. Maybe he should check before getting on. But only Markus knew . . .

* * *

"There's no answer, sir."

"Thanks for trying." Markus hung up the phone and continued to read the file. "Crap. Axyl Houston. Did I ever choose one."

A skinny med with dreadlocks detoured around Markus's cubicle. "What's up?"

Markus looked up. Luke was one of the few guys at the center that he liked. They knew without saying so that they shared the same view on the whole dumping business because they both avoided those cases. He'd seen Luke clock out and leave when he saw a case come up. But that didn't mean Luke would help him out. "Axyl Houston," Markus said, as if it were an explanation.

"The senator. What about him?"

Markus wasn't into secrets. The more news he made of it, the less of a burden it would be in his mind. "His kid just got stolen."

"Seriously?"

"Yeah. Guy posed as a med and took off with it."

"Wow. Tough break. The cops in on it?"

"Not yet. But they will be. Wow. I wonder if the Alligator knows who she's dealing with."

The younger med grinned. Only Markus dared call her the Alligator. "Huh. I hear the senator's a hard rod, but you know Ms. Gatryl. Nothing scares her." He chuckled and moved down to his own gray cubicle.

Markus tapped his pen on the desk, thinking things through, then continued to read.

* * *

A security guard, anxious to relay his findings to the Administrator, reached over the depot counter and grabbed the phone. "Ms. Gatryl, we located his reservation entry. Rex Montane left the depot at 2:35, headed to the airport. Not doing much to hide his tracks. He must be pretty stupid."

"Have you notified airport security?"

"Yes, ma'am. They were notified at three-twenty. You should be getting a report from them anytime."

Allison grabbed a notepad and began to scrawl. She would need a press statement ready.

* * *

Anne stood outside the Gift of Life Center debating what to do. She normally wasn't a person who made demands. She never questioned authority. But the previous hours had brought her new vision—as the senator's co-hab, she *was* authority. These people should be serving *her*!

She wavered as to which entrance to use.

As she watched a med scan his ID to enter the back entrance, she went with her gut, grabbed the door before it clicked shut, and stepped into a long, polished hallway lined with office doors on one side, and wide swinging doors emblazoned with "Laboratory Transfers" to her left. She took a few hesitant steps down the hall and opened an unlabelled door on her right.

The man peered over his glasses at her. "May I help you?"

"Oh. No, excuse me."

She closed the door and went back to the laboratory transfer doors. She pushed one open just enough to peek through. Several gurneys, neatly made up, lined one side. Glass medicine cabinets and a vacated counter lay beyond. Bright lights illuminated a far corner through the glass window of an

operating room. Voices drifted from behind a curtained parti-
tion, but no one stood in the main room, and the end of the
room receded into a hall.

Anne strode through the room, her feet arched onto tip-
toes to keep her heels from clicking against the linoleum. She
could feel hives breaking out across her back and thighs.

Heavy steps moved across the room. "Who are you?"

Anne twisted around. She wanted to demand information. Instead she withered. "I was sent over for some records."

The man glowered at her. "How did you get in? You can't
come through here. Take the next hallway and follow it to the
front entrance."

Anne let her heels flop to the floor and tapped her way
across the room. Beyond the door lay a hall of hospital rooms
and a busy nurses' station. She debated. It would take forever
to check every room. And how could she find an infant she
had never seen?

Squaring her shoulders, she stepped up to the counter.
"Excuse me. This is an emergency. An infant was sent here by
mistake. He must be located immediately."

Black eyes in a dark face full of intelligence and control
turned to survey her, annoyance flaring over the interruption.
"Says who?"

Anne knew at a glance that she had to use a name this
lady would respect. "Doctor Kim Lui."

The black eyes stared through her a moment, then
relented and turned to the computer system. "What's the
number?"

"Number?"

The nurse's resentment went into every staccato syllable. "The patient number. I don't call them by name."

"He wasn't assigned a number yet. He would have just been admitted during the past hour or so."

"You're in the wrong place. New admits are down the hall and to the left." With that, she turned her back on Anne.

Anne hurried down the hall. Halfway, she stopped as the unmistakable sound of a child's scream tore through her body.

* * *

Trudy was still waiting for her rental car when she heard the page for Rex Montane.

A security guard looked up from his post by baggage check, cocked his head as if to hear better, then grabbed the reservationist's phone and punched a button. Trudy stood up and moved to the counter, feigning interest in a pamphlet about the airline.

The guard chomped on a wad of gum as he waited for an answer, then pushed it to the side of his cheek with his tongue. "Hey. Polaski here. We're looking for that guy you just paged. Who paged him?"

Trudy couldn't hear the response.

"I can't believe you didn't ask. Don't you have procedures? What did he look like? . . . No visual? You people are pathetic. Follow up on the system and see where he called from. And page me immediately when you have some answers."

He dialed another number. "Polaski here. That Montane guy was just paged, but Mike doesn't know who wanted him. He's doing a check now. I'll get back to you."

The reservation clerk stepped up. "May I help you, ma'am?"

Trudy pulled out her ticket. "Can you tell me how much I'll need in tolls?"

The clerk studied the ticket. Trudy studied the guard. Polaski, badge number 55643. She tapped the info into her cell.

"You've rented a hydrogen car. No pollution tolls at the booths, and the highway tax is included in your charges right here."

"Okay. Thanks. Is it almost ready?"

"Let me check."

The guard had returned to the baggage check, examining each tag as the luggage passed through.

"One of the drivers is bringing it up to the loading dock, just through that door. Will you need help with luggage?"

"No, thank you." She smiled her best political smile and took the ticket back. With one more look at the security guard, she headed out the door.

As she slid behind the wheel, she patted the sleek upholstery, glad she had splurged. Not many people could afford to rent a hydrogen car, but working for the senator definitely had its perks.

Her mind remained occupied with the mystery of the Dominian. Despite his explanation, she had no doubt he was still a Dominian, especially now knowing officials were searching for him. She wondered what had happened to his family—if that part of his story was true—but whatever had happened, she felt sure he was outside the Dome illegally.

He could be exactly what the Liberty League needed—someone to act as a liaison with the Christian underground, to unite the two in a plan to restore liberty to the nation. Both factions had been collecting data for years, working themselves into positions of power as quietly and unobtrusively as possible, aware but mutually suspicious of each other. Now they needed to work together to take things to the next level.

She couldn't jump the gun, though. First, she intended to find out who he really was and what he was up to.

She pulled out her cell phone and hit a speed dial number. If Marty Young didn't already know what was up, he'd find out. Ferreting out the truth of what was going on behind any given news story was his baby. "Hey, Marty. Under the radar, here: What's the word about a guy named Rex Montane? Is he running from something?"

His voice sounded much deeper over the phone. No one would ever suspect he was a scrawny 16-year-old kid. "Just got a flag about that. Some disturbance at the medical center."

"Stay on it and get back to me." She hung up and revved up the car. Gas-fueled cars weren't allowed within city limits, but with a hydrogen car, detouring back to the office first wouldn't be a problem. She could look the info up on her cell, but the senator's system could access much more information. Something was going on with that Dominian and she intended to figure out what it was. Marty might get the truth of the news story, but she wanted the truth about the man.

*   *   *

David let the girls and grandmother pass, then sidled past the oncoming passengers, back to the waiting area. A security guard was waving toward the door, hurriedly explaining something to the ticket clerk. ". . . a guy alone with a baby. Rex Montane. He's wanted for kidnapping."

They were on to him. David ducked into the restroom.

He shuffled through the contents of his duffle bag, pulled out the freebie airport hat, and tucked his hair up into it. Then he pulled half the diapers out and stacked them by the diaper changing station. Very gently, he laid Frankie in the bag and zipped it half-closed—the tube of thick white diaper cream caught the zipper. Grinning, David pulled it out and smeared it across his nose and cheeks like the thick sunscreen he'd seen on others. He slid the tube under Frankie, then zipped the bag closed again, all but two inches.

* * *

Holding Anne's file, Markus shook his head and muttered, "What have I got myself into?"

The phone rang.

"Hello."

"Markus, is that you? Turn on the visual."

He flipped the switch. "Yes, Ms. Gatryl?"

"These nurses say this Rex Montane fellow has brown eyes. Are you sure they were blue?"

"Yes, ma'am. I talked to him for quite a while. Pretty sure they were blue," he lied.

"You looked right at his eyes, did you?"

"Yes, ma'am, I did." Markus held himself in check, trying to sound sincere. "Good-looking fella. Hard to take my eyes off him."

Allison hung up on him, and the phone buzzed again. "Dr. Holmes, we need you in delivery. Stat."

"Get Luke," he replied. "I'm going home."

* * *

Anne stood transfixed in the Gift of Life hallway, bound by the wailing and unable to move her body, unable to proceed around the corner. A nurse whirled past her with a tray of injections and entered the room. Again a high-pitched scream filled the air, and then silence.

Anne fairly collapsed with relief.

Two nurses emerged, one holding a bag of fetid greenish-black bile, her nose wrinkled in disgust.

"Next time, don't let the morphine drip run out. I won't stand for screaming."

"I'm sorry. But why don't they just declare him used up. He has hardly any functions left. What else can they get from him?"

"It's his blood type and crossbred genetic structure. He is one of those genetically altered kids who are supposed to never get sick; that's why his limbs and face are so deformed. So they want to max out his use. I heard Rytter say his eyes were next, and then some ancient politician is supposed to get his cerebral fluids. I guess that will end it."

"Well I wish they would hurry up about it."

Anne rushed down the next hall, her hand over her mouth.

* * *

The policeman peered at Allison Gatryl over his reading glasses as he tapped his cell, entering notes as the Administrator talked. At her first pause, he looked up. "Well, Ms.

Gatryl, I'll file an APB on him, but kidnapping really isn't our jurisdiction."

His partner, Dink, was touching things on the desk with his bony fingers. He mumbled something that sounded like a garbled mix of English, Chinese, and Spanish. Allison glared back at the first policeman, her expression demanding a translation.

"We'll station a few men around the airport and depot, but Dink and I can't see no reason for roadblocks or nothing yet."

Allison rolled her eyes.

* * *

Betty Holmes met her lover at the back door. The house smelled of apples and cinnamon, his favorite scent. She'd put the silk sheets on the bed and pulled the covers back artfully, invitingly. Candles burned in the bedroom. Soft music drifted from the radio. And she wore a black gown she'd bought during better times for a glitzy fundraiser. Anyone would have thought the preparations were for a special occasion, and they were. Every tryst with Robert had to seem like paradise, if she was to pull him into her web. If she was to get one day closer to freedom from Markus.

Robert stepped inside, dressed in business clothes: expensive black suit, pale green shirt, and solid black tie.

Betty loved the square firmness of his face. She was tempted to reach out and stroke him but resisted. It was important to let him make the first move, to let him feel like the conqueror.

She handed him a glass of wine.

"I only have an hour," he said.

She posed against the counter so that her cleavage showed. "Then let's use the time wisely."

He tossed back the wine, set the glass on the counter, and then took her hand and led her up the stairs to the bedroom.

* * *

David strode out of the restroom, past the clerks, and behind the second security guard who was still checking tags on baggage. As he rounded the corner, there was Jessica, still slumped at the counter waiting for her boss.

She perked up as David came into view, nudging Clara, the reservation clerk. "That's him. Rex. I think. Look. Right there."

Clara kept typing, only half-listening to Jessica's moon-spun tale. "Where?"

"Just at the end there, going around the corner. Did you see him?"

She shot a brief glimpse in the general direction of the end of the corridor and then back to her screen. "No."

"Oh well. There's Ms. Jones. I'll see you later."

As Jessica jogged off to her boss, the phone intercom released three short beeps. "Attention all personnel, please be on the lookout for this man." Clara glanced at the visual that popped up in the corner of her screen. The voice continued, "His name is Rex Montane . . ."

Clara dialed security. No matter that she didn't actually see him. This would make her look good. "He just went by here. That guy. Rex something. I just saw him not half a minute ago heading to the main entrance. He looked just like the photo and he had a baby in his arms."

The main intercom came on. "Security code seven. Security code seven. Zone three."

David sensed the commotion and bristled. They must have spotted him. He had been heading for the Taco Shack, thinking there would be an exit nearby, but now he stopped and sat at a table with his back to the crowd. A security guard intent on getting to the main entrance passed within five feet of him.

David moved to the food line and counted to thirty, every second passing to the thump of his pulse as a loud murmur spread through the room and then turned into a hush. David froze before a dozen staring eyes, but the fear that cringed on their faces went beyond him. He turned, ever so slightly, watching the people and looking over his shoulder.

Two men in black uniforms approached the far counter. Not police: on their uniforms were the UO emblem and red Population Control patches.

David, forgetting his own predicament, squinted at the scene. The officers approached a food counter, one of them holding up some kind of license and the other carrying a device that blinked red. They stopped in front of the cashier, a young woman, maybe twenty, still blemished with teenage acne, and very pregnant. She stared wide-eyed at the men and began to back into a corner. Her thin arms instinctively crossed in front of her face and then thrashed uselessly at one of the men, but only for an instant. The other officer stepped in and thrust a hyposyringe into the side of her neck. Her arms dropped. Her face relaxed into a zombielike stare.

A voice whispered beside David. "Some people think they're above the law. Think they can fill the world with more brats for my tax dollars to feed."

"Serves her right," said another, with unchecked scorn.

An elderly woman beside him said nothing, but David thought he could read sympathy on her face. The only one.

David closed his eyes and said a silent prayer, then slowly, while the crowd remained transfixed, moved through the maze of onlookers toward a hall marked "Office Staff Only." The end of the hall opened to a lounge where two men sat with their feet propped up, one staring at the compupanel, the other blinded by his movie visor.

Frankie began to whimper.

"Oh no, not now, Frankie." He opened the duffle bag, stuck his finger in the baby's mouth, then slung the strap over his shoulder in one easy motion.

An exit gaped open right beside the employee lounge; now if he could reach it without raising alarm . . . Slow, easy, nonchalant, shuffle the feet, no big rush, just taking an out-of-the-way exit.

Everything happened in slow motion. The first employee looked up from the computer, turned his head to the door, and stared him straight in the eye, steady, thinking split second thoughts in a second-by-second play; he turned to his co-worker still blinded with the visor, slapping his shoulder and starting him out of his seat.

David's heart raced. His head pulsed. Sweat beaded on his brow. He fixated on the exit, willing it closer, picking up his momentum just slightly, wanting to run but holding back. Any minute they would see him. They would react.

The first employee was on his feet now, looking again at David curiously, cocking his head. Staring.

David was within three feet of the door, ready to plunge.

The employee reached down beside the door.

David inhaled, expecting a shock or a thump but pressed forward to the exit.

The employee slumped back down in his seat with a bag of raisins.

David escaped out the door.

A security guard stood twenty feet away, talking to a policewoman.

* * *

Markus walked straight out the main entrance, his heart in his throat. The Alligator wouldn't fire him. She couldn't fire him.

Sure she can. Everyone's disposable, including me. But I don't care anymore.

He timed his departure perfectly, meeting the bus at the corner without having to wait, and sat seething among the homeward bound group, half listening to their mundane discussions. None of them cared. How many helped in the slaughter every day? None of them cared.

He slammed the door as he entered his house, rattling the dishes in the cabinets.

"Is that you, Markus? Home already?" Betty's voice was shrill and wavering, a sure sign that she had been dozing. His wife had to have her afternoon nap.

"Yes, it's me. Who were you expecting?"

"Well, no one," she said as she entered the kitchen clad in a bathrobe, slightly dazed with sleep, her blond, coifed hair mussed and flattened on one side. "Not you." She seemed confused.

"Hmmph."

"Is something wrong?"

"There's plenty wrong, but nothing I can fix."

"Oh. A bad case again."

Markus was fed up. "They aren't just bad cases, Betty. They are dead babies." He screamed it at her in an effort to propel it into her brain. She never understood. The subject was long worn out between them, a divider that should have been met before marriage.

"But Markus, we've discussed this, dear. They're much better off. Who would want to be crippled? Abnormal? It's for the Good of the Nation."

Markus leaned wearily on the counter. "Are you so sure about that? How can you have such strong opinions when you spend your days lolling around with your high-class snobs and writing your pathetic little fashion blurbs? You have no contact with the real world."

"What do you mean, the real world? I keep up with everything."

"That's not the same as experiencing it, Betty. Spend a week in the Family Counseling Center, just one week, and then see what you think."

She wrinkled her nose in disgust.

"Afraid of what you might see?"

"No. I just wouldn't want to be around those low-class people with all their problems."

"They aren't 'low-class.' Just people being told . . . forget it. I'm not going to go into it again, because you won't believe me. You'll say I'm twisting figures around and that it's all for the best, that they go there by choice." He looked defeated.

"All right," she said finally, determined to mollify him to keep things on track. "All right. You could arrange for me to volunteer, couldn't you? I'll do it tomorrow. Right away, so I can get it over with. In the morning, if you can arrange it, okay?"

He nodded, his forehead furrowed in mistrust.

"I'll have to call Jennifer. She's holding the Ladies Guild, you know. That's all right. She has the worst cook." She interpreted his silence as things being settled between them. "Now where is my other earring? Must be in the bedroom. Let me fix my makeup before I get on the visual."

Markus picked up the receiver, shoved the visual to Off and quickly made arrangements with the center before Betty could change her mind. He should have thought of this years ago.

* * *

Three officials had taken over the Administrator's office. The first to arrive was a spindly bookworm named Rand Williams. Rand the Tracker could dig up record origins faster than anybody in the country. He knew exactly who they were dealing with and where he had been. The suspect had been to the depot.

Allison rolled her eyes again. She already knew that.

What Rand didn't tell her was that they were dealing with a Dominian: a Dominian kidnapping an Outer Citizen.

Allison paced. She couldn't get near her phone or her paperwork. If those nurses hadn't bungled everything up with their big mouths, she would have handed Ms. Shelton a dumping order and let the neonate go for lost.

Then came agents Tracy Studler and Dean Floyd, who had quickly hustled Allison out of her office.

"Are communications secure?" Studler asked. He was six-four and muscular, a former pro quarterback used to taking charge.

Rand linked a pocket computer to the Administrator's desktop system. "Yes, sir. Checked out fine."

"Good. Now you two go find me a pitcher of water and some cups. And don't come back in until the door is open."

Agent Studler settled himself at the desk and nearly gagged at the smell of musky perfume that wafted from the soft seat cushion. He pulled out his cell and swiped his finger across its screen.

"Yes?" came a reply on the other end.

"Got an incident."

"Who?"

"Under the arch." Everything had ears listening for key phrases—the phones, the computers, the television screen, and he wouldn't let anything out that he didn't have to. Agent Studler wouldn't say "the Dome."

"Sure?"

"According to Rand."

"Go on."

The agent summed it up in one word. "Kidnapping."

"Who?"

"Senator Houston's baby."

"Houston?"

"Yes." Studler twisted the wedding ring on his finger. "A neonate meant to be disposed of."

"Go on."

"They're not within grasp yet."

"How many on it?"

"Three of ours. More outsiders."

"Are they aware of the arch?"

"Ours are."

"Let's keep it concealed . . ."

"It might not be anything," Studler interrupted.

"We can't take that chance. You concentrate on following him. We've got to get him."

"Right."

* * *

Anne was halfway to admissions when she passed an open door. She quickened her steps to get by it, but she couldn't keep from sneaking a glance. What she saw froze her.

The little girl was probably three, maybe a small four-year-old. Her blond hair was dull, matted, and chopped unevenly within a couple inches of her head. She lay sallow and pale, staring blankly with one eye. A patch covered the other eye. Tubes invaded her body at multiple points: two tubes in her arms and two running from beneath a crumpled disarray of gown.

Anne stopped and stared.

The one eye blinked.

Anne turned away, focused her eyes on the middle-aged nurse at the Admissions desk at the end of the hall, and strode purposefully toward her, head erect, expression commanding. "I am Senator Axyl Houston's co-hab. The obstetric department has lost our baby. Rita said I should come check over here."

The nurse looked doubtful. "Rita, hmm. Male or female baby?"

"Boy. Frank Shelton."

"Numbers, not names. Couldn't look it up without a number. Anyhow, no males have been admitted today. I've been doing admission entries since I got here. No male neonate."

Anne's poise melted. "Are you sure? Maybe before you came on? Last shift, maybe? I don't know his birth time."

"No, ma'am. Can't check back records for you. That would be against policy. As it is, I shouldn't have answered your questions."

Anne's inner strength wavered. "Please, couldn't you? You don't understand. Senator Houston is not going to like it when he finds out that you have lost our baby." She knew what he would actually do was make a statement about her incompetence and leave her looking like some raving idiot to her friends, showing up without a baby after all her talk. She wondered what heart-rending story she could conjure for her circle of friends.

The nurse yawned, not bothering to cover her mouth. "Go get a warrant, then I'll get my D. H., and then you can see some records."

"Who is the department head here?"

The nurse scowled.

"Get her on the phone now."

"Don't need to. He's right there, coming up behind you."

A short, balding man approached and nodded toward Anne before addressing the nurse. "Louise, let me know if a Ms. Shelton comes by here asking questions. Seems the Administrator is looking for her."

The nurse cocked her head.

The man looked surprised, quickly assessing Anne with a frugal eye. "Ah. Ms. Shelton. Pardon me for not recognizing you. I'm a big fan of the senator." He waved his hand before him. "Mind if we take a little walk back to the Administrator's office? I believe she will be able to answer your questions better than my nurse."

"Somebody needs to." This man respected her position; she felt full of authority again as she stepped off beside him. "I have a few for you, too."

* * *

Marty Young rocked back in his chair, his dirty-blond hair spiked on top and his tee shirt wrinkled, as he munched on contraband homemade potato chips. Miss Brenda cooked them in batches and bartered them out to the community in exchange for small jobs, including the computer fix he'd done for her that morning. What sat in front of him now was more to his liking—following a news story incognito. He watched the cops' every move and made notes for two reasons: to protect his friends in the Christian underground but also for the dirt that he would share with his buddies in the Liberty League. The Christian underground was a group of peaceful people just trying to preserve their faith, but the Liberty League was intent on taking the nation back to freedom.

He was sure that day was fast approaching, the day when the timing would be perfect to step out of hiding and bring liberty back to America. And he intended to play a part in it.

* * *

David saw the policewoman turn to look at him, but she didn't react. Maybe the cap helped. He walked away with his back to them, feeling pins and needles as they stared at his back, but their voices were still low and steady, intent on their conversation. He made it as far as the edge of the parking lot, where he had to climb three steps to the street. He held the bag as balanced as possible, but it bumped his leg on the third step.

Frankie wailed. A newborn's cry. In an instant he was given away.

"Hey, you. Stop! Police!"

He broke into a run. Frankie's crying stuttered at every jolt.

The laser light was on his left shoulder. He couldn't feel it, but he knew the shock would come. His back was tense with anticipation of it.

Five more steps.

"Stop."

It stung. Burning, stinging, intense pain. He grabbed at it with his right hand, giving support to the weight of Frankie, until he finally heaved the strain of the bag to his right arm.

The beam broke. The current was gone, but the pain thumped through his shoulder and down his aching arm. David grimaced.

The officer raised the power level on her weapon. But by law she had to call out to the suspect before firing again. "Stop. Stop now. Police!"

Their voices were moving, bobbing, breathless.

The road lay ahead. A depot van, a bus, and . . . a Freedom Rider taxi. Yes! Twenty yards, around the slight curve of building.

The beam couldn't bend. It could only hit building building building building, then his hip, his back, his leg.

"Lock on, Shalayka. Lock on."

"I'm trying."

David felt the burn hit his side. He could smell it as he dove into the taxi.

"Get me out of here."

"No way. I'll get burned up." The driver turned alternately between the police and the squalling baby.

I've got two hundred to debit if you'll get me around that next corner."

The taxi screeched away, leaving a taxable exhaust trail behind.

"Scan your code or I slam on my brakes."

David abandoned all worry about using his code. They knew who he was. He waved his card in front of the reader. "Done."

"Right."

The car whipped through a yellow light, around a corner, down a mile, and then suddenly its power cut out. There was a sound of whining gears as the cab coasted to a halt in front of a busy food court.

"It's not me, man," the driver screamed. "*They* stopped it."

David climbed out and limped into the anonymity of the crowd.

The taxi driver grabbed his phone and ran from the taxi. "This is one-twenty. I just got jacked by a guy with a gun. The cops used Safe-Stop on it. It's parked until I get clearance. Corner of Halifax and Armstrong." He took refuge several hundred feet from the vehicle and waited for the police to catch up.

David ducked out of the crowd, slumped among some bushes, and anxiously unzipped the bag. Frankie seemed unhurt, and he quieted as he was lifted up into David's cradling arm and found the waiting bottle. His sucking was as vigorous as his wailing had been, and the bottle quickly emptied.

David searched the crowd for police. None. Yet.

He removed the hat, grabbed the red shirt from the bottom of the bag, and tugged the burned shirt over his head, wincing at the wound on his side. He couldn't see his back, but was sure the setting had only been on stun because the pain was fading already. The one on his side hurt, though. Luckily, only the edge of the beam had caught him. Painful, but not deadly. He smiled grimly. *Conveniently sterile, and self-cauterizing too!* He gritted his teeth and eased into the red shirt. A minor change, but if they were looking for green, it might give him an extra second. He couldn't move fast anymore, but at least Frankie was quiet now, as he stepped cautiously into a back alley.

What on earth would he do with Frankie now? How could he possibly get back to the Dome? He couldn't go back to the Depot to rent a car. There were bound to be officials crawling all over it. He had to lie low for a bit and figure things out. But where?

He stumbled forward, watching in every direction for signs of being followed. Through the alley, down the next block, he stopped. A department store. He debated the risk but decided he had to do more to disguise himself or he'd never get away. He walked through the automatic doors, his hat pulled low, trying to appear casual and unhurried to the cameras that greeted him on each side of the entrance.

He perused the unfamiliar layout of the store, struggling to walk without favoring the pounding ache in his side. Quickly glancing down each aisle, he found what he needed. He set a nondescript beige shirt and a pair of brown pants in the cart. Then scissors, a razor, and blond hair dye.

This time there was an automated check out. No problem, unless it set off some type of alarm. He had no idea how quickly the system could pick up a code and react to it.

He ran the items through, and then hesitated, wondering if he should use his real code instead. They wouldn't be looking for David Rudder, just Rex Montane. It was a hard choice, but he went with the card. Right now they didn't know he was a Dominian. If they figured that out, he could endanger all his friends and family if they decided to make a national issue out of it. You never could tell.

He held his breath as he passed the card over the scanner.

"Thank you, Rex," it said. "Shop with us again."

Back in the sunlight, he stood hyperventilating. He hadn't counted on anything like this.

He had to find someplace to hide and come up with a new strategy.

* * *

Trudy checked the messages on her desk. One taken at 2:30 canceling a Monday meeting, and one from Axyl in her assistant's handwriting. She glanced at the pale-freckled man through the office window, sitting at his desk fidgeting with the heavy heirloom ring he wore on his left hand. Axyl had one, too. They were fourth cousins or something ridiculous. She couldn't stand Norman, but with him being related to Axyl, there wasn't much chance of getting him fired.

She stepped out the door, waved the note in her hand, and spoke softly for fear he would fall into some strange fit if she got him upset. "Did the senator say why I'm setting up this conference? I'm surprised he didn't call me about it."

Norman moistened his thin lips with his snaky pointed tongue. "He said your phone was off since you were in the med center. He said you're supposed to find out what Senator Gonzales needs and have the information on his desk before he arrives."

"Arriving when? He wasn't coming back to the office until tomorrow."

"He's stopping in tonight."

Trudy ran her hand through her hair but withheld any sign of frustration. She handed Norman a note. "I've written out a document under this filename, some memos, and some legal data. I need you to pull this up and get them into form."

Norman made a face of obvious disgust at actually being told to work. "Yes, ma'am."

Her watch said 4:30. At his speed, he would easily be busy for the next thirty minutes. "I don't want any interruptions. If you're done, you may leave at five. I'll pick up the calls after that."

"Yes, ma'am."

Trudy escaped to her office and debated a moment whether to research the records Axyl wanted or resume her search for the Dominian, but there really wasn't any choice. She knew she had to do Axyl's work first.

She settled down to business at her terminal, flipping through records related to Bonita Gonzales in less than ten minutes. She knew what Axyl wanted—something to bribe this senator into backing his bill. She reviewed the state records, pulled out a couple of Senator Gonzales's most repetitive pressing proposals, and set them aside for Axyl. Then she turned to locating Rex Montane's record.

She skipped through barriers with a flurry of key strokes: access code, distribution priority, security level admittance, and UIC. So easy once Marty taught her how to do it. She'd invaded the system dozens of times. Marty embedded a key-memory program to record all of Axyl's keystrokes and sorted out the security passes.

Voila! Citizen records right at her fingertips. Everything you ever wanted to know about a person could be found through their Universal Identity Code, with the highest priority access code, that is.

Unfortunately, she didn't know his code, only his name, and she suspected that was probably an alias. Rex Montaine. No find. Phonetic connections. Maytayne and Montane. Try Montayne, R. Bingo! Randall? Hmm. Visual. No. Other listings. Montayne, Dexter. Dex to Rex? Could be. Petty theft. Illegal possession of firearms. Hmm. Visual. Not her man.

Montane. Three of them. Cheryl. No. Jack. Maybe. Number three, Rex! Visual. Yes! The address, probably fake. Employment: Public Medical Physician. Tour duty. Health (brief): Excellent.

The identity had to be false. There was no mention of Dominian stature.

She picked up her cell and flipped to the data she'd
scanned from Jessica's phone. Only a dozen phone contacts,
most of them tied to the PMS. But her name and UIC were
easy enough to retrieve.

Norman knocked on the door. "I have a delivery for you."

With a keystroke, she dropped the information to the
status line, out of Norman's view. "Thanks. Why don't you
call it a night? I'll catch the phone." She glanced at the hand-
delivered envelope. Campaign fund deposit notification. She
locked it in a drawer and turned back to the computer.

Jessica Main. Visual . . . yes. Fat face, no makeup. Looks
like her. Criminal record: Insufficient tax fund. Some time in
Work Camp. Address: 120-3 Gray Square, Government Block
2342, Apartment 3.

No mention of marriage or civil partnership in either record.

She sat puzzled over it a moment, then had a thought.
Medical records. "Had a baby, Jessica?" Health records, security
code. List to screen. Medical jargon. Let's see. Nothing that
looks like maternity. Boring. Down, down, down. Hmmm. Year
2017: vaginal fetal termination. Uterine something or other.
Infection? Hysterectomy in 2017.

"Hysterectomy? That baby can't be hers. Okay, Rex,
where are you really hiding in this thing?"

She looked at her phone and thought of checking in with
Marty, but no—not until she knew whom she was dealing with.

* * *

Anne walked stiffly beside the Gift of Life Administrator, hovering at least a head over him, following his lead through the
maze of PMS halls.

"I went in one of the rooms."

"You shouldn't have done that, Ms. Shelton. You may be carrying contaminants."

Anne stumbled and gasped. She hadn't thought of that. "I'm sorry." She picked up her stride again, but less forcefully. "I saw this poor wisp of a girl strapped to four machines and drugged out of her wits. I can't get her out of my mind. It was so upsetting. She looked so pitiful."

He breathed deeply. "I'm sure it was unsettling for you."

"I heard the nurses talking . . . I wondered . . . Is she a donor or something?"

"Probably not."

"Because donors are like brain dead or something, right? Or so deformed and retarded they aren't aware of what's happening?"

"Certainly."

Anne weighed his response against his bland expression. "How about the screaming I heard farther up the hall?"

"Screaming? Are you sure?"

Anne half-laughed. "Yes. Screaming."

"Oh, I'm sure it was just a child having a tantrum. Children do that, you know. Some just hate taking medicine and go into absolute frenzies."

"A tantrum?"

"Certainly."

"If he was screaming, he could hardly be a brain dead donor, could he?"

"Exactly."

Anne tried to dredge up the memory of the wail, but it faded dully behind the urgency to see Frank. Of course he was telling the truth. People would know if children were slowly being taken apart. Axyl would know. *Axyl wouldn't let that happen.*

The nurses' conversation slipped from her.

Anne cleared her throat. "I hope your Administrator found my Frank."

* * *

Markus pulled his phone out and wondered for the umpteenth time that day why he hadn't gotten the Dominian's number. *Stupid.*

He tossed the phone on the counter and headed to the family room to see if they were reporting the situation on the news.

* * *

Marty watched captured footage of the chase from police cameras. He had a hard time bending his mind around this one. Why did the guy steal a baby?

There was definitely something deeper to this story.

He kept the system recording on one half of the screen while filtering through the footage on the other side, looking for clear shots of the man's face. There wasn't much to go on. A couple side views. But he didn't look like a maniac, or like he had some evil intent. It wasn't that kind of expression. If anything, he looked scared. So what was he up to?

Ransom? Enough people were suffering from poverty to make that a possibility. And that would explain the look of fear. Could be he had a family to feed and no income. The soup kitchens were overrun with people. So many cities crippled with unemployment and crime. This guy wouldn't be the first or last to do something desperate.

Marty munched on another potato chip, realizing how lucky he was to have found refuge with the Christian underground or he'd be in the same spot. He'd had to go into hiding when he escaped from the UO Institute and was lucky that the Christians had taken him in, given him a place to stay, and kept him fed.

He leaned in, pressed a key, and backed up the audio streaming between the officers till he picked up the name: *Rex Montane*. That gave him someplace to start.

He knew Trudy was probably digging around, too. Between them, they'd figure out this guy's story.

* * *

Joanne watched her back carefully as she made her way from the social services building down the street to the bus stop. When she got off the bus, she observed her surroundings carefully before she set off down the road. She shopped at three stores and sat in a coffee shop to eat a sandwich before she finally slipped in the abandoned apartment building and took the fire exit to the basement.

Faces turned as she entered the room, arms enfolded her shoulders, children hugged her legs.

Stoop-shouldered Heidi Craigs shuffled over. Her aged voice crackled over her words. "It's almost seven. Father Simeon is about ready to say grace. Could you fetch Marty? He's all wrapped up in some news story and won't come out of that dungeon of his."

"Certainly, Miss Heidi." She really wanted to talk to Father Simeon about her exchange with Rex Montane. She'd been waiting all day to tell him. But she could hardly ignore Miss Heidi's seniority.

She patted five-year-old Katie Smith on the head and pried her from her legs, then hurried across the room to the far exit. Halfway across the room, she spotted Jessica Main. "I need to talk to you, Jess."

Jessica stepped over to her. "Tomorrow. I'm going home." She hated to pass up the weekly community meal, but her raging headache had returned. "I felt bad all morning and it seems to be flooding back over me again. Mental, not physical. Nothing you're going to catch."

Joanne nodded and clasped her arm. They weren't bosom buddies who had confessed life secrets with one another, but they often chatted during social hours. "Next time, then," she said, and pushed on through the crowd.

Katie remained on Joanne's heels and was joined by her brother Jeffrey.

"Where you going?" Katie asked

"To get Marty," Joanne replied. "Go back, Katie. Your father will worry."

"No he won't. I'm with you."

Joanne touched the little girl's curly locks, then took her hand and continued down a hallway with Jeffrey tagging along behind them, through two more doors to the room Marty Young considered his office.

He twisted in his chair as Joanne entered and waved her to a seat. Katie ran to him and climbed in his lap. "Got any chocolate?" she asked.

"Shh," he responded. "You know the drill. Silence."

Joanne leaned in to watch more closely. "Who are they looking for?"

Marty sighed, tapped a spot that raised a picture of Rex, then flipped back to the police camera view.

Joanne jumped up. "That's Rex."

Marty shot her a questioning look but turned back to the screen to watch as the police talked. "We've lost his trail, but he can't be too far away. The taxi is back there."

The camera jolted around as the policewoman twisted and turned, presumably looking for some sign of him.

"Are they after him because of the baby?"

Marty narrowed his eyes at her. "Yes. How did you know?"

"Because I told him to do it. The baby was going to be . . ." she let her words trail off as she looked at Katie and Jeffrey.

"Euthanized," Jeffrey finished.

"For the Good of the Nation, for the Good of the World," Katie tagged on.

Jeffrey whacked Katie. "I told ya to quit saying that." He turned to Marty. "Is the baby deformed? Missing his arms or got a squished head or something?"

"People like him could ruin our country," Katie said.

Joanne stared at the children and bit her lip. She'd hoped their father would have countered the propaganda they were getting at school. Her mother had done so when she was alive, but she'd died over a year ago.

Jeffrey moved closer. "Can I see a picture of it? Does it have guts hanging out or anything?"

Marty waved Jeffrey away. "Get your morbid mind out of here and find me some pizza."

"And get Father Simeon, too, Jeffrey," Joanne said, taking a seat again. "Tell him it's urgent."

Jeffrey frowned but obeyed.

"You too, Katie. Go. And you stay with your father," Joanne ordered.

"You can't blame them," Marty said when they were out of earshot. "It's pounded into them for eight hours a day, and George is reluctant to say much against it. He looks at what I went through, and it scares him to death. What's he supposed to do?"

Joanne didn't know the details of Marty's past, except that he'd been placed in a government institution at a young age because his parents continued to school him even after homeschooling was outlawed. He escaped the system during a transfer when he was fourteen, made his records completely disappear, and had been living in their community ever since. His parents had been released from prison, but to return to them would jeopardize both him and them. No one, not even Father Simeon, knew his real name. He hadn't become a Christian, despite the community's gentle urging, but the underground was his only refuge. Everyone treated him as an equal. Joanne never ceased to marvel at his natural strength of character.

"They don't know who Benjamin Franklin is, but they can tell you when Change came to America and how much *better* things are now," added Marty with a snort.

He pulled the picture of David back up on the screen. "Anyway, what do you know about him?"

Joanne focused on the screen. "He's the one we've been waiting for." She explained about his visit to her office. "He's a Dominian."

"I know." He didn't tell her how he knew. He had ways of finding out whatever he needed, and no one questioned him. Most of them didn't want to know how.

Joanne thought about her own involvement with this running man. Hers and Markus's. Then something dawned on her. "Markus!" She stood up, appalled that she'd forgotten him. "I've got to make sure he's okay."

* * *

Anne perched on the edge of her chair, staring at the Administrator. "What do you mean my baby was *stolen*? One minute I'm being told he had some deformity, then that he was taken to the Gift of Life Center, and now you want me to believe somebody *took* him? Really, Ms. Gatryl. Pardon me if I'm reluctant to believe your story."

The Administrator moved from behind her desk to prop on its edge, looming over Anne. Anne was all model—fine high cheek bones defining her frail, strawberry-blond princess looks. She despised such women. She envisioned crushing Anne with a twist of her arm.

"Ms. Shelton, I know you were led astray by the nurses. They weren't aware of the situation and will not be apprised of it even now. We don't want to cause any undue publicity.

"As to your neonate's condition, he is afflicted with Down's, which is debilitating and irreversible. Why this man chose to kidnap a mutant is unknown. I would only be making a guess, and I prefer to leave that to the police who are now handling the case.

"My advice to you is to forget about it. The criminal will be caught and dealt with. What you need to concentrate on is a healthy baby. Dr. Lui tells me they still have several frozen specimens and a surrogate she can contact right now, for your approval."

Anne continued to stare at her, close-mouthed, unable to collect the thoughts railing through her mind.

"Perhaps you'd prefer to wait until tomorrow." She tossed a look to Kim and received a nod. "The surrogate will still be prime then."

Anne found her voice. "I need to make a phone call."

"Of course. We'll wait outside."

Anne pulled out her cell. Axyl wouldn't answer if he was in a meeting. If she was lucky . . .

"Yes, Anne."

She fell apart at the sound of his voice, barely able to bite back tears. "Axyl, can you come home tonight? The most awful thing has happened, and I need you here."

"What is it?"

"Our baby. It's lost. Or dead. Or something. They keep telling me different things. Can you come?"

"I'll be there in three hours. Meet me at the office."

She hadn't expected him to come; he *never* changed his plans for her, and he had a dinner meeting in Washington that evening. "Yes, of course. Thank you, darling."

She stared out the window. *Axyl is coming home because I need him.* She stepped into the hall. "The senator will be here in three hours. He'll handle this." Without waiting for a response, she headed out the front entrance.

* * *

Several miles down the road, through whatever camera-free alleys and passageways he could find, David found himself in a seedy area that probably wasn't safe even in broad daylight. A couple of ragged bums stood fighting over scraps from trash cans. Voices raised in an argument emanated from the broken window of a building off to his right. In the doorway of a pawn shop stood a storeowner looking for business. In front of him was the Virginia Goodman Motel, and there was nothing good about it except that the walls were still intact. He could slip into one of the abandoned buildings and just hide, but he needed running water if he was going to change his appearance.

He fingered his Rolex. There was really no choice. He couldn't risk scanning his ID again. They would track him. He would have to barter with the watch—it was all he had. At this dump he could likely strike a deal without raising any questions. He shook the watch from his arm as he pushed through the door.

Dangling the wristwatch from his fingers, he leaned on the grimy front counter, concealing the baby below. "I need a room."

The clerk, a short, swarthy fellow slouching half-asleep in his chair, sighed, pulled himself from the chair, and took the watch. He flipped it back and forth, examining it. "Fake," he said dismissively.

"It's not," David said, his shortened temper clear in his tone. "And how would *you* know?"

The clerk seemed to consider that and shrugged. He flipped a key across to him. "One night."

Two drunks lay asleep against the corridor walls. Several doors stood open to the light breeze, some emitting shouts, others ribald moans and expletives.

David double-locked his door and stripped the brown coverlet from the bed, hoping the sheets beneath were semi-clean. The room reeked of sweat and black-market tobacco smoke. Nevertheless, David felt safer. He could contact the Dome again, change his appearance, and then make tracks. And he had an idea of who could help him . . . if she was willing to risk it.

He crouched down and stared at the infant. He'd fallen in love with him during the past few hours. His tiny lips. His almond-shaped eyes. His wide, flat nose. "How can you be so cute when you're not even a day old?" he asked. A part of him knew he ought to rush through the task of changing and feeding him, but he also wanted to savor every moment; there might not be many to share. He changed the diaper in a hurry but lingered over his toes and little fingers, the wrinkled red face and dark fuzz of hair. "I don't suppose you can tell me what we're supposed to do about all this attention you're getting, can you? Do you still want me to go for it? Keep running to get you out of this loony-bin town?"

Frankie cooed.

"I should have known you'd answer in a foreign language. I need an interpreter." He picked the boy up, and softly, like the whisper of a breeze, he sang to him until the baby's eyes fluttered and bubbles of formula gathered on his lips.

He laid Frankie on the bed and watched as his gaze fixated on a dark beam running the length of the white ceiling and knew sleep was only minutes away.

Lord, please lead us to safety.

He wondered if the news had reached the Dome through the Internet, and if so, what kind of spin the media had put on it.

He pulled out his cell and stared at it a minute. Even though it was tied to a local number so that it wouldn't be tracked to his identity, all calls to and from the Dome were monitored, so if someone noticed an outer state call into the Dome, it might still raise alarm. He couldn't risk it. Instead, the council had set up a system for sending an SOS but told him only to use it in case of a dire emergency.

It was time. He had no more options. He had to chance it.

He'd memorized the sequence. He tapped in a number, waited while the temperature and time were repeated three times, followed by silence, then entered a series of numbers and hung up without speaking. The entry would trigger a subroutine that would post a bulletin to an obscure weather-charting Web site that someone in the Dome checked every day. When they saw the storm warning with the code, they would know he was in trouble.

What they could actually do for him was uncertain. They could track him by the his cell location to hone in on where the call was made, but it would take a day or more for help to reach him even with a car, presuming someone else could get out of the Dome quickly. All he could do was stay out of sight and keep looking for a way home.

In the meantime, he was about to become a clean-shaven, short-haired man.

* * *

Baby Frankie had lifted Jessica's depression, but she still had a headache.

It was a relief to be back home. She crawled between the sheets, a luxury in the late afternoon. She'd taken her reading panel to bed with her, intending to relax a little with a murder mystery novel. Instead, she curled up around her pillow, closed her eyes and conjured up images of Rex and Frankie. She smiled sleepily in a haze of make-believe family life.

The love she imagined seemed too real. At first she could feel its warmth envelop her, but as sleep pulled her into dreamland, she shivered with cold. Fear wracked her as she fell into the dreaded track of life relived.

In her dream-state, she was 13 again, sitting on an orange plaid couch, watching her mother pull a little box from her purse. Mama and her diets. Mama and her exercises. Eventually Mama had guessed what she herself had at first denied and later hidden out of fright.

Mama shoved the home pregnancy test at her.

She didn't need to do the test. She had known for six months. But the baggy styles hid the small lump of belly. Jake, the boy, had only laughed when she told him. He knew the course. "So?"

Mama screamed when the stick came out positive, shaking her and yelling and throwing things, calling her a whore, wanting to know what boy had wanted such a stupid girl, and telling her to take care of it that very day or to not come back home.

Jessica could have done it on her own. Everyone knew what to do. The teachers had explained it year after year, where to go, when to go. It wasn't the knowing what to do, it was having the nerve to go. Anne took care of that; she always did what was right. Mama considered Anne to be very responsible and a good influence. And in this case, Anne had continually quipped what Mama said: *Make the Right Choice.*

So Anne and Debra walked with her to the clinic and waited patiently, reading magazines and chatting about nothing while she went in to get rid of her problem.

They hadn't planned on it taking two days. Just a prick of a needle, the lady had said. Some fluid removed, a little saline solution injected.

But the nurse never explained that the saline would burn the baby, nor that he would fight against the deadly fluid, swallowing it in his effort to escape, choking on it as it burned his skin and throat, until it burned the very life out of him.

Little sporadic movements of infant limbs that she had never fully recognized as alive hammered against her, turning, pounding, trying to escape. He was trapped in a pool of death with no escape, betrayed by the very person who had given him life.

She cried at the truth of the torture she was making him endure. She could feel his struggles, his kicks, his panic. She wanted to stop the process, to change her choice, but it was too late.

While she cried, Anne and Debra sat in the waiting room, reading and gossiping and watching the clock. Finally they got bored and went home.

She remembered his final movement, a pointed knot of limb rising beneath her flesh. His fight for life ended. He was dead.

But that wasn't the end . . . Her labor started. Not just a few contractions, but intense labor for twenty-five hours, her body trying to push out a baby who couldn't help with his delivery.

She was alone when he emerged burned from saline but perfect in his small, lifeless premature form . . . a beautiful boy with grayish-blue eyes staring dully out from his wasted body. She wanted him to see the love she felt for him, to see the tears she was crying for him.

A nurse entered, grabbed him away, and threw him into a plastic pan.

The nightmare nurse strangled Frankie and threw him in, too.

* * *

Anne checked her watch. She still had an hour until Axyl would arrive. She needed to talk to someone. Immediately. She thought of Debra. She had lots of society friends but never had a closer confidant. Their friendship had endured despite their changing lives. Well, at least enough to be a shoulder to cry on. After all, Debra was expecting a baby, too.

As she directed the taxi down the middle-class roads of her youth, Anne's eyes welled with tears. Much as Debra could get on her nerves, she was glad she had stayed in touch occasionally. Funny she never thought of how superficial her other friendships seemed compared to her high school days. No one else confided secrets or called in the middle of the night or listened intently to dreams or helped with problems. She and Debra hadn't shared that way in eons, but somehow she felt compelled to go to Debra. Debra would understand, and the years would melt away between them.

She pulled up to the brick transitional with its rounded windows and angled roof, green lawn and privacy fence, and actually envied Debra for a second. It all seemed so homey. Even a dog barked in the backyard.

Debra answered the door in a white cotton nightgown. Her breasts, swollen with pregnancy, showed bare beneath it. Her mouth fell open. "Anne? Come in."

A dirty-faced boy ran crying down the hall, naked.

"I was just trying to get that boy in the tub."

"Oh." Anne stepped in. "I . . . I just needed to talk."

Anne pointed to the hallway. "Do you need to catch him? I can wait."

Debra shook her head. "That's all right. What's up?"

Anne wished they could sit down. She couldn't have an intimate conversation standing in an open foyer. "My baby. I think they killed him or lost him or something."

"They terminated it because something was wrong, or what?"

"I'm not sure. They said something was wrong with him, but there wasn't. I had all the tests done. He was perfect. But they can't find him and someone told me he was dumped."

"Well, you know the drill," Debra said. "You give the speeches often enough."

But this was different. "But . . . But Frank, he was perfect. I know it. And I looked everywhere for him. Even the Gift Center. Gee, it was awful. Kids strung up on drugs with parts missing. If you'd seen this little girl . . ."

"What did you expect it to look like?"

"You mean you know what goes on there?"

"It's no secret."

"Oh."

"If a body is going to be terminated, it may as well serve the common good first."

Of course, she knew that was right. It only made sense. Her concentration was scattered. She refocused on herself. "But my baby—what should I do?"

Debra raised her hand in a questioning gesture. "Ask Axyl. He's the big senator, right?"

Anne nodded, too emotional to speak.

Debra softened. "I'm sure the authorities will find the baby."

"What if there was something wrong and they didn't tell me? I just can't bear to think of him that way."

"Did you watch Axyl's speech yesterday? This is exactly why he's pushing so hard for the Better World Bill—so you won't have to think about things like that. The system will take care of it for you. You wouldn't want it. It would be a monster, right? Let them solve what happened and then look to the future, to producing a healthy infant, one you can truly love."

The steady crying in the hallway came to an abrupt end.

Debra cussed. "Look, silence means he's into something. Tearing off my wallpaper, or worse." She glanced toward the hall and back again, anger glowing red in her face, frustration showing in the sweep of her hand and rush of her words. "Do you want to come in and visit a while?"

Anne shook her head. "No, that's okay." She moved her rigid body out the door. She would go wait at Axyl's office. Axyl would take care of everything.

* * *

After several hours of fruitless sleuthing, Trudy arched her back and stretched her arms. "I know you're in there, Rex." Aggravated, she reached for her phone to call Marty and noticed the time. "Eight! No wonder my stomach is screaming."

She reached into her drawer and pulled out a commercial dinner pack, peeled the cover back, and clicked on the central state news site. She gasped at the headline story.

In local news, a man is wanted for the abduction of a PMS neonate. The kidnapper was posing as a med when the abduction was made. He is said to be armed and dangerous. Police have no leads as to why the neonate was kidnapped, though one source claims it is a plot against Senator Axyl Houston. Senator Houston, however, denies any claims to the neonate.

As if drawn by the news story, Anne appeared in the office doorway. "Trudy! What are you doing here so late?"

Trudy hastily switched to another story. "Just the usual." She pulled a chair out and waved Anne into it. "What are *you* doing here, is the question."

Anne collapsed with drama into the chair. She considered Trudy to be a great listener, even though she wasn't really a friend. She was so professional, she would never think to gossip or make snide remarks. Finally, someone who would listen to her with the attention and compassion she deserved.

"Oh, Trudy. You wouldn't believe it. Our baby is missing. Or stolen or lost. I don't know. They're all a bunch of liars."

"Whoa. Start over again. The senator didn't even tell me the baby had arrived."

"Frank was delivered sometime this afternoon. Axyl didn't know until a couple of hours ago. He's on his way back from D.C. as we speak."

Anne gave a brief description of what she had overheard at the nurses' station, seeing the dumping bin, and her search through the Gift of Life Center.

"Now they're trying to tell me someone stole him. Can you believe it? They lose my baby and blame it on a kidnapping!"

Trudy remained silent through the explanation, wondering how Axyl would react to the events. He would make sure the baby was euthanized, of course. No Down's baby could be connected to the author of the Healthy Selections Bill. Had someone really kidnapped the baby, or was PMS trying to cover something up?

Trudy thought of the child she herself was carrying and the implications of what could go wrong. She hadn't had time to research *that* yet. "Oh, Anne. I'm so sorry for you. You've lost your child before you even laid eyes on him. Let me think. Maybe there's some way to get to the bottom of what happened." She thought aloud. "We can't look it up on the computer—he wouldn't have an ID chip. Hmm."

Anne checked the time on her cell. "Axyl should be here any time. He'll know exactly what to do."

No doubt, thought Trudy. *But not what you're expecting, Anne.*

* * *

David had just stepped out of the motel shower and pulled on his clothes when he heard sirens. Faint at first, but definitely getting closer.

He had no idea if they were after him or someone else. Anything could be possible in this neighborhood. Maybe there was some deal going down nearby that the cops had gotten wind of.

He wasn't going to wait around to find out.

He dashed across the road in the graying light. Fifteen, maybe twenty minutes until dark overtook the town. He fled down a side street, Frankie bouncing in his arms, Joanne's crucifix bouncing against his chest, Frankie crying, the crucifix urging him onward. Then he saw it. A miracle. A white building with five triangular protrusions across the front like the folds of a giant concrete fan. To the far right were two heavy black doors and a sign overhead: *The World Church Welcomes You.* A church! An evening service! He could hear voices inside.

David slipped through the metal doors to the safety of the vestibule. Voices raised in song filtered through the wall: *We are one in the spirit, we are one in the world.* It echoed around in the cavernous building, subdued and hollow, filling David with a sense of security until the words settled in his head and he realized what they were singing: *We are made into a perfect body / Through our universal unity / We live and love without borders / By the grace of the Unified Order.*

He hesitated. A World Church of the Unified Order— what exactly did they *believe*?

David held a pacifier to Frankie's searching mouth, quieting him as he stepped into the main room. It was built like an ancient amphitheater. At the far end of the room, a preacher stood at a shiny gold podium at the center of the sanctuary— more of a stage, carpeted in green—with rows of seats rising around it. The place looked like it could hold several hundred, but there were only about seventy in the congregation, most of them bunched together toward the center aisle, with their hands joined and eyes cast to the ceiling, which was painted like a star-studded night sky. The pale blue walls were unadorned, except the wall behind the preacher, which bore a portrait of the earth encircled with hands of every color and illuminated by seven beams of light.

David slipped into a seat on the back row near a brooding man who sat with his face cupped in his hands as if suffering some inner turmoil.

The congregation's voice rose and fell in incantation:

Praised be to the Holy One, immanent in all.
Awaken our minds to our inner power.
Praise be to the earth, the sun, and the moon.
To you we pledge to be servants and friends, nature and
    humankind as one
Praise be to peace and unity
And our place in the circle of the eternal world.

David shivered.

The Reverend's eyes were closed, his head dropped in meditation. Slowly his head rose, his body stiffened, his eyes opened like an antenna rising from the altar. His gaze halted on David.

* * *

Trudy felt Axyl Houston's presence before she saw him; she had senses like a deer. She modified the end of a probing question into sympathy for Anne's predicament. "Isn't it . . . terrible, but maybe it's all for the best."

Anne, totally self-absorbed and her back to the door, leapt at the touch of his hand on her shoulder.

"Oh! Oh, Axyl, it's you."

"Who else would it be?"

"I don't know. I'm just such a bundle of nerves."

Axyl watched Trudy gather her notes into a folder. "Isn't it time you went home, Trudy?"

"It is late, isn't it? I was working on that news release about your trip next week. It's all written. I just have to go over it once more and post it." She smiled with ain't-I-a-hard-worker innocence.

Axyl was unimpressed. He took Anne's elbow. "Come into my office."

Before Axyl was fully in his office, Trudy had exited the UIC search and pulled up the news release she had written that morning.

Picking up the office phone, she feigned dialing out, then sat pretending to type while eavesdropping on Anne and Axyl's conversation. The bug was a rudimentary system, but Marty had guaranteed it would work and that it was simple to install. He was right on both counts. She could hear everything Anne and Axyl were saying.

* * *

Chills ran down David's spine and sucked the breath from his body as the preacher stared at him. He reached forward and pulled a prayer book from the seat in front of him. *The Unified Bible.* The notation barely registered as he flipped it open to look busy, but the words before him gradually started taking shape. Matthew

13:36: And the leaders gathered around the Minister and asked, "What was the meaning of your story of the field?" The Minister answered them saying, "The field is the world and the seeds are the citizens who live according to the authority of the world to bring peace. The good seeds are citizens who live according to the Minister and leave judgment to those in authority. The bad seeds do not strive for peace and are enemies of the world. They will be gathered up and killed."

David felt his throat tighten at the distorted verse. He set the book down and watched a group of five parade up the aisle. They assembled on the altar and began singing and dancing. The congregation joined in, clapping their hands and swinging their hips.

The preacher closed his eyes and extended his arms outward as if he were physically absorbing the energy around him. Minutes wore on. A mist of something odd wove into the air. Not incense. More of a chemical. A drug?

Music rising and falling, people joining in, swaying, singing, moaning.

David watched, astonished, feeling lightheaded as he tried to focus.

The preacher brought his hands together above his head, and cymbals clanged. The room fell silent.

"We must remember that although each one of us exists as a separate entity, we are also a member of the human body as a whole. We are one. And it is with that awareness, with perfect peace and unity with the world, we will reach our immortality. For as surely as our bodies perish, we will be reborn into another cycle of life.

"We are the universe. Everything we do is related to everything around us. The world does not act upon us; we act upon the world."

There were nods and murmurs of approval. A few people let go of their neighbors' hands to clap.

"When we live each moment for the good of the universe, when we grasp the power of peace and unity, we become one with the Holy One. We *become* the Holy One!"

Soft music began to play. The preacher's voice dropped to a soft beckoning whisper. "Surrender yourselves. What could be greater than the final unification?"

David perused the room. He had to find another way out. On the far side of the room, there was a door, but he wasn't sure it was an exit.

They all closed their eyes again as a woman in the front row approached the podium and began reading Scripture, or at least something like it.

"What about Jesus?" David muttered under his breath.

He didn't think his words were audible until the brooding man turned to look at him. The man's face paled and then lit up. He clambered onto his seat and raised his arms in the air. "Jesus!" He screamed. "Jesus!"

The congregation turned in one wave of crooked necks and bodies to stare at him.

He jumped from his seat and went running out to the street, hollering all the way. "Jesus, save us!"

The congregation followed him out, crowding out the door and into the street to see what he intended to do.

David slipped out the side entrance, but he could hear the commotion. He edged up to the corner of the building and peered around the edge. The man had climbed on top of a parked car and stood there with his arms outstretched, preaching. "Wake up, people! Jesus is Lord and Saviour. He alone can lead you to salvation. Come to the Lord! Come to the Lord!"

People stopped and mingled around him. Shopkeepers came to their doors to investigate the commotion. Others from the service gathered around, explaining to people in the crowd what the man was saying.

A siren blared as officials approached, ignored by the crowd until the car was right upon them. Loudspeakers roared, "You are in violation of the Tolerance Act. Desist before we take action."

"Jesus! The Lord is our Shepherd, and we his sheep. Have faith in the Lord."

With the officers' attention on the man, David withdrew into the alley and dashed between buildings. He crouched a moment, panting. "That man is braver than I am, Frankie." He peeked around the corner once more at the street preacher. The beam of a Guglioman gun shone a bright orange spot against the navy of the man's shirt for a mere instant. His last word, "Praise," fizzled from his lips as he collapsed, a disjointed, limp figure, and rolled off the roof, down the windshield and across the hood to the ground.

Three people rushed to his side. A matronly woman stood in front of him and faced the crowd. "Do you see what they did? They shot him for praising the Lord. Where's the tolerance, sayin' he can't speak out?"

One officer aimed his gun at her while another yelled out. "Disperse! Disperse or we'll use gas!"

A small group to the right began to chant, "Nobody moves! Nobody moves!" People near them struggled to get away, pushing their way through the crowd, knowing what was coming. David leapt to his feet, tucked the baby in his arm once more, and dashed down the alley. Behind him, people screamed as shock waves struck them, and Liberty gas released into the air. Frankie's wails as David jostled him along was a mere whisper beneath the noise of the crowd.

* * *

Marty cracked his knuckles and frowned at the screen. The police had temporarily lost their hold on the guy, but they were sure to figure out who he was and track him by his identity. He needed to find out what Trudy knew, because he hadn't found a Rex Montane who matched. It had to be a fake identity, and he was willing to bet Trudy knew more than she was telling.

As he reached for his phone, Father Simeon entered, a gaunt, elderly man who stooped with the weight of his sheep upon his shoulders. He'd been in earlier to glimpse some of the unfolding scene but only stayed a moment. Marty knew he didn't want the rest of the community to become alarmed over something that might not have anything to do with them, but the dinner was over now, so Marty knew he was ready to talk.

Marty pulled a pile of papers from the old upholstered chair in the corner and shoved it closer to the screen. "Have a seat, Father."

The priest eased into the seat. "Who is he?"

He explained what Joanne had told him about the baby.

"A Dominian risking his life to save a baby. How do we locate him? We need to get someone out there to intercept him. Before they shoot him."

* * *

Two blocks away from the church, David spotted an open-air transit bus: public transportation had been provided free of charge in major cities around the country, ever since the federal gas tax had been increased to 300 percent. He slowed to a normal walk and tried to board like he hadn't a worry in the world. But he wondered if anyone could sense his intense adrenaline high and the pounding in his chest.

At the front of the bus, a compupanel flashed to a segment on him, or rather the bearded, long-haired man he'd been the day before, but after a few moments it switched to the scene unfolding around the street preacher. He watched carefully. He wasn't in any of the shots, but how long would it be before someone in the church mentioned seeing him?

He couldn't try contacting the Dome again. He couldn't get through the airport. He couldn't rent a car; that would require his UIC, which they were bound to be tracking now.

He was still frantically seeking a solution when two stops later the five people in front of him stood as the bus came to a stop. He had barely caught his breath, but he stood as well. He could see the driver watching them in his mirror and couldn't chance having his face studied too intently.

He moved down the road behind the others just long enough for the bus driver to pull away and lose sight of him, then he veered down the first side road so he could think without being watched.

A little girl approached on a bicycle.

He turned and retraced his steps and took the next left, his mind whirling. He could ask Markus, but authorities may be watching him as well.

Day One

He stared into space as he moved onward. People ⟨
back and forth in front of him, but they didn't even glanc
way, and he barely noticed anything about them. He cross
a busy intersection and stood before the entrance to a grassy
park with overgrown brick pathways and paused to stare at a
park bench. Surely he could sit for a few minutes. The park
appeared a natural sanctuary for a parent with a child.

He pushed himself forward the last few steps and sank to
the bench, feeling utterly alone. "Dear God, what should I do?"

A hunched, elderly woman wearing a black net hat from
another lifetime doddered down the sidewalk. Just the sight of
her tenacious effort took his mind off his dilemma. Pain etched
her eyes and mouth. Arthritis curled her fingers and her left
wrist. She made him think of the old woman he'd given the
pill to that morning in the Life Continuity Center. How long
ago that seemed.

She stopped in front of him, and without a word, pulled
the blanket back to inspect Frankie's face. Her every movement
took so much exertion, he couldn't bring himself to stop her.

"He's a beautiful boy." Her voice was as husky and unused
as her hands.

With concentration, she maneuvered her left hand into a
large apron pocket and pulled out a tiny brown paper bag. "A
gift," she said, holding it out to him.

He took the bag and watched as she moved down the
road with interminable slowness until she reached a crowd on
the sidewalk.

Spell broken, he opened the bag and peered inside. A
piece of paper and a key.

Propping the baby across his legs, he pulled the key ring
from the bag and read the label: Midway Inn, Room 133. He

dropped it back in and pulled out the note. Tight scrawling leaned heavily across the page: *For I was hungry, and you gave me to eat; I was thirsty, and you gave me to drink; I was a stranger, and you took me in* (Matthew 25:35).

David folded the note into Frankie's blanket with inspired calm.

He searched the area for any sign of the old woman. Where did she go? How did she know he needed help?

Frankie whimpered in his arms. "I know, little guy. You are being such a good soldier in all this. But you know what? Sure as you are breathing, the Lord is with us. He was in that church. He is in this town. And he's walking this path with us. . . . *he who endures to the end shall be saved*, Frankie. I just have no idea when or where the end is. I don't even know where we are. But we're going to find that hotel."

* * *

Joanne called Markus's phone for a third time. She imagined he was standing in the kitchen staring at it, knowing it was her, and wondering how he could take the call with his wife standing across the room.

It wasn't like *that* with them, though. She loved him, but she would never interfere with his marriage. She could never be closer than an arm's length away.

But she had to know if he was safe or not.

* * *

Trudy was disappointed. Anne's explanation to Axyl revealed nothing new. What a credulous idiot Anne was. What a typical head-in-the-ground citizen, not to know what was going on in the Gift of Life Center. *Organ donation and experiments!* No one had said anything when embryos, then fetuses, were created and used for research. Now she pretends to be shocked?

Axyl responded with his typical closed-mouth silence. Anne would be sent home to bed with a sleeping pill or something stronger.

Disgusted, Trudy hung up the phone, and cleared her desk. As she turned to pick up her purse, a man stepped up.

"Excuse me, Trudy."

Trudy spun around, startled by the tall, black-suited man.

"Is Senator Houston in?" he asked.

"He's in his office, Mr. Uh. . . ." She shook her head. "I'm sorry."

"Don't be. We haven't met." He waved a badge. "Agent Tracy Studler."

He reached out and shook her hand. She smiled and nodded. She knew exactly who he was.

"I'm working on the kidnapping. I was told the senator would be here."

She would love to have five minutes alone with him to ask questions, but she maintained her professionalism. "Yes, of course, Agent Studler. Ms. Shelton is terribly upset by it all. The senator is calming her down. I'm sure it would do them both good to hear if you have some news. Just a moment."

Trudy buzzed Axyl. "Agent Studler is here to see you."

Anne's whimpering meshed with his reply. "Send him in, and come take Anne home."

Trudy bit back a curse. She was being sent away as a babysitter for delicate little Anne. She hid her exasperation and motioned him to follow her. "This way, please." She led him into Axyl's office.

Despite the noise of her whimpers, Anne's perfect face was unmarred by tears. She clutched a tissue dramatically in one hand.

Trudy touched her shoulder. "Come on, Anne. Come with me."

Anne, not especially interested in hearing any more confusing details, willingly followed Trudy out.

"The senator asked me to take you home, but would you mind if I called my roommate first? I had just told her I was on the way, and she'll worry if I'm late," she fibbed.

"No, go ahead. I need to visit the restroom anyway."

Trudy sighed with relief, took up the phone and listened in to the conversation in Axyl's office.

Agent Studler took a seat across from Axyl. "Do you know anyone by the name of David Rudder?"

Axyl furrowed his brow. The name sounded familiar. No one recent. The name flickered before him, disappearing before it formed. Maybe it was something from his childhood. He never could recall much before the UO Institute.

He shook his head in frustration. He just couldn't stick the name to a face. He knew so many people. "No. But everyone knows who I am. Is it someone trying to threaten me through the kid?"

"That's what we're trying to determine. Perhaps a Dominian?"

"A Dominian?" Axyl said. "Why would a Dominian be out to get me?"

"Jack mentioned . . ." He let his words trail off to see where they may lead.

Axyl maintained a neutral expression. *Jack Friday had a loose tongue.* Sure, they both knew Studler, but their discussion about the fate of the Dome was top secret. Jack Friday had no business mentioning it to anyone. It was one thing for Jack to threaten him for self-gain, but leaking plans to some spook? Jack underestimated his determination to achieve a perfected citizenry. He'd made a mistake in crossing him. "I have no idea what you're talking about. But someone got to this baby, right? I think they're trying to make a point, which is exactly why we're not going to react the way they expect us to."

"So what do you want done?"

"Find him," Axyl said.

"Find the kid. Right," replied the agent. "Big search, lots of attention. Everyone wants to know why the guy stole the garbage baby. Don't you think that will make the situation worse?"

"Find the Dominian. Trash the kid. It's an imbecile."

"So what do we tell the press?"

Axyl smirked. "PMS is about to find my kid. I told a certain person to replace him with a new one. Some surrogate is about to have a bad pregnancy terminated, and there's Senator Houston's child, safe in the hospital after all." He paused to check his watch. "Should be happening about now. Old story never took place."

"So what do we do with the Dominian?"

He smiled as an idea formed in his head—the perfect way to begin the destruction of the Dome. "Put a gun in his hand and create something more threatening. Something that will turn citizens against him."

"Frame him for a bomb threat somewhere?"

"Exactly. Use him as an example of what happens if they try to interfere in our world."

"The problem is we can't find him."

"When has that ever been a problem?"

Agent Studler nodded. He knew what Axyl was suggesting. Just get somebody charged with it and say it was the Dominian. Axyl didn't want justice. He wanted publicity. The *right* publicity.

Anne came back down the hall, her heels clicking on the hard floor like pop guns.

Trudy hung the phone up with great care. *David Rudder.* Trudy wanted to dive into the system to check out the lead, but it would be too risky just then.

"I'm ready," Anne said. She looked back as if she could see through to Axyl's office. "I thought he was going to be so understanding. He flew all the way home, left a meeting and everything, and all he says is to just go home to bed and see what they find out in the morning."

"Well, that's probably best." She wanted to get free of Anne, go back to her investigation.

"I can't go home. He's my baby. Why does everyone think I can just forget about him? Imagine what my friends are going to say when I turn up without a baby."

Trudy sighed. Anne would use the pity party to keep attention on herself for as long as possible. Immediately she felt bad for thinking that. Certainly Anne cared about her child, too. "Let's go by the PMS and talk to the Administrator to see if anything has turned up."

Anne nodded. "Okay. At least I'll feel like I'm doing something," she said, but in reality shivered at the idea of facing the hard-shelled woman again.

As they reached the car, Marty called. Trudy ignored it. She couldn't risk their association with Anne at her elbow. She would call him back when she was alone again.

* * *

Markus's phone vibrated around in circles on the counter for a third time. Betty picked it up, glanced at the number, and tossed it into the basket with the keys. She wished he would go out so she could call Robert, maybe even go meet him somewhere.

She pulled a glass from the draining tray, filled it with water, and leaned against the counter. Maybe she could give him an errand to run. But what?

As she thought about it, she turned and stared at the basket, thinking about what the cell display said: *Korany/Social Services*. What dealings did Markus have with Social Services? Maybe that would get him out of the house.

"You got a phone call," she hollered.

"I don't care," he said.

"Maybe you ought to call back. It might be an emergency."

He fidgeted with the remote, afraid of what a phone call might mean—something about that Dominian and the baby. He'd seen the news. He kept expecting officials to come knocking on his door any minute. He had no idea this thing with Rex and the baby would end up being such a big deal.

He shoved the remote aside and strode to the kitchen. He had to get out of the house. It was after eight. He'd go listen to the guys' lame jokes and watch the game.

Betty eyed him with disdain. She wanted him to go but couldn't help scoring a point off it. "The man is headed out to the bar. Surprise, surprise."

"Got better plans for us?"

Betty turned her back on him to set her glass in the sink.

He didn't have anything to say to her. There was a time he would have rubbed her shoulders and asked what was wrong. Now they lived like strangers. The fight had gone out of him. It was easier to follow the path of least resistance.

He grabbed his keys and cell and headed out the door. There would be nothing in life to encourage his heart to continue beating in his chest if it weren't for Joanne, and tomorrow was their day together, volunteering at the retirement home; the only day of the week he looked forward to. Until then, there was one place he could go to forget about life: Happy Zack's.

* * *

Set back from the road, the Midway Inn stood between a shopping center and Memorial Park, giving it an odd, unbalanced look of green shade to one side and lifeless cement on the other. A circle driveway looped by the front door, but David veered across the shopping center parking lot to the hotel's parking lot and followed the sidewalk that wound around the Midway Inn until he found Room 133 on the far side, by the park. He shifted Frankie to his left arm. "Here goes, Frankie-boy." Every nerve was on edge as he fitted the hotel card in the lock and held his breath a moment, debating, seeking courage. In one motion, he turned the knob and opened the door.

Nothing happened.

No bomb. No agents. No strangers.

He stepped in, shut the door, and locked it.

On the bed lay a suit of clothes and a tray of food sat on a small table in the corner.

He peeked into the bathroom and small closet. "Hello?" he asked softly. No one answered.

He laid the sleeping baby on the bed and stretched his weary arms out, massaging them up and down to loosen the stiffened muscles. Frankie stirred. David grabbed the pacifier and eased it back into his mouth until his breathing settled into a rhythmic, slumbering reflex.

A note on top of the clothes bore the same scrawled handwriting: *For you.* He stared at it, then at the clothes. Tan walking shorts and a pale oxford shirt, tan socks, and even a pair of underwear lay across the bed. They weren't brand new, but they were clean and the shirt was pressed. A diaper bag, carefully packed with lotions, diapers, and a dozen disposable bottles of ready-made infant formula, sat at the head of the bed beside a small pile of blue, yellow, and lavender baby clothes. And a baby sling. "Wow. Look, Frankie! This is fantastic. You might be light, but I'm not used to propping something in my arms all day. And my shoulder's killing me."

Answering his growling stomach, he approached the table to eat. Green bean casserole, baked fish, and apple sauce. "Thank you for this, Lord," he said, "and whoever you are that left it here for me."

* * *

Trudy stood behind Anne in the PMS Administrator's office, not wanting to draw attention to herself. The cheap furnishings echoed Trudy's image of the Administrator. She had dealt with women of her sort plenty of times. Egotistical and lewd.

Working in politics had exposed her to a plethora of power-hungry people, but she had never felt inferior to any of them. Afraid, maybe, but not inferior; it sounded contradictory but wasn't. She knew many people in politics who had no hesitation about using their power to crush anyone who got in their way, but she viewed them with disdain. They were like thugs hanging out in alleys using force to get drugs or whatever else. She knew she was smarter than them. Perhaps not as physically strong but definitely more able to outwit them.

She felt neither fear nor inferiority toward Allison Gatryl and stood off to the side as Anne was offered a chair.

"I'm glad you came by," the Administrator began. "I just tried to reach you and the senator. I have wonderful news."

Anne twisted her hands together. "What?"

"We have found the baby."

"Found him? Is he hurt? Did that man do anything to him?"

"Sit down, Ms. Shelton, sit down." Allison looked Trudy up and down like a steak, then waved her to a chair in the corner.

Trudy deflected the dour assessment with a haughty tilt of her head and remained standing behind Anne.

The Administrator took a seat behind her desk before continuing. "It seems you were right after all, Ms. Shelton. After you left, Doctor Kim Lui and I reviewed the entire case, and she solved our little mystery. Apparently, someone not only confused the baby's files but also the baby. Your son is perfect. Let me buzz the nursery and have him brought in." She pressed a button on her phone. "Gatryl here. Bring Ms. Shelton's baby to my office, please."

Allison's hard face looked morbid even with the effort of a smile. "You have named him Frank, have you?"

Anne's hands shook. "Yes, after my father and grandfather." Nerves put her in chatter mode. "I like the new tradition—you know, using one parent's surname as a first name since co-hab rights mean a child only bears one parent's name. Wouldn't Houston be cute for a first name? But the senator didn't like it."

Allison sat on the corner of the desk and tried to look interested.

"So I decided to honor my father. Not that I really like the name Frank, but it is a good, solid name and not too popular anymore. I don't like popular names. Too trendy. I want him to stand out."

Trudy smirked. Stand out? Anne kowtowed to every social whim there was. She didn't even know how to be an individual, let alone stand out. How unlike his mother such a son would be.

"Frank Robert Shelton. Nice, isn't it? I do hope he looks like a Frank . . ."

"Ah, here's Dr. Lui now." Allison slid into the chair behind the desk and breathed a sigh of relief. "Give him to Ms. Shelton, please."

Anne took the bald-headed boy into her arms like a piece of glass. "Oh, he's beautiful."

Her voice dropped to a whisper. "Hello, Frank darling. Mama was so worried about you. I knew you were here somewhere." She looked at Trudy. "Isn't he beautiful?"

Trudy smiled weakly, then turned her attention to the doctor. Kim Lui's jovial softness looked dumpy next to Anne's porcelain-molded face, but Kim's eyes had a glint to them—two hard spots of dark brown in place of Anne's empty blue ones.

The forced smile on Kim's face did little to disguise the irritation in her high-pitched voice. "If there's nothing else you need . . ."

Anne looked flustered. "That's it? You just hand him to me and leave? I don't know what to do with him."

Kim stood motionless, her motherly smile properly in place as she blinked at Anne. "Did you take the parenting classes?"

"Of course I did."

"Then you're all set." She spoke with such a kindergarten-teacher pleasantness that a person couldn't argue with her. She glanced at the Administrator, then left.

"But I don't know what to *do* with him," Anne said.

Allison stood. "I'm sure you'll do fine."

Trudy saw where that was going and took precautions to keep herself out of it. "Certainly you know what to do. First give Senator Houston a call and let him know all is well. He can come pick you up, and you can all get home to bed."

"I forgot to call Axyl!"

Allison sat back down. "I already notified the senator. As I said, I had called various numbers trying to reach you."

"True. I'll just call and see when he can pick me up." The baby had begun to fuss and squirm. She looked from Trudy to the Administrator trying to decide who might take him, but neither moved.

Allison stood again. "Let's take you both down to the nursery and see if someone there can help answer your questions and get you ready to go home. You can call the senator from there."

"Good idea," seconded Trudy. She began moving toward the door, talking all the way. "I'm so glad everything worked out. I'll call tomorrow to check on you." She slipped through the doorway, turning her head over her shoulder as she did so. "Congratulations!"

She reached the hospital exit. The Dominian and the real Frank were still at large, and she intended to find them.

* * *

With a full stomach and the baby fed and clothed, David's state of mind improved. He didn't know what else he might expect from his secret benefactor, but his course of action seemed clear: he had to seek out the only sympathetic person he knew in town: Markus. Remembering Markus's words, he decided to try the bar.

Guided by his cell, he walked about thirty minutes down side roads, emptied as dusk fell, and arrived on a main street beside Happy Zack's, a brick building with dark windows and a sagging awning. Only a few pedestrians were in sight, but just to be safe he stepped back into the dark alley, pulled out his shirttail, and hid Frankie in the sling under his shirt like a fat stomach. He was sleeping soundly, David hoped it would be dim enough inside that no one would notice his belly was actually a baby.

He took hesitant steps through the door and came to an abrupt stop. Light wafted from tiny spots in the ceiling, high-lighting pinpoints of table tops. The barstools and tables were jammed with patrons, music rising and falling amid the spurts and lulls of conversation. A large group of cheering men sat watching a baseball game on a television that covered nearly the entire back wall.

David perused the faces, hoping he'd find Markus at the back but nervous about Frankie, about being discovered. In fact, now that he'd made it through the door, he couldn't imagine what he hoped to accomplish by talking to Markus. He had to get out.

He passed between couples, his head ducked down. A woman stepped into his path and touched his arm. David jerked away and bumped into a table. Frankie mewed in protest, unheard above the raucous noise. He adjusted Frankie. "It's okay, buddy. Just a few more minutes." He skirted between tables to avoid the crowd standing at the bar and searched for a back exit.

He avoided the flecks of light bouncing from the antique mirror ball hung over a tiny dance floor and made his way between two other couples before reaching the back wall.

Markus sat alone at a corner table, near the baseball fans but not joining in their howls and cheers. His hands lay spread on the table top, his eyes fixated on some indeterminate spot in front of his nose.

David sat down, relieved to let Frankie settle on his lap under the table, and turned to the game for minute. He would have liked to watch it, to have been a normal guy having a normal night at a bar after work.

He shook Markus's arm. "Markus. *Markus.*"

Markus blinked but didn't move. "I guess you bet on the wrong team," he said, and laughed at his own joke, but Markus didn't respond.

David waved his hand in front of Markus's eyes and sniffed the half-empty glass. It didn't smell like liquor, but that didn't surprise him. Alcohol had been banned in 2018, replaced by a government-sanctioned drink popularly called Jack-Up Juice, which supposedly provided mild euphoria while improving brain function. But who knew what kind of designer-chemical concoctions you could get at a place like this?

Markus turned to look at David, but his eyes still seemed fixated beyond David, unable to focus.

"Markus, come outside so we can talk. We need to talk. Can you come with me?"

David stood up and tugged on Markus's arm. Markus continued to peer at him, his expression unchanged, but after a minute he became less rigid. David put his arm around him in a knowing gesture and led him out.

Markus walked easily beside him, like a dog on a leash, but it was awkward trying to maneuver him and keep Frankie from bouncing too much in the sling. Out the exit and away from the lighted archway, he pulled Markus to a stop and retrieved Frankie from under his shirt. He felt the baby's head and placed a hand against his tiny chest to make sure he was breathing normally. "You sure tolerate a lot, boy. You're going to be a rough and tumble kid, aren't you?" In answer, Frankie flicked his eyes open and shut, flung his fist out and luckily managed to land one knuckle in his mouth. David sighed. "You're worth all this, buddy."

Again, he led Markus forward, off the sidewalk, down the alley way to the back parking lot.

Several government-run taxis were parked along the sidewalk in the best parking slots, clearly designated as *Parking for Runners*. Three drivers leaned against one of the cars sipping at canned drinks and laughing. David avoided them and kept Markus to the side of the building.

Still, they spotted David. "Hey mister!"

David ignored them and continued to walk, not daring to look in their direction.

After a minute, the Runners' conversation resumed, more intent on their own camaraderie than saving some drunk a long walk home.

David searched for privacy, maybe a small stretch of green grass where they could sit, free from hidden ears or eyes.

The odd companions moved in and out of the bright circles of streetlights to the end of the block. There David spotted a restaurant closing up, its outer lights flicking off one by one.

David hurried Markus to the side entrance, to a patio of indestructible cement tables and benches.

"Markus, I'm going to sit you at this table, okay?"

Markus gazed at David, recognition slowly lighting his eyes while his face relaxed into tired folds of sadness. He didn't respond, but he voluntarily took a seat. David risked holding Frankie out to him and Markus responded by taking the baby onto his lap and gently stroking the few strands of silky hair.

"I'll be right back."

He jogged to the front entrance and pulled open the door. The manager, busy producing reports from the register, looked up and shook his head. "Closed."

A homely waitress in an ugly brown apron uniform stepped up behind the manager. "Want any coffee before I toss it?"

"No," he replied curtly, without looking at her. He pulled keys out of his pocket and turned to David. "We're closed, mister. Try us tomorrow."

"All I wanted was a cup of coffee for my friend out here. He seems to have had a bit more fun than his system can stand, and I'm trying to get him home."

The manager shook his head. "It's nine o'clock."

David raised one eyebrow.

"Business Safety Act?" the man said, implying whatever the law was, it was common knowledge to a normal citizen.

The waitress elbowed her boss. "Aw, let me give him some for free, Steve. I'm just putting it down the drain anyhow."

The manager shrugged. "Go on, but lock the door after him."

The waitress disappeared behind a door and returned a minute later with a paper bag. She took the keys from beside the manager on her way to the door and whispered to David. "I put a cup for you too, and some sweetener, creamer, and a couple of pastries we was going to toss out too."

"Thank you."

"Ain't nothing. You remind me of my Bob when we was dating. I guess if we'd had a son, he'd be the spitting image of you."

"And he would be a lucky man to have such a kind mother." He held up the bag. "I thank you."

He heard the lock clank shut behind him as he rounded the building but was sure two eyes watched until he was out of eyesight, thinking of him with memories of youth. Funny, he felt 90 years old.

At the table, he passed a cup of black coffee to Markus and took Frankie onto his own lap. The city was asleep around them. A car puttered past and paused in a quiet hum at the corner signal. A trash can lid clattered to the ground across the alley, causing a barking frenzy to break the dark silence.

Markus looked toward the dogs' rally and then to David as voices came out the back door of the restaurant. David held his finger to his lips, then sipped at his coffee again.

A shrill voice rang out behind them. "Good night to ya, Bobby-boy."

He turned, his hand raised. "Good night, sweet Mama."

She chuckled and followed the group of diminishing voices.

Time for business.

Markus was peering into his coffee. "You look different. Great disguise."

"I'm glad to see you're back with us."

Markus looked at him resignedly. "Yes. I was in Heaven, and you brought me back to this hellhole."

"It's not that bad, Markus. Besides, you can't get to Heaven until you've dealt with earth."

Markus twisted sideways to face David. "You know all about Heaven, do you?"

The dogs quieted. David's heart throbbed in his ears. He knew what was coming—the doubts, the questions, the same ones he carried in his own head and had to fight back with blind faith. "Yes, I know my faith."

"So where is God? Why did he abandon us?"

"He didn't abandon you. He was thrust away. All you have to do is open your heart and he will be with you again."

Markus was reflective. "I have. I prayed to him to save the babies, and then you showed up. At first I thought you were Christ. But I see you're not. And I see you've brought the baby back."

"No, I'm not Christ, but I am his servant, and I am not returning his child to a slaughter house. I think God intended for us to have this meeting."

"It's illegal, telling me about God without my permission."

"Only if you say I'm violating your rights."

"True." He paused. "My parents gave up everything to help the Church fight that bill."

"I'm sure God rewarded them."

"They're dead."

"You just said you'd rather be in Heaven."

The dullness had faded from Markus's eyes. Instead, they were overly bright. His face was intense with varying emotions: happy, scared, angry. "I was raised to know God. The new churches preach about universal connections or something."

David thought of the World Church's prayer and shivered. "If you can't find a church, you'll just have to seek him in your heart. Like Joanne." He touched the crucifix she had given him. "You're a good person, Markus. And brave. You put your life on the line trying to save babies like Frankie from death. I believe you are really a Christian. Your faith has just been dormant."

"Four. I've saved four. But do you know how many I've killed? Eleven newborns. Ten of them looking at me and wailing as I pushed that button. And in the other departments, the ones they killed or carted off, the children, the infirm, the elderly that I did nothing to stop. I'm not brave and I'm not good. I'm a coward. And I told them all about *you*. If they ask me, I'll turn you in again. I'm nothing. I'm not worthy of fame or power, and I'm not worthy of salvation. The only noble thing I've ever done is uphold my old-fashioned marriage vows, and Betty says I'm a selfish pig for that as well, thinking my pitiful soul might be redeemed for it, while her world is a torturous curse of having to endure me."

The coffee cup crumpled in Markus's hand.

"You risk your life to save children. That shows how noble you are."

"No. I'm a coward because I can't kill them. Stealing them is just a way out of killing them."

"You place your life in jeopardy because the very core of you knows killing is wrong. You refuse to do it because it is morally wrong, and your soul is worth more than your life."

Markus squared up to David and leaned forward a little. "Don't make me sound grand. I'm not. I'm pathetic." He gritted his teeth a moment before continuing. "My parents came to my door, and I slammed it in their face. They stood on street corners like beggars—my father, an esteemed doctor!—handing out fliers about Jesus, pamphlets that exposed some conspiracy plot against Christianity. They said the World Church was out to eliminate Christians. I told them they were idiots and to leave me out of it. I had a good medical career ahead of me, while my father's was in ruins. Everyone laughed at him."

David could see the pain in Markus's face. He wanted to clasp his hand but knew Markus would withdraw from intimacy.

"What happened to your parents?"

"You remember how it was back then: They said that Christians were troublemakers, terrorists who used violence to impose their judgments on everybody else. You could get arrested if you tried to convert somebody or spoke out against homosexuality or abortion. But my parents, just had to 'spread the word of God'"—Markus's voice took on an ironic edge, but to David it sounded forced—"so they joined a protest group in front of a UO church to tell people the only way to Heaven was through Jesus. They thought they could make a stand. A couple of extremists showed up in hoods, started shooting at them and killed most of them, but the news reports said the Christians had fired the first shot. The few Christians that survived were sent to jail for intolerance. The killers got off on technicalities."

David was familiar with the scenario. His mother had shared those stories over and over again: how Christians were persecuted for things they didn't do; how it became acceptable to attack Christians in the street and vandalize their homes and churches; how tolerance laws protected everyone except those who believed in Jesus.

Markus continued. "My parents didn't survive."

David let the words, the horrible truth of it, settle around them. He could see tremors flow over Markus.

"They killed my parents!" He started crying, his whole body shaking with the effort. "I let them kill my parents. I should have convinced my father to stay out of it."

"You couldn't do that, Markus. They felt a calling from God."

"My dad used to get all worked up about these people and their agenda to destroy Christianity, but I thought it was a bunch of crap. I mean, come on, who would really believe that?" He stopped talking and sat staring at his crumpled cup.

"Your father was right, but we both know they aren't all dead," David said. "The Dome is full of Christians, remember? And there are others, but they're like you. They're sleeping, needing a nudge to wake them up."

Markus looked at him dispassionately. "So I'm awake now. What do you suggest we do—storm the capital? They would lock us up and throw away the key. Or they'd blow us away like that preacher on the news a few hours ago."

David gazed at Frankie. "You saved him. I believe that one small act will ripple, and ripples grow. The rest will come, I promise. God is here for you. He has a plan for you."

Markus sighed. "We'll see." He nodded toward the baby. "And him. I hope you and God have plans for him."

"I have to believe he does." The thought fed his dwindling courage. "If nothing else, we have made a statement."

"A five-second blip on the news. That's hardly going to change anything."

"That depends how many sit up and listen, how many think about having the courage to do the same thing, how many think of saying *enough is enough—we want God back in our lives and we want to stop this massacre of God's creations.*"

"Not enough people did it even back when they had churches preaching it to them," Markus protested. "Most don't even have the notion in their heads anymore."

He thought of Markus's true heart. And Jessica's. And others he'd glimpsed in the past weeks. People were still people, with the same emotions, the same capacity for reason and goodness that they'd had since the beginning. "You underestimate love. There is still a lot of love in this world. And that is the very definition of God. Love must win in the end."

Markus set his jaw tight. "We'll see."

* * *

Axyl dialed the number.

The Minister of World Peace answered. "You took your time."

"I'm sorry, sir."

"Explain yourself," The Minister said.

"A mixup. I have it under control."

"Rumor says it's a Christian or a Dominian."

"Still working on it."

"I am confident you will solve it."

"Yes, sir," Axyl replied.

"Does this affect the big picture?"

"No, sir."

"Your colleague laughed at your solution. A poison injection? That's the best you can do?"

Jack Friday laughed at me behind my back? To the Minister? "Not my final solution, sir. I will have a report ready for you at the meeting."

"I trust you will."

"The Better World Bill, sir . . ."

"I'm aware of your work. Carry on."

The call ended.

Day Two

July 3, 2042

Trudy skipped down her apartment steps to the walkway that led to the parking lot. The street lights were still on as the blush of the rising sun lit the clouds hovering on the horizon, and the air held the fresh aroma of morning dew.

Once she had David Rudder's name, accessing his records had been child's play. She knew everything there was to know about him. He wasn't a criminal or a Dominion official. His status listed him as a doctor on temporary leave. The only inkling of suspicion was the death of his wife and their newborn infant daughter.

She and Marty had talked far into the night about the possibilities. Marty told her that he and the underground church had made contact with him, set him up with some clothes, food, a hotel room. But they wanted to watch him a little more before deciding what to do. They had the same questions she had. What was he doing here to begin with? Could he possibly be crazed with grief and in search of a baby to love? Why would he come to the outer states?

167

And then in the wee hours, she woke with alacrity: the Dome didn't allow abortions or dumps. He must have figured he could come out and steal a dump kid and never get caught. He could be expressing some vendetta against the outer states, but if that were the case, wouldn't he have made a huge scene? Maybe choosing the senator's baby was just dumb luck. And now getting away with the baby was almost a *fait accompli* since Anne had taken the replacement child . . . but why did Axyl want to hush the whole thing up? *Because it would draw attention to what the Better World Bill was all about.* How did Jessica figure into the picture? Was he living with her illegally in government housing?

Now, at the crack of dawn, she shook with adrenaline, anxious to take action. She clicked on the note in her cell phone. Jessica Main. *Start there.*

* * *

The dressing room was obviously the most important upper room in Markus Holmes's house, at least to the extent of space and time that Betty had allotted to it. With two guest rooms and no children ever expected, the entire fourth bedroom had been converted to a vanity closet with a full-wall mirror, perfect artificial lighting, special detailed shelving for proper makeup storage, and a comfortable swivel office chair for the hour-long makeup process. An array of beautification tools was carefully stocked in the cabinets.

By 7:45, Betty had begun her morning ritual, sitting in front of her mirror, carefully creating her face. If Markus insisted she go to that degrading Family Counseling Center, she wanted those people to understand they were dealing with an upper-class woman, a contributing writer for *World Beauty* magazine, at least occasionally. Not some two-bit tech school nurse with bedpan hands.

Betty's goal in life was to look as if she was prepared for a modeling shoot every day, never a hair out of place, never an age line visible that could be cosmetically or surgically disguised. Her nose was naturally flawless, coming to a delicate point over a wide mouth and dimpled chin. Her skin stretched taut over high cheekbones, and when high collars hid her neck, she could pass for being in her late twenties.

She pulled the long bristled brush through her thick honey-colored tresses, convinced this morning, as every morning, that she had been the sole voice responsible for women's return to long hair. She had proclaimed the new fashion in her articles and pictures because long hair would make her look younger, and before she knew it, the trend seemed to cross the entire nation. How dare Markus consider her contribution to society to be puny and worthless!

Markus's heirloom grandfather clock began its bonging count in the entrance hall. Seven thirty. Betty perused her large appointment calendar lying open in the corner. She was supposed to be at the center by 9:30, which didn't leave much time.

There was something else marked on the calendar. Oh, great. The star. She was ten days late again. She'd been hoping it was the onset of menopause, but she didn't have time for a PMS appointment. She stared at the star trying to remember if she had taken care of that yesterday when she noticed it or decided to stick to the schedule.

She took the pill case down and dumped the pills on the counter. Eight left. Did she have ten to start with, or eleven? She fingered one pill for a minute, deciding she would have had cramps, or started, if she had taken it, then popped it in her mouth and swallowed some water. Better safe than sorry. She sure didn't want a baby, and she would never want one of those disgusting vaginal abortion procedures done on *her*.

She hid the pills back on the shelf. Markus would be furious if he knew about the pills. She laughed, remembering when he warned her they could cause a heart attack. Like she'd believe that! She hadn't had heart problems in five years.

She returned to penciling a dark, blackish-green line around her hazel eyes.

* * *

Jeffrey was standing by the front door waiting for Katie when their father rushed past him with a pat to his back. "Don't forget to lock up, son. See you tonight."

Jeffrey watched his father run down the hall to the stairwell, footsteps echoing down behind him. He wished he had the courage to play hooky. Spending the day with Marty in the underground control room would be a lot more fun than school. He wanted to know what happened to the man Marty was tracking the day before and what was wrong with that baby. He'd heard stories at school about kids missing body parts.

Katie finally joined him at the front door. "Your books, Katie. Where's your bag?"

"Oh, yeah." She ran back to their bedroom and returned a minute later, panting.

"It's okay. We've got time," Jeffrey said. He made sure they headed out to school with a bit of time to spare, to allow for Katie's dawdling. Katie always moaned about going to school. She was always talking about attending one of the special schools where students got swimming lessons and band and real art with sculpture and everything. Instead, they both attended the Anne Frank City School, a sprawling building with strict rules and a hard-nosed principal who didn't like either one of them.

Fifteen minutes later, Jeffrey left her at the kindergarten entrance and trudged to the middle school building.

As Katie walked down the hall to her classroom, her knee socks jiggled down her calves and sagged around her ankles. She hiked them back up to her knees; straightened the pleated skirt, vest, and blouse that made up the school uniform; and continued down the hall to the principal's office. Procrastinating, she turned to stare out the lobby window at the early morning sunshine, dreaming of long summer vacations like her mom used to talk about. She liked to dream about going to a ranch and riding a horse. She thought it would be worth the carbon footprint to own a horse, and that maybe if she gave up eating all meat she could apply to have one. She would spend all the rest of her days horseback riding. But her daddy insisted even a dog carried too many points for their family to maintain.

Three second graders jostled by her and knocked her books to the floor.

It was going to be another bad day.

* * *

David slouched against the pillows in bed at the Midway Inn, bleary-eyed. Frankie had chosen midnight to announce his discomforts. David yawned, exhausted from efforts of lulling the infant back to sleep for short thirty-minute catnaps.

He finally turned on the compupanel to see the top stories and determine if he was still considered a hot item.

The newscaster clasped her hands in delight. "Here we have a happy ending to our story about Senator Houston's missing baby. Apparently the baby was never stolen."

Her partner smiled like a brainless mannequin. "That's right, Marge. The baby was right there in the hospital the whole time. The records had been confused."

The camera flipped to a clip of Anne at the hospital holding a blond baby.

"Ms. Shelton, how do you and Senator Houston feel about the hospital's treatment of your baby?"

Anne looked like the perfect mother engrossed in her infant as she recited the words Axyl had prepared for her. "We're just glad he's been found."

"Do you plan to press charges for medical misconduct or neglect?"

Anne looked confused for a moment. Axyl hadn't answered that one for her. "Uh. No. I think they have corrected their mistake. Everyone makes mistakes. And Ms. Gatryl has assured me the parties involved have been dealt with."

The camera switched to Allison Gatryl, the Administrator. "Is that right, Ms. Gatryl?"

Hate seemed to bleed through the calm expression. "I run this medical center to my utmost ability, with a proportioned balance of reward and punishment as I see fit according to the laws of our nation. This incident was merely one case in the many thousands we handle, which is a good record by any standards, but we continue to strive for perfection."

The clip swung back to Anne and her baby for a five-second span, and then back to the news lounge.

"It certainly is nice to report happy news, isn't it, Harrison?"

"Yes, Marge, it is. And for an explanation of the man being chased as the kidnap suspect, we turn to Charlie. Charlie?"

"Thanks, Harrison." The screen split, showing a reporter with a backdrop of David's race to the taxi. "Yesterday, police and airport security personnel chased this man, suspected of kidnapping. That, however, was not his crime. Officials have released a statement identifying the man as Rex Montane, and according to the cab driver he assaulted, he was in possession of a gun. It is suspected he had plans to hijack a plane. He is under further investigation."

David leaned his head against the wall and moaned. If the authorities were only onto his old description, he was safe.

He pounded his head against the wall three times in exasperation. Distracted, Frankie let go of the nipple and wailed until David lured him back to it by lightly touching the nipple to the tiny circle of lips.

He doubted the PMS's word of dropping the case. If the authorities had discovered his Dome status, they were out to get him behind public view.

First things first. He couldn't risk trying to get through airport security with the baby. The only solution was to find another way to get Frankie to safety. Markus was still figuring out his path; he wasn't ready to help beyond the risk he'd already taken. David understood that. He almost envied him for it. But either way, Markus couldn't help beyond what he'd already done—pushing him down the road with Frankie.

David's only other connection in this city was Jessica Main.

The thought of her produced a smile.

With the heat off his trail for kidnapping, it shouldn't be too risky to contact her. He had it all worked out.

With Frankie once more settled for a nap, he reached for the hotel phone and dialed the airport.

The phone immediately went to a menu, but he took a chance and pressed zero in response. Thankfully, it connected him to a live person. "Airport Information. How may I assist you?"

It was a woman's voice. Perfect.

"Good morning. I really need to have a message delivered to my . . . co-hab. Could you possibly do that?"

"Is she an employee?"

"Yes, she is. Jessica Main. She works in the janitorial department."

The woman considered his request. She knew Jessica and didn't recall her ever mentioning a boyfriend, but now that she thought of it, Jessica rarely mentioned anything about her personal life. "Well, sir, I would like to help, but it's really against policy."

"Oh, please. I know you must believe in romance."

He could hear the quiet sigh. "Yes, of course."

"Well, I've been gone for two months, and I'm just on my way back and have a fabulous surprise for her. I just want her to meet me at the Shadow Café for the Unity Day Parade."

Bekka the receptionist sighed again, but this time with resignation. "I really shouldn't, but since it's Jessica, I'll make an exception. I know your Jessie. Not real personal or anything.

In fact, I didn't know she had a boyfriend. But she's a hard worker and I admire that. I won't page her or nothing, but she's due by here in an hour, and I don't mind just slipping her a note."

"Thank you. It will mean so much to us." He'd decided to use the baby's name instead of his own. No one knew the baby's name except her. "Tell her to meet Frankie at the Shadow Café on Liberty Street at nine in the morning for the parade. She'll know where I mean. It's her favorite spot."

"Okay. I will. You be good to her, you hear?"

"Yes, ma'am. I sure will. Thanks again."

He hung up, relieved.

With a turn to the mirror, he scratched at the new brown growth on his face, wondering if he should bother to shave it. He was hotel-bound for the day for safety's sake. Until tomorrow. Until Jessica.

He knelt beside the bed and began to pray.

* * *

Markus took the bus across town. Most weeks he looked forward to the one day a week that he volunteered at the retirement home because Joanne volunteered there, too; that's how he had first met her.

This week, he really needed it—time away from the hospital, away from the news of that Dominian and the baby. He wanted to shut himself away, disentangle himself from the whole ordeal.

* * *

Standing by a cluttered fold-out table in the back corner of his office, coffee filter dangling forgotten in his right hand, Marty stared deep in thought at his compupanel. He'd seen Anne Shelton on the news, and what she'd said was still playing through his mind—her baby had supposedly been found. Senator Axyl Houston's baby. The Dominian still had that baby, and both the Dominian and the baby were still holed up in the hotel room that the Christian underground had provided. *Unless something had happened during the night.*

Not a possibility. His contact would have told him. Unless something had happened to his contact too.

He dropped the coffee filter on the table, pulled out his cell, and entered a number.

"Anything change?"

"Far as I know, just the one outing. Problem?"

Marty frowned. He and Rand had followed him the previous night to see what he'd do. They'd been so relieved to see him return to the hotel that he'd been tempted to approach him right then to talk to him, but they decided it would be better to observe him a bit longer, to see what other contacts he had. Everything was at risk. They didn't know for sure he'd been honest with Joanne, or what his true motive might be. So they'd let him sit. If he was gone now, he'd kick himself.

"I told you to call if he moved. I'm coming."

"Stay put. Too many and we'll raise alarm. I'm sure he's still there. I'll get back to you."

Marty shoved the cell in his pocket and stared at the screen again, putting pieces together in his mind. Deviant kidnapped, big chase, not caught, case dropped as if baby has been found. Different baby. Healthy baby. So what was the deal?

Deviant. Healthy.

The Better World Bill.

Houston was the one behind the infamous Better World Bill they seemed helpless to prevent. That put a different twist on it. Especially seeing how the senator managed to conveniently *fix* the situation with a replacement baby.

Somehow, it all tied together: the Better World Bill taking steps to eliminate all deviants without an option to keep them, and the senator's kid falling into that category. Wow. This could be the break the Liberty League and the Christian underground had been waiting for. It would take careful handling to get it out without being censored by a government watchdog. And it had to create enough stir to really expose the full corruption of the system, a practically impossible feat. But he loved a challenge, and this would be something fantastic if he could pull it off. Insane even.

The thought made him grin. If there was one thing he loved, it was doing something insane. Infamy!

He planned to talk to that Dominian first thing this morning, but they had him hidden and under surveillance. He had to act on this opportunity to destroy the Better World Bill while the situation was still hot.

He looked through his files and found exactly what he needed to get it going: an interview with the executive director of the Gift of Life program.

* * *

Fred Mannsey, principal of the Anne Frank City School, walked into the teachers' lounge and clapped his hands to get everyone's attention. "I know you all saw the news clip yester-day about the Christian getting shot for preaching from the roof of a car. I want you to raise the subject with your students today. You know what to watch for. Send me any names that need follow up."

Van Fenmore touched the principal's shoulder with obvi-ous intent as he passed by. "I'll see what I can do for you, hon."

Two other teachers shot glances at each other as they headed to their classrooms. "Fat chance," one mouthed.

* * *

Betty Holmes sat in her car and groaned at the thought of actu-ally entering the National Family Counseling Center, an ugly glass-and-cement fortress that once had been considered mod-ern. Betty much preferred the sleek gray law office two blocks down, constructed of recycled plastic that gleamed beneath the summer sun. Betty had seen the view from the top floor on Monday when she'd met with her attorney.

She wished she had done it years ago, but Robert hadn't been around back then.

She laid her forehead on the steering wheel, moaning epithets for Markus. She would skip this stupid volunteer stuff, but he would be sure to ask probing questions and check with the director. She couldn't afford a fight if she wanted to pull off this divorce without a hitch.

Her eyes brightened. She could use this forced work to her benefit: make herself look like a good concerned citizen work-ing for the good of the state. *Betty Holmes, not only a fashion icon but a selfless volunteer.* The judge would leap to her side.

She glanced in the sun-visor cosmetic mirror, lightly touching her hair with her right hand but not adjusting a thing; she was perfect. Her lips were ruby red, her nose duly powdered, and her lashes thick and brows perfectly arched.

She forced herself from the comfort of the car. Fatigue had plagued her lately, perhaps a sign of the onset of depression. Not unlikely, with what she had to endure.

Inside, the center was just coming to life. Secretaries were looking over the day's schedule, several meds were milling around the coffee machine discussing their golf game, and two technicians were comparing their graphic booth experiences in the Football at Home series.

Betty stood inside the door a moment, surveying it all. Much to her surprise, the waiting area was tastefully decorated in Ever-Wear fabrics of ecru and hunter green. The cushioned chairs were spaced by formulated-wood tables strewn with UO health and population control publications. All three secretaries were well-dressed women in their thirties, with desks that spoke of either organization or strict rules. This place was not the cesspool she had expected.

A teenager, her hair bound up in a net and her clothes hidden beneath blue coveralls, concentrated on mopping the last stretch of green and beige speckled laminate. Betty disregarded the wet gloss and strode across the floor to the nearest secretary to introduce herself, not caring a whit that she left footprints in her wake.

"Good morning, Ms. Holmes. Have you ever helped out here before?"

Thinking of her day in court, she gave a cat's smile. "No, but I may become a regular."

"Wonderful, wonderful. Let's get you assigned to a counselor, shall we?"

Brooke Evans was hidden in an office down the first hall. She was busy shuffling papers when Betty was ushered in. Brooke was slightly overweight, had dark circles under her eyes, and no makeup other than a spot of concealer on her chin. Her damp, cropped hair and her brown dress blended in with the office furniture. To Betty's trained eye, Brooke's bone structure was exquisite, and her heart-shaped face was endearing. Photogenic dark brown complexion. She could make her into a beauty queen. It took great willpower to suppress the urge to pull out her pamphlets on beauty tips and fashion sense and perform a miraculous make-over as she listened to the girl's instructions.

By the time the doors opened at ten o'clock, Betty had reviewed procedures for accepting a child into custody. She couldn't counsel anyone, but she could assist in processing the paperwork. It seemed easy enough, if not tedious.

Brooke led her to a desk in the lobby, supplied her with pens, and helped her greet the first "customer."

Betty was astonished. The patron wasn't low-class, and indeed not even female, but the best-looking man she had seen in a long time. He could only be in his thirties, much younger than she, but of course she didn't look her age.

He sauntered up to her desk—silky blond hair, green eyes, beautiful teeth, and nonchalant charm. He carried a young child, her little hands clinging to his shoulders and big green eyes just like her daddy's peeking out beneath a pink bonnet.

"Good morning, sir. How can I help you?" Her simple greeting was heavy with implication.

The man was unaffected. He was totally absorbed with sorting out his day and was hoping to find a good babysitter.

"My co-hab left me last night. The sitter won't answer her phone—she is best friends with Lacey, you see, and has no desire to help me out. Anyway, I'm late for work and I've got to have someplace for Carey to stay. I was wondering if you could provide a list of babysitters or make some kind of recommendation?"

Brooke and Betty looked at each other, and then at the patron. Brooke replied, "You mean a private babysitter? Any of the UO day cares can offer perfectly adequate care, sir."

He tensed, his scorn visible in the set of his face.

"No way. All those other children with their runny noses, and who knows what else, breathing on her? Never."

"Really, sir, the day cares are top-notch. Do you have her UIC? I can check for an opening for you," Brooke said.

"No, thank you." He turned to go.

Brooke took a step toward him. "I think, sir, you should use a qualified, registered center. Let me write down her UIC and I will check tomorrow to see if you've registered her with a suitable caregiver."

He braced himself, as if he felt an invisible noose tightening around him. He turned to face her with a most gratifying smile and twinkling eyes full of charm. "Oh, I know you mean well, but I couldn't ask you to go to such trouble. Do you have children?"

"No."

"What a shame. Such beautiful women as yourselves really ought to have daughters replicating your genes." He lavished his best smile on Brooke.

"She's a beautiful child," Betty interjected, trying to rouse attention.

He embraced them with his twinkling eyes. "Thank you. Thank you both. You've been a great help."

As the door closed behind him, both women smiled like schoolgirls.

Betty swooned. "This volunteer work may not be so bad after all."

The next encounter wasn't so pleasant. A stocky woman entered the building pulling on the arm of a girl perhaps five. The little girl's black hair was done up into a dozen beaded braids and tied with bright ribbons. The woman's anger filled her face, as she snatched at the girl's arm.

"Come on," she said. "I told you I wouldn't tolerate your mess no more, and I ain't. You gonna go to one of them special schools I heard 'bout on the radio."

"I don't want to, Mama," whimpered the girl, "I won't be bad no more. I pwomise."

She gave her a brusque shove. "You right, you won't do it no more."

The girl grabbed her legs and wailed pitifully. "Mama. Please, Mama. I'm sorry. I won't hide in your closet no more. I won't eat none of your chips. I won't come in your room. Nothin', Mama."

The woman pried the little girl's fingers loose from her trousers and lifted her by her wrists. "Hush up."

Betty greeted the stocky woman with an understanding smile. All babies, in her mind, grew to become these awful, uncontrollable monsters. Brooke handed Betty a lollipop from a drawer, which she passed on to the wailing girl, and waved the distraught woman into a seat. The girl huddled under her mother's seat, secretly unwrapping the candy, and stealing glances at her mother, fearing she would snatch the treat away.

"How can we help you?"

"I need help with this young 'un. She's got outta control and I can't be dealin' wit her no more. I heard about them schools that help kids like her. I heard they's free."

Betty glanced at Brooke for reassurance, then down at the Ten Steps to Admittance sheet.

"Would you like to schedule an appointment with a counselor?"

The woman grunted. "I have to have an appointment? I thought I just had to sign some papers and you all would help me know what to do wit' her. I heard tell you got some special school that might could help her get some respect."

Betty glanced at the paper again, sure she was skipping some steps or something. "Let me record your UICs and check guardianship records; it won't take long."

"Better not take too long," she muttered looking at her girl's sticky face, "cause she's bound to start up again right soon as that candy's gone."

Another young mother entered with a small toddler propped on her hip. She held her head high with pride, but her eyes were puffy from recent tears. She looked from the letter in her hand to the labels over the two hallways.

Brooke approached her. "You must be Sarah, my ten o'clock appointment."

"Yes, ma'am," her voice cracked. "Sarah Chance."

"Great. Come on back."

* * *

Marty set off down the road toward Miss Yancey's diner for a bite to eat, thinking about how to proceed. Watching the officers pursue the Dominian had stirred something in him. Everything the Liberty League and the underground Christians had said about the Better World Bill hit him as he watched that smug Anne Shelton drool over that baby as if it were her real son— when she *had* to know that her real son, her defective son, had been kidnapped, and if he hadn't been kidnapped, he would have been thrown away like a piece of trash. How warped was that? Why, if Axyl Houston was so set on passing this bill, would he not make a public example with his own deviant kid?

Because it would make it too real. It would make it too clear what the Better World Bill means.

And then here was this man, this Dominian. He must have known. The Dome must have figured out that the senator's kid was a deviant and set out to make a statement by stealing it to bring attention to it.

What did that say about him—Marty—and his fellow lovers of freedom? A new conviction flowed in his veins, pounded in his heart, churning with all the animosity he harbored for being interned in that UO institute all those years. He wanted restitution. And was tired of waiting for it.

He was ready for a revolution. And he had a plan. For starters, he had set up an interview between Gift of Life Chairperson Shyla Hillis and newscaster Henry Burth—easily accomplished by making a few calls impersonating first one side's assistant and then the other's, then hacking the station's production schedule.

But the Gift interview was only the setup. The news team would never tell what really went on. They'd feed the public the same Good for the Nation song and dance that they always spooned out. He intended to bleed a bit of reality into it: show the world what really went on inside the Gift Center and what the Better World Bill actually meant.

He stopped short. People knew it was a donor center. Or at least they ought to know. It wasn't a secret at all. His plan was just to give them a graphic reminder. *But where did all those donors come from?* There couldn't be that many brain-dead people, especially brain-dead children. So where were they getting them?

Then it hit him: the National Family Counseling Centers had to be involved in the process. He'd read the documentation and never made the connection: parents gave up all parental and medical rights.

He turned around. Food could wait. He had to check out the Counseling Center first.

* * *

Jessica heaved the mop ahead of her, into the lobby, past the airport information desk. Bekka was talking into the phone and punching buttons. Jessica waved to her with mop in hand before flopping it down and pushing it between the bolted chairs.

Bekka paused between buttons. "Jess! Come here." She waved a paper in her hand, pushed a button, and muttered into the phone.

Jessica laid the mop across the seats and stepped up to the counter.

Bekka covered the mouthpiece. "You didn't get it from me, hear?" She went back to the business of flashing buttons.

Jessica stared at the folded paper, walked away a few steps, and unfolded it.

Meet your fella Frankie at Shadow Café
For Unity Day Parade at 9 a.m.

Jessica stared at it, puzzled. She read it three times, glanced back at Bekka, who took the curious look to be pleased surprise at the prospect of seeing her boyfriend again. Bekka grinned and continued mumbling into the phone.

Jessica read it once more. Her fella? What kind of bad joke was this? Her fella?

A warm feeling flowed through her. It couldn't be . . . Rex? A little voice in the back of her head giggled. It was rusty from disuse, a little tingly, somebody-likes-me feeling from back when she was a kid.

Why would Rex call himself her fella? To joke? To continue the farce for some reason?

She shoved the note to the bottom of her pocket, making sure it was deep enough not to pop out during work.

She would go. There was no indecision. She had no reason not to go. No other person in her life. Nothing pressing to do. Another empty Saturday. Just laundry and a good book. She would definitely go.

The mop seemed much lighter as she pushed it across the floor.

* * *

Debra shifted her pregnant frame in the chair of National Family Counseling Center, uncomfortable with the weight of the overdue baby. It was a last minute decision to bring Johnny to the center, but now that she was here, talking to these people, she was glad she'd come.

Initially, she'd come in anger to take revenge on Harve, to find a way to hurt him the worst way possible because she was sick of him. Every last thing he'd done the night before had gotten on her nerves until she couldn't stand it, until she'd screamed at him and he'd yelled back, and they'd gotten in the worst fight ever, and he left.

On her own, she couldn't afford two kids, and there was no way she'd let Harve have Johnny. No way. *Nothing* would hurt him like losing Johnny.

"I like this place, Mommy," came his squeaky baby-talk voice. "Good lollipops."

Debra sighed, relieved at having made the right decision. He would receive a top-notch education and become a Peace Patroller for the state, or a soldier, maybe.

Johnny tugged on Betty's arm and pointed to the acrylic prism paperweight. "Can I touch that thing?"

Betty Holmes looked at the sturdy boy. He had actually asked first instead of grabbing for it like the last three children brought in. She mused a moment. Actually, the little red-headed girl hadn't grabbed. She had fingered it softly without picking it up.

"Well, it's not mine. I'm just helping out here today," said Betty.

The little boy stood stock still, gazing at it.

Betty gave in. "All right. Go ahead, but be careful with it, okay?"

The boy grinned and took it in both hands, turned it from side to side to watch the colors shift.

Debra snatched it away. "Crap, Johnny. You've got that sticky lollipop drool all over it." She pulled moist wipes from her purse, wiped it clean, and plopped it back on the desk, remembering in a flash why boys irritated her so much. Dirty, noisy, and disruptive. "Sit down and don't move. Now!"

The boy puffed out his lip and sniffed but dropped obediently on his bottom. Betty looked at him and then at his mother with approval. "Good kid."

"He'll make a good soldier." She shifted her heavy body to give him room on the floor.

Betty looked at him on the floor again, then held out the next form. "If you're sure you don't want counseling before terminating your custody, you'll need to sign here. It says I've explained the counseling program that's available and that you have chosen not to talk to anyone."

"What's to talk about? The UO Institutes are fantastic. Look at what they turn out. Did you know Senator Axyl Houston wasn't much older than my boy when he was sent there? Maybe Johnny might be a senator one day." She signed the form with a flourish.

"This next form is the actual termination of custody. By signing this form, he becomes property of the state. If his physical condition warrants it, he may be euthanized according to standard medical procedures or otherwise handled as seen fit by the state according to health and mental standards. Fill out his name and UIC here, birth date, and your name and UIC here. Then sign the bottom."

Debra held the pen poised in the air. She knew how the system worked, but she asked just the same. "Like if he was harmed in a war and was brain dead or something, right? Or his arms got blown off?"

Betty looked from her to the paper to the little boy. Everything Markus had ever said to her came flooding back, but she pushed the memories away. "I'm not a doctor, so I really couldn't say." She set the paper in front of Debra and handed Johnny another candy. He bore a resemblance to a little boy she'd played with as a kid years ago.

Debra read the words through several times until they blurred in front of her as her resolve wavered. She contemplated his future: dressed in a miniature uniform, seated at a desk being obedient, marching in line with hundreds of other children, saluting the UO flag. He brushed against her leg, but she kept her eyes trained on the paper and contemplated *her* future. She couldn't raise two kids. Impossible with the economy the way it was. And she wanted her baby girl.

Johnny pulled at the hem of her maternity dress. "I want my daddy."

His sticky hands moved from the dress to her leg. Messy. Messy boy. Messy men. Harve had left a path of turmoil in her life, making her lose sight of her career goals, making her lose her determination to succeed. He made her become less than she could have been.

And he'd betrayed her. She was sure of it. She was sure he'd had another affair.

His name rose like a curse in her mind. *Harve.*

Hurting Harve was reason enough. It would kill him to find out she'd sent Johnny off to be a soldier.

A *soldier.* She gripped that image as she gripped the pen and swirled her name across the black line.

"Am I done?" she asked, picking up her purse.

"Ah, yes. I believe so. Let me see." Betty read over her list of procedures. "Yes. Yes you are." She filed the papers into a folder and stood. "Come on, Johnny," she said to the boy, holding her hand out to him. She hadn't taken the others back. Several had gone for counseling, and a nurse had taken the little girl. She wavered, unsure where to go until another worker pointed to a door off to the side.

The little boy reached for her hand, his sticky fingers clasping her own.

* * *

Van Fenmore, kindergarten teacher, watched the children's faces closely. "Who thinks the man shouldn't have been shot?"

Three kids raised their hands.

"Katie. Tell me why, hon. Tell me what you think."

"He was only talking. Why'd they shoot him?"

"Because he was talking about hateful things that could hurt people," answered Preston Malloy without waiting to be chosen. Preston could get away with it because he was Mr. Fenmore's favorite. He got treats all the time.

Seymore Blaine waved his hand wildly in the air until Mr. Fenmore pointed to him. "The man was telling what he believed, trying to make other people believe it too. That's not right."

Mr. Fenmore nodded. "Do you understand that, Katie?"

She pursed her lips. "He was just talking about Jesus. What's wrong with that?"

"Jesus is made up," Prissy said.

Mr. Fenmore leaned forward. "Do you think Jesus is a myth, Katie, or real?"

"Real," she replied. "Otherwise they wouldn't shoot people for talking about him."

He tapped a button on his computer. "What do you know about Jesus?"

Katie hesitated. She wasn't supposed to talk about God in school. Her daddy told her not to.

"She don't know nothing," Seymore said.

"Be quiet, Seymore. What do you know, Katie?"

* * *

Trudy drove up to Jessica's apartment, uncertain what she expected to find. David? The baby? Jessica? Or all three? She wasn't even sure what she planned to say to them, if they were there. She just wanted to confirm her suspicions.

The complex was typical for government housing: single-story concrete apartments with plain white doors and one small window centered to the left of the door. Every painted surface was peeling. Trash fluttered around the walkways. The parking lot held three cars, probably supplied by the government for government employees. Almost everyone else used public transit. Trudy pulled into a slot near the entrance to the complex and walked to Jessica's front door.

The place was practically deserted. One woman at a distant apartment stepped out to shake out a rug and disappeared inside again. A cat dashed across the road. But nothing else.

Trudy ignored the front door and walked purposely around back, walking confidently, like she belonged there, like she was used to following the long cement walkway edging the six-foot-wide strip of common area that was more dirt than grass, which ran the length of the building. She would peek in the window to assess the situation. Then she would go back out front and knock on the door.

She heard muffled music and voices coming from the first apartment, second one silent, third one was Jessica's. No one anywhere in sight. She peered between the bars of the one back window. No one inside. Silent.

Now what?

She stepped up to the back stoop, ground level with only a single patio block laid as a step in front of the plain, white door with an old-fashioned keyed lock. The door frame was rotted and the bottom of the door was swollen from rainwater settling on the cement. She puzzled over what to do. She wasn't a burglar. Her daddy had taught her a lot of things but not how to pick a lock.

She looked around, hoping to spot some place that a key might be hidden. Everybody kept an extra key somewhere. To her right she saw a ceramic yard turtle. Too obvious. No one would really put a key in a commercial key hider. Instead, she reached over and checked out an old pair of running shoes. Nothing in them. Where else? Off to the left, she spotted a plastic plant pot with the remains of a flower withered to a pale brown stem and shriveled blossom. She lifted it up full of hope, but the only thing under it was a family of grubs. She turned back to the turtle. Still disbelieving, she picked it up, fiddled with it and opened the key compartment. Surprise, surprise, there was a key.

Trudy was slightly disappointed at Jessica's lack of ingenuity . . . until she tried to insert the key. It didn't fit. She tried it upside down, just in case. Not a fit. She laughed. A decoy key. How funny. Or maybe the key to the front door?

She turned and headed to the sidewalk but stumbled on a broken bit of cement, nearly tripping. She righted herself and looked back at what she'd almost tumbled over: the corner of the patio where a triangular piece had broken loose and had been planted back in place without meeting the edges smoothly. She cussed and kicked it just for good measure, then really looked at it. The broken piece looked like it hadn't been disturbed in ages. Dirt had settled around it. Grass had sprouted in the crack. But the door looked like it hadn't been used in ages either. It was worth a try. She leaned down and pried the corner piece from the clutches of the earth. There beneath it, pressed into the dirt, lay a key.

She pulled it from the dirt, wiped it off, and fitted it into the lock. After fiddling with it, the doorknob turned in her hand, but the door wouldn't open. It had to open if the doorknob turned, didn't it? The swollen door . . . she put her shoulder into it and shoved as hard as she could. The third try, it finally swung open.

Stunned, she stood there a second, then quickly stepped inside and pushed it closed behind her.

She was in a long laundry/storage room with a bathroom to one side. She stepped through to the main room, a family room with a kitchenette to the left, a sparsely furnished bedroom to her right, and a second bedroom strewn with sewing projects and crafts.

The living room couch sagged but had recently been recovered with yellow-and-green-flowered material, an amateur attempt at a slipcover using sheets instead of upholstery fabric. An old walnut rocking chair, a shelf of books and magazines, and a scarred wooden chest completed the room.

Trudy crossed the room and peered at the spines, curious about Jessica's interests. Dickens, Shakespeare, Bronte. Modern works of Candace Fenn. *Politics and Policies of the New Millennium.*

Old stuff and new, all requiring some decent range of intelligence—and all in old-fashioned paper book form. She might
have underestimated this girl. *Moby Dick. Gone with the Wind.
The Scarlet Letter. Little Women.* Hmm. A Bible. A Bible? Not
the authorized UO version, but an old one—the Douay-Rheims.
In government housing! How daring! Trudy touched the spine
but passed over it for the next book, a plain brown volume worn
and cracked from attention. As she pulled it from the shelf, it
fell open to text marked by an old photo of an elderly man and
woman surrounded by a brood of children, one of which she was
sure was a teenage Jessica. Lifting the picture, she read words
that were highlighted in garish yellow on the page beneath it:

> *We are not our own any more than what we possess
> is our own. We did not make ourselves, we cannot be
> supreme over ourselves. We are not our own masters.
> We are God's property. Is it not our happiness thus to
> view the matter? Is it any happiness or any comfort to
> consider that we are our own? It may be thought so by
> the young and prosperous. These may think it a great
> thing to have everything, as they suppose, their own
> way—to depend on no one—to have to think of nothing
> out of sight, to be without the irksomeness of continual
> acknowledgement, continual prayer, continual reference
> of what they do to the will of another. But as time goes
> on, they, as all men, will find that independence was not
> made for man—that it is an unnatural state—will do for
> a while, but will not carry us on safely to the end.*

> *—Cardinal Newman*

Stunned, Trudy read the passage three times, thinking of how alone she was, thinking how she'd strived to be independent for so long, so unattached to anyone or anything. Was this Cardinal Newman right? Is that what her life was missing that no amount of work seemed to fill? The emptiness that no adventure chased away? She needed something. She thought a baby would help. But God?

Her eyes were drawn to the wall at back of the room, to a sketch depicting a homeless family of the late nineteen-hundreds crouched beneath a bridge.

Trudy shuddered. The image carried her back to the day that changed her life, to when she was a little girl crouched under the sagging porch of her parents' house, smelling the damp earth, her back against the cool roughness of the cinderblock foundation. Father, demanding she not make a noise, tripped back up the steps to the house as Mother's screams filled the air. And then, through the checkerboard holes of lattice, she saw Grandma being led to a black UO car, her morning apron still tied around her, and her hands wet with dish soap, being led away for violating Freedom from Religion legislation.

That was the day Mother had her breakdown.

How could she have forgotten? She almost fainted with the memory, catching her hand on the side of Jessica's couch, breathing deeply to control the explosion in her head. With clarity, she pictured her reclusive mother who said little to anyone. Her mother had become a shell. She tended her garden. She never read, watched news, or listened to the radio. The reason and change had existed too long to attribute to anything. It was as if the earlier mother had never existed. Mother is as Mother had always been. And explanations had died with Father years ago. But now she remembered the happy mother who had laughed and celebrated. And prayed reverently.

She remembered it all through a fog of denial and years of dire warnings against professing any belief in the Trinity. God lay dormant in her mind like childhood dream waiting to be pulled from hiding by cue of a smell or a touch. Or the right words.

She gave the rest of the room a cursory glance. In contrast to the used furnishings, a fairly new computer was neatly arranged in a built-in desk cubby. Computers were considered a human right, as essential as a telephone or refrigerator, and therefore included free of charge in government houses across the nation, but not without infringement. Every transmission was tracked.

The kitchen, tidy but not especially clean, disappointed Trudy. A few dishes lay spread on a towel to dry, a few others were stacked in the sink, but there was no sign of baby bottles or nipples.

No crib in the bedroom. No baby toys or clothes.

She moved to the computer, woke it up, and scanned the files. So easy—files were barely even coded. Pay info: Airport Janitorial Services.

She called the main operator. After three recordings, she reached a person. "Hi," Trudy said. "My sister works there and I forgot what time she said to pick her up. Could you tell me what time the current shift ends?"

"One o'clock."

"Thank you." She glanced at the time and slid the phone back into her pocket. "One o'clock. I'll be there." Work first, but she'd find some excuse to leave before one.

* * *

Marty had walked by the local National Family Counseling Center often enough, but he'd never been inside. Large bushes grew along the parking lot, blocking the view from the office building next door, lending a sense of privacy to the cement sidewalk that led past windows to a glass door. Everything about it beckoned with a message of *Welcome*.

The lobby area was empty right then, but he could hear soft sounds, farther back in the building. Crying.

A blond lady greeted him. "Can I help you?" she asked.

He shrugged at the lady. "My sister said to meet her here. I'm early. She's always late." He laughed at his own joke and took a seat in the waiting room.

The lady returned to her work.

He figured it was worth an hour of his time to eavesdrop and see what went on just in case his hunch was right. He pulled out his cell and surfed the Internet while he waited.

* * *

At eleven o'clock, Axyl entered his office, settled at his desk, and picked up the phone. He began to speak, first in generic pleasantries, then in a businesslike tone. "The situation, Mr. President, is that Jack Friday suggested negotiations. It's important that I keep this bill on track . . ."

It took him about twenty minutes to settle the matter. Axyl was a key component in fitting the last of the UO pieces into place, in creating true Universal Unity by setting an example of full compliance to the UO ideology, and he wasn't about to be stopped by Jack Friday—whether the root of Jack's sudden hesitation was greed or doubt, he didn't care. He would pay him off and keep his bill rolling.

He had one more deal to confirm that afternoon. Bonita Gonzales was playing the populist, arguing against the bill in public. He picked up the phone again, this time skipping the small talk. "Bonita," he said, "I think it's time to show that change of heart. We're getting down to the wire."

"Sure," she replied, "when you deliver."

The connection went dead. Axyl cussed. She hadn't even given him a chance to respond.

Trudy, seated at her desk, pretended total concentration as he walked by. Working for Axyl provided access to information she would never have been exposed to otherwise, but her stress quota had reached its peak. She had spent years working her way into this position so she could report to the Liberty League on the inner workings of the senator's office. The mixture of power and danger had always intoxicated her. But now a new, reality settled over her: she had to think of her own unborn child. Knowing Axyl had no qualms over killing Anne's baby, Trudy felt sure he would try to influence her decision—if she let him know. Maybe she could keep her child's health a secret. She and Axyl certainly never spoke of family or personal lives anyway. She stared at the screen trying to read the words to edit the document, but her mind remained distracted.

She pulled the medical form out of her pocket and stared helplessly at the meaningless words and codes that defined her baby's condition. She had accessed a medical dictionary and confirmed that the chromosome structure showed slight deviation from normal but could find no indication of what it meant. She wished she knew a doctor, a real obstetrician or geneticist who could explain what the mutation meant.

The twelve-week ultrasound confirmed two arms and two legs and ten fingers and ten toes and all the proper organs. Was the problem mental?

Axyl's voice on the intercom broke her train of thought. "Trudy, come in to my office, please."

He never waited for a response and expected an immediate appearance. She gathered a notebook and pen and entered his office with her usual dignified grace.

As she took a seat, she concentrated on keeping her breaths shallow. "Sir, did you retrieve the file from my desk last night?"

"Yes, Trudy, I did. Have you written the press release I requested?"

He had forgotten his decision to assign that to Norman. Sloppy, Axyl. Sloppy. "No, sir. You assigned that to Norman, and he has not passed it on to me. Would you like me to request a copy from him?"

He stood up and moved to the front of the desk to prop on the edge. Trudy couldn't breathe.

"Do you know what the Better World Bill entails, Trudy?"

"Yes, sir. You wanted a bill written to expand Healthy Selections to other phases of healthcare."

"To *all* phases of healthcare!" Axyl smiled as if relishing the thought. "Perhaps I should have involved you in its development a bit more. You see, A Better World will extend the Health Continuity Councils to include health viability even before birth. Right now, in the case of births, we only have that control over government surrogates, but with this bill, we'll mandate that every birth be governed by the same strict guidelines of health and productivity, every child's score evaluated by the Healthcare Continuity Counsels. By eliminating *all* deviants at birth we will save hundreds of billions right from the start, and allow all the time and medical attention currently wasted on their care to be directed to more beneficial ends. And generations from now, the entire nation will be healthier, free from genetic disorders. A Better World will mean the end of all deformity. It will ensure that our country is a nation of perfection.

"There will be other social benefits, too. Think of all the suffering and expense currently saved by government intervention in surrogate births, and expand that to all births. No longer will *anyone* have to decide the fate of a deviant. The government will lift that burden from all parents and take care of the problem. We will relieve individuals of the horrible stress of making the right decision."

Trudy rarely expressed any opposition to Axyl's comments; he was the boss. But this involved her personally. Still, she had to be politic. "How does this influence the definition of parental authority? Currently, under Healthy Selections, parents may opt to keep their child."

Axyl shook his head. "People are too emotional. They have trouble making decisions with their heads instead of their hearts. That's why there are still so many defects, too much money and time spent on the chronically ill and the mentally feeble. Think of how families suffer to support severely handicapped family members. It can bankrupt them. People *need* the government to help them make the right choice.

Trudy tensed.

Axyl's eyes never left her face. "We both know this concerns you, Trudy."

Trudy raised her eyebrows, but said nothing. With effort she could be as cool as him.

"Your fetus. You refused to stay and have the termination done yesterday."

It took everything she had to keep from shaking. She knew what was coming.

"I cannot promote my bill while one of my own staff carries a deviant."

Trudy continued to stare at him.

"You know what to do."

She had the wild thought of asking him if he knew what was wrong with the baby but didn't really want to hear it from him. He wouldn't care, anyway. Any imperfection would be intolerable to him. Besides, she feared her chin would quiver. Silence stretched between them. Finally, she stood. "Will there be anything else, senator?"

"Just one thing." He picked a note up off his desk and handed it to her.

His handwriting was tight contortions:

PMS appointment, 2:00, Gyn Center.

She spoke through stiff lips, "Thank you, sir," and retreated to her office where she succumbed to the shakes. With effort she mentally forced her body to relax: one arm, the other arm, her spine, her legs, until the quaking dissipated. She had to think rationally.

She wouldn't let him force her to abort her baby. She had some money tucked away. She would use it all to survive until she found another job, if that's what it took. And if she had to, she would go back home to live with her mother.

Her phone said noon. She forced herself to sit quietly in her chair. She supposed he was watching her door, waiting to see what she was going to do. No, it wasn't as simple as quitting her job. She knew too much. Axyl could make a phone call and have her arrested on some false charge and locked up for life. Or worse. Her stomach knotted with fear and uncertainty.

She heard footsteps in the hall. Without thinking, she turned to her computer and began flashing through commands and screens, without much conscious thought of where she was going. She just wanted to look busy.

He paused by her office window, then continued down the hall.

She picked up her writing panel, tucked it into a briefcase, and left her office. Stopping at Norman's desk, she presented her most normal smile. "I'm leaving for the rest of the day. I have an appointment. Axyl insisted . . ." She let her voice trail off. It didn't take much to make her voice emotional. "I probably won't feel up to working tomorrow, so please take care of my calls. I'll see you Monday."

Norman looked at her inanely. "Okay."

The secretary, though not a close friend, eyed Trudy. "Is everything all right?"

She wanted to scream *No*. Instead, she nodded, strode away, and tried to keep from breaking down as she waited for the elevator, descended to the lobby, and escaped to the street beyond.

She walked a few blocks in the direction of the PMS, then ducked into a tiny store that sold old books. She knew the owner had what she wanted. She'd seen it several months before—a small journal titled *Inside the Dome*. She gave him her best smile. "Mr. Redd, remember that old silver coin of mine you admired so much?"

The old man looked up from the novel open on his lap. "Why yes, Miss Trudy. I surely do. You ready to sell it to me?"

She slapped the quarter on the counter. "I'm making you a trade. The coin for this book."

He didn't even glance at the title. His fingers worked to pick the coin off the scuffed linoleum counter. "You made an old man happy today. Take whatever book you want."

"Thank you, Mr. Redd. Enjoy." She slipped the book into her pocket and rushed out the door, no computer, no television, no cell the wiser of her purchase. There was something to be said for old coinage.

* * *

Harve Johnson stormed into the National Family Counseling Center and went straight to the front desk, his huge body dwarfing the woman behind it, his face a physical growl.

Betty Holmes, overwhelmed at the man's size and obvious vehemence, blanched. "May I help you?"

"You better. I want my boy back."

"Excuse me?"

"You heard me. Debra Sykes brought him in here and signed him over. But I'm his dad, and I want him back."

Eyeing the teenage boy reading a magazine in the waiting area, Betty fiddled with her pen and tried to sound official. "I'm sorry, sir, but that's against regulations. If she had custody, which I'm sure she did or I wouldn't have processed the work, she has rights over him."

Marty Young, sitting in the waiting area, slipped his camera out of his pocket began recording. His hunch was paying off at least with a nice emotional battle of the co-habs.

"No way. Just because she put claims on him when he was in utero, when I didn't even know him, doesn't mean she can decide to terminate parental rights without even consulting me."

Betty grimaced as a pain gripped her abdomen. *What timing. I've got to finish with this guy and go home to bed.* She swallowed the pain, then replied with cool reserve, "We are a counseling center. We help make informed decisions about a child's care, and the guardian has all rights over that decision."

"He's not property. He's a person. A child. He has his own rights."

"No, sir. Not until he's age five. And then, sir, after age five, he has absolute rights, and you have no control over his decisions." She had heard Markus fume over this dilemma so many times, his explanation came to her naturally. Perhaps this time with more understanding.

He leaned forward into the woman's face and spoke quietly, brusquely, each word emphasized. "You go get my son for me or I'll make a lot of trouble."

"Look, mister . . ."

"Johnson. Harve Johnson."

"Mr. Johnson. Tell me your son's name. Better yet, his number."

"Johnny. Johnny Sykes." He rattled off the 16-digit number.

She didn't have to look at her list of names. She remembered him. The sweet one. The one with the sticky hand that she had led to the back herself. "Yes, he was brought in and processed in to the program. She refused counseling."

"Well, un-process him. I'm taking him home."

"I can't do that."

"You can do that, or I'll break every bone in your body."

"I'm sorry, Mr. Johnson. I'm just a volunteer here. I don't have authority to take action."

The word volunteer screamed in his brain. Why would anyone volunteer to help steal children away?

He pushed her desk several inches into her. "Then I'll get him myself."

He strode past her desk, long, heavy steps, clomping down in his construction boots, straight to the admittance door as if he worked there himself.

Across the room, an administrative clerk assessed the situation and pushed a silent alarm button to summon the director and the police. The procedure was routine.

"Stop, Mr. Johnson," Betty yelled as she trailed behind him in her high heels. As another cramp knifed her abdomen, she paused, then hurried to catch him. "You can't go back there."

He ignored her, shoved the door open, and stopped a few paces down a hallway to where it joined a large holding room full of dazed and sobbing children. He stopped, horrified. Small cubicles lined the walls of the room with privacy curtains pushed aside. Every examination table held a little hostage, with technicians drawing vials of blood and filling out screens of data.

Betty had only been as far as the door, where she had pressed a buzzer and was met by a technician. She went charging after the man and halted at his side, sharing his vantage point. She moved past him to see Shanna, the little girl she had processed, lying drugged into an unseeing daze. Johnny was two cubicles over, curled up in a ball. Three vials of blood hung from a rack beside him, and a tray of needles and empty vials lay on a moveable stand by his head.

Johnny whimpered, a cry of despair without the energy to cry anymore.

Harve Johnson crossed the room in two steps and lifted Johnny into his arms. Shock, surprise, and relief passed over his childish features in waves. His tiny arms reached for the familiar neck of his daddy, a neck as large as his little toddler waist. "Da! Da! Da!"

A technician turned. "Put him down this instant."

"Fat chance," Harve said as he struck the man square in the face and then lunged for the hallway and door.

Brooke was there now, blocking the door. "The police have already been called. I suggest you put the boy down and wait peacefully. We don't let unauthorized parents come in here and bully us."

"Get out of my way, lady," he said, kicking her in the stomach with his heavy boot and bolting for the front exit.

Betty moved her hands from her throbbing head to the tingling developing in her left arm.

Police sirens approached, their squeal filling the lobby as Harve Johnson pushed through the glass doors.

"Stop and put your hands up!" yelled an officer.

Harve never paused. With Johnny hugged to his chest, he ran down the sidewalk toward a taxi. People stopped in the street, summing up the scene in an instant. Those in the lobby held their breath.

The officers aimed their beams for his calves, since the boy was in his arms, and he stumbled, but kept moving. He was close enough, though, that he was an easy target. They hit his thighs and his right hip.

"He's my son!" he screamed. "My son!" He floundered for a step and collapsed against the car. "I just want my son."

They finished him with a ray aimed at his head.

A technician ran out the door with Brooke. "Get that boy back into the room."

The technician dragged him from the car and carried him screaming back to his cell.

Marty Young quickly concealed his camera and slipped through the crowd gathered around Harve Johnson's body. He knew an official news team would arrive in minutes to expose Mr. Johnson as a traitor to the Unified Order. The story would surely be that he was a wife-beater, a child-abuser, a tax cheat—somebody who got what he deserved. But Marty would stifle that. He would bleed the video into the news with scenes from the Gift Center. He would show these ignorant people what really went on in the system.

And then, he would watch the results.

* * *

David paced back and forth in the motel room patting Frankie's back. The baby had fussed most of the night, and David had walked the floor so long, stared at the walls so long, he couldn't stand it anymore. There was nothing he could do until the rendezvous with Jessica. He couldn't contact the Dome, and even disguised he couldn't risk too much public exposure, but he had eaten the last of the food that morning. He was hungry and grumpy and yearned for fresh air.

He stepped cautiously out the door and headed toward the back of the motel, away from the main road. From the sidewalk, a path led through a small patch of trees to a park where the old woman had met him with the key.

He settled on a bench in the sun and watched as a group of school children disembarked from an elementary school that backed up to the park. They looked like a miniature army standing at attention, twenty identical robots in their uniforms, until the teacher clapped and the children dispersed across the playground equipment, squealing and yelling. As they moved closer, David could see their individuality: rosy cheeks, curly hair, an afro, a bob, a chubby face and scarred knees, a sly grin, a bossy scowl. They were all so alive and carefree—and so unexpected. He had imagined all this world to be as miserable as the adults.

"You see those kids?" he asked Frankie. "You're going to run around and play like that some day."

He sat on a remote bench, relishing the sunshine and clear blue sky, as the children's happy noise washed over him. He closed his eyes, imagining himself a child in their version of tag. "Zap, I got you," they called to one another. He opened his eyes and watched the zapped kid crumple to the ground and lie there until a girl, flapping her arms like a bird, pointed to him and declared, "I release you." A new version of freeze tag. Some things never changed. He touched Frankie's nose. "Zap, I got you. But let me tell you, buddy, it's not so fun when you really get zapped." His shoulder was fine, but the wound on his side still throbbed. He closed his eyes again, relishing the slight breeze on his skin, and didn't see the little figure approaching.

* * *

At the retirement home, Joanne leaned close to Markus as they helped an elderly man into a wheelchair. "I feel like we abandoned him."

He knew she wasn't talking about the patient. "We did what we could. Let him handle it from here."

"But they're after him."

Markus tucked a blanket around the man's knees and stood up. "What do you expect me to do?"

"I don't know," Joanne said as she took hold of the wheel-chair. "Something."

* * *

Marty, feeling good about what he'd recorded at the Counseling Center, strolled across the back alley and down two blocks, then ducked into a small diner. "Hello, Miss Yancey."

"Hello to you, Marty-boy. Will it be the usual?"

"A whole one. I'm sharing today."

She nodded. "And what have you for me, dearie?"

He pulled a silver barrette from his pocket.

"My land, how beautiful. Where on earth did you find such a thing?"

"Can't tell that now, can I?"

She laughed. "Get on with ya. It will be ready shortly."

He moved to a corner table where a group of four young boys sat arguing good-naturedly. "You don't stand a chance," one was saying.

Marty slapped him on the back. "Whatever it is, I'm up for a wager."

"Of course you are, Marty," said another. "And no doubt you'd win."

Marty settled into a chair to wait for his food.

* * *

Katie walked up to the man with the baby and peered into his face. "Hey mister, are you asleep?"

David jerked. "Whoa. You scared me. I didn't even hear you walk up."

"I'm very small so I don't even crush the leaves when I walk. It creeps out my brother."

She *was* small, with huge brown eyes and a head full of curls. Adorable. "Aren't you going to be in trouble coming way over here?"

"Naw. Mr. Willis and Mr. Fenmore bring both classes out for recess at the same time so they can talk over by the trees and touch each other. It's really gross."

"I bet."

"Can I see your baby?"

He wasn't sure what to make of this little sprite. "If you don't wake him up." He peeled the blanket back, and she peered over his arm to look at him. She made some cooing whispers to him, then, satisfied, looked up at David. "You're the guy on the news, aren't you?"

David's heart stopped.

"Don't worry. Jeffrey told me it's all a secret and not to talk about it."

"Who's Jeffrey?"

"My big brother. He wants to be like Marty when he grows up, learning all the secrets and stuff. He's always try-ing to act like Marty, whistling, and doing this weird wink." She tried to demonstrate, but it turned into a lopsided, twisted smile with her tongue stuck out. It took everything David had not to laugh at her.

She gave up on the wink. "If you saw him, you'd know it by his green ball cap. Marty gave it to him, so he never goes anywhere without it on."

David nodded even though he had no idea what she was talking about. "So are you going to tell Marty and Jeffrey that you saw me here?"

"I have to tell Jeffrey. He makes me tell him everything."

"I see." David leaned in conspiratorially. "Maybe just this once you could keep a secret from him?"

"Maybe," she said, "but he can usually tell."

A whistle blew, calling the children back to order.

Frankie squalled at the noise.

"I gotta go," she said. "Nice baby."

David watched her run back to her classmates, then hustled back to the confines of the room to gather his stuff. He had no idea where he would go now. But he couldn't stay in the area. Whoever Jeffrey and Marty were, they knew who he was and where he was hiding.

He shoved the hotel room door closed, locked it, and took three steps into the room before he was struck by two things—the aroma of pizza and a scrawny teenage boy sitting at the small table by the window.

* * *

Home at last with her new baby, Anne sat in the nursery, rocking him, replaying the previous day's events in her mind. The irresponsibility of the PMS staff! How dare they make her think that her healthy, normal baby was deformed.

The rocking lulled both her and the infant, her mind moving in waves with the rhythm of the seat. Normal, deformed, normal, deformed, normal.

The fuzz of his hair, his puckered lips, his itsy-bitsy fingernails. Everything was perfect. Perfect, perfect, perfect, perfect.

She had expected him to look like Axyl. At least his eyes. Or his hair. But he had none of Axyl's features at all. Not like Axyl, not like Axyl, not like Axyl.

She tried to picture him years ahead, a grown man, standing a head taller than his father, thick and wiry, with silky blond hair, but had a hard time with the image. She couldn't picture Axyl with an arm slung over his son's shoulder. Maybe stretched out in a formal handshake? Formal handshake, formal handshake.

Not bound together. Rather detached. They might not even know each other by the time the boy grew to adulthood. Axyl might pass them on the street and never recognize them. It seemed a miracle they'd been together for two years. She could never get too comfortable.

Losing Axyl would destroy her. At his side, she had risen to the height of society. Axyl was her life. Her claim to fame. His baby would keep that connection alive. Her baby. So beautiful. So perfect. Perfect, perfect, perfect, perfect.

She forbade the other images from entering her mind, but she was too tired, too weak to push them away. The dead babies in the dumping bin, the little girl in the Gift Center. The man's hand around the leg of the infant girl. Piles of babies. Death, death, death, death, death. Dead babies, dead babies, dead babies.

And what if they called her tomorrow and claimed he had Down syndrome? What would she do? What would she do?

She couldn't answer that. Things like that wouldn't happen to her. Or to her baby. Not this baby, not this baby.

His whimpers subsided. His eyes finally closed.

She heard the garage door close. Axyl, home for a shower. He did that sometimes on Fridays. To the club to work out and then home for a shower. To relax, he would say. Late meetings on Friday nights, he needed a midday break.

He walked past the nursery to the master bedroom without seeing her. He slammed the bedroom door so hard that the walls shook.

The baby wailed.

Anne cussed.

Back to rocking. Back to sleep, back to sleep, back to sleep.

* * *

Betty Holmes closed the back door with her foot and threw her car keys at the kitchen table as she doubled under the pain of a cramp. Cursing, she headed for the living room and dug out a prized possession—an old, savored bottle of black market vodka. After a shot straight up, she flipped through the computer looking for music that would rock the house. Hard-core, full blast, to chase her desolation away. The windows vibrated to the blaring rhythm. She downed two more shots of vodka and threw the crystal glass at the wall as if it was Markus. She wished he had been home waiting for her.

"I didn't need that in my life. I'm not a savior like you," she yelled at him, though he wasn't there to hear it. "I don't want to know about the horrible things people do. I just want to get away from you and get on with my life."

She grabbed the bottle, gulped three more mouthfuls, and staggered up the stairs to the master suite. The music rose with her, into the bathroom where she set the whirlpool tub to fill, and into her vanity room. She stripped as she went, set the bottle on the counter with a clank, and leaned closer to the mirror to examine the reflection blurring before her. Her appointment book, lying open on the counter, stuck to the moistness of her hand. She stared at the page, at the star, wondering in her muddled mind what it meant, then moved like a disjointed robot to pull the pills from hiding. Dumping them onto her palm, she stared at them quizzically, plucked at one, popped it into her mouth, and dropped the rest on the counter. She took another slug of vodka.

Stockings. She sat and worked each stocking off her legs with the exaggerated care of drunkenness until her feet were free of them. Then the slip. Standing, wobbling, she pulled it over her head.

A pain shot through her chest, and her stomach heaved. She leaned against the door jamb waiting for the nausea to subside. Sweat poured from her pores.

A new song started up. She grabbed her liquor and danced, twirling and side-stepping into the adjoining bath where the rushing water quieted to a steady stream as the tub filled. Dipping to the side she shut the water off and slipped into the foam to numb her mind with her poison pleasure.

The heat enveloped her, pulling her into its relaxing prison. The blood pounding around her injured heart rushed to the extremities of her limbs. Agonizing pain tore through her chest and down her arm. The liquor bottle slipped from her hand and crashed to the floor, glass and liquid sparkling against the tile.

Betty Holmes went limp.

* * *

The policeman hung up the phone. "I just got a call from a teacher out at Anne Frank City School. He says one of the kids at the park was lured over to talk to some guy sleeping on a bench."

"A perp. You'd think they could get it at the Fun Houses, but no, they got to have the challenge of the draw. Send Dink and Mack out that way. He's probably gone by now, but if not, pick him up for vagrancy and we'll have a little fun with him."

"You don't think it could be that guy that's on the run?"

"Sitting in the sun on a park bench? Right."

The officer shrugged.

"Well, if you pick him up, run his prints and check."

"Will do."

* * *

David stopped midstep. "Who are you?"

"I could ask you the same question."

"Uh, you're in my room."

"True. Name's Marty Young. And *you*"—he pointed his finger at David with a little smile—"are a Dominian."

David stood his ground despite an aching desire to run. "How do you know that?"

"I make it my job to know."

His brain finally connected the name. "That little girl . . ."

Marty frowned. "What girl?"

"She just ran up and talked to me. She said you know secrets."

Marty shook his head. "Wow. Katie." He'd be giving her a talk after school. He picked up a slice of pizza and motioned to David. "It's gonna get cold." He took a bite, then through a half-mouthful asked casually, "So, why'd you steal the baby?"

David didn't see any harm in telling the truth. It was better than what was being said about him. He moved to the bed, sat down, and uncovered Frankie. "Look at him. He has Down syndrome. They were going to kill him.

"It's a plot against the Better World Bill, right?"

"What?" There was nothing complicated about what he did. "They were going to *kill* him."

Marty felt his phone buzz. It was Trudy. He wasn't letting her in on anything yet. Not until he had it all figured out.

Before he could slip his cell back in his pocket, it lit up again. A police alert. He looked up at David. "Were you sitting out in the park?"

David nodded. "Nothing happened."

Marty waved toward the box on the table. "The rest is for you. Stay put. They're on your trail. Let me go check what this is about and see if I can throw them off track."

David picked the baby up. He wasn't about to be surrounded and trapped.

Marty held up one hand. "No, seriously, *don't leave this room.* I'll be back in a bit."

David eyed the door after Marty left. How could he trust the word of a teenager?

He couldn't. He couldn't trust anyone.

He moved forward, locked the door and leaned against it. *Help me, Lord. Should I trust Marty?*

He laid Frankie on the bed and caressed his cheek. "I wish you could talk to me, Frankie. I wish you could tell me what to do." Frankie cooed, the night-long fussing and whimpers forgotten.

David eased his tired body onto the bed and stretched out beside the baby. "From the mouths of babes," he said. "You're bound to have some wisdom to share." He raised his eyes to the door once more as he strained to listen for every tiny sound, for any indication that someone might be coming for them, and back to Frankie with a deep cleansing breath. He tucked the blanket around him and ran his fingers gently over the fluff of baby hair, long, tender strokes as the liquid gray eyes blinked heavily with fatigue, once, twice, five times, until David's fluttered too, his hand pausing a little longer each time before stroking the baby fluff again. He thought of the little girl's head of curls. *Katie's* curls. Her image swirled in his mind's eye with their conversation: she had been told he was a secret and to not tell anyone. Surely that would mean Marty was with the good guys, not setting him up. *Please, Lord*, he prayed, *let it be so.*

His eyes wanted to remain shut, to dwell on Katie, but he forced them open to gaze at Frankie again, his baby chest rising and falling, his baby lips parted in sleep. *Frankie. Katie.* Katie's impish smile teased at his thoughts. He let his eyes close once more, just for a second so he could think about her, mixing her image with Bethany, until Bethany grew in his mind from the infant she'd been in the hospital, to being a toddler of two, crawling over him, sitting on his stomach as he lay there so she could peek at Frankie the way Katie had, then slipping off to crouch over Frankie, patting his head with her pudgy toddler hand before kissing him on his soft spot. Then wiggling between the two of them, her body cuddled up to him, squirming until she was comfortable, finally still. He could feel her slow, sleepy breaths, her warmth spreading through him, slowing his racing heart to a steady beat until his own body relaxed, until his eyes couldn't open, and he drifted into deep, sound sleep.

* * *

For the fourth time, Anne rose slowly from the rocking chair, careful to move fluidly, to not jolt or bounce or move any part of her body too quickly. She held Frank aloft as if he were perched on a cloud in front of the rocking chair and moved with infinitesimal steps toward the nursery, watching this time that she didn't stumble on one of the cats, that she didn't catch her toe on the rug, that nothing would jar the sleeping baby boy. Finally in the nursery, she stood at the crib, held him over it, hovering just above the mattress, lowering him with more care than the finest crystal as flesh met blanket. She eased her arms out from under him, slowly, imperceptibly, not letting the finish line rush her progress as it had last time, until her arms were free and he was there, in the crib, asleep and she was no longer bound to him. She crept across the room to the spare bed, curled up, and with a long sigh, slept.

* * *

At 12:45, Trudy eased the rental car into a parking place near the bus depot and waited. Jessica had arrived on the bus, so she was fairly sure that's how she would leave work as well.

She turned on the radio and reclined her seat, tingling with the fun of playing detective, at the idea of actually tailing someone. She had no idea what it may prove, but she'd run into a dead end in trying to locate the Dominian, and she felt sure that eventually, one way or the other, Jessica would lead her back to him.

While she waited, she pulled out her cell and flipped to the news in case there were any updates. Top story: man shot for attacking technician at a National Family Counseling Center. No clear picture of him, just a spokesperson from the center. And a name: Harve Johnson.

She stared out the window and thought it through. First off, what was reported probably wasn't what happened, so what was the real reason this man was shot? She puzzled over it. If a child was taken away, remanded to a UO Institute, they weren't processed through a Counseling Center. If he'd taken the child there of his own volition, he wouldn't have attacked a technician. Maybe he'd gone there for counseling and things had become hostile?

Or maybe David Rudder had someone else working with him to bring the system down.

She glanced at the time. Fifteen minutes till Jessica got off work.

She needed to talk to Marty. He had to know something by now. She pulled up his name and called.

* * *

Marty knew all the shortcuts. First, he had taken the path through the wooded area of the park, to a side street. Sometimes he jumped on the bus when it was there, but today he'd had to keep going across the road, down the alley and along Hannity Avenue, which paralleled the main drag but was lined with small businesses that dwindled into a smattering of homes and two apartment buildings before reaching the string of abandoned buildings that stretched over the Christian underground. More than once, he wished he'd ridden his bicycle, but he wouldn't have been able to carry the pizza.

He rushed through the echoing hallways to his office, threw down his keys, woke up his computer system and turned on his police monitor. He had to create a diversion to keep the cops from figuring out that the "perp" in the park was actually the missing Dominian.

As an officer's voice rose from the monitor, his cell vibrated. Trudy. Again. He'd put her off too many times. He answered, "What's up?"

"We've got to talk."

He used his free hand to continue pressing buttons on his system. "I know. Too much happening right now."

"Do you know anything about the guy shot at the Family Counseling Center?"

"I was there, but I don't know who he was."

"Is he connected with the Dominian?"

Marty hadn't considered that possibility. "I don't think so. He was ranting about his co-hab."

"Well, tell me what you do know."

Another cop's voice came over the scanner. Marty turned one ear to it. "I will. Tonight. I promise."

"I might not be able to tonight. I'm on a stake out." She loved how that sounded.

"Okay, okay, I'll get back to you, but I can't talk right now. In a bit. Gotta go."

He hung up. He doubted she had anything to tell him that he didn't already know, so she could wait.

He turned up the volume and prepared what he was going to say about the perp, the drunk on Sixth Street who was about to become a decoy.

* * *

At the Midway Inn, the maid heaved her cart from room 131 to room 132. The parade had brought more people to the hotel than she'd seen all year, and her cart was heavy with dirty sheets and towels. Four more rooms and she would finally be done. None too soon. Travelers were coming back to their rooms, and new arrivals were anxious to get settled in.

As if he could read her thoughts, her boss-man approached with long, pounding strides. "Speed it up there, Lolita. We have people lined up in the lobby."

She nodded, avoiding conversation with the brusque man.

He continued past her as she knocked and unlocked the next door. It hadn't been used. A quick walk to the bathroom to make sure supplies were there, and out again, one less to clean.

She heaved the cart forward again and stopped. Light knock, unlock the door . . .

Her boss-man had turned and headed back toward her. "What are you doing? Don't you look at your list? Both of these rooms are empty. Hurry and do the next, the one with two queen beds. I have a family waiting in the lobby."

She was too weary to rush. She turned and reached for the doorknob to pull the door closed and stopped. "*Señor. ¡Mira!*"

Look? Look at what? He peeked in at the man sleeping beside the infant. "Go," he said, waving her away. "Finish the last two rooms."

He slipped into the room, stared long and hard at the man, then pulled out his cell.

* * *

With the diversion successfully accomplished, Marty checked the time. He wanted to head straight back to the Midway Inn, but he had to get the interview and program feed ready for the morning news. He set to work on the pictures first, transferring them from his camera to his computer, and settled into artfully arranging them for maximum impact.

The Dominian would have to hold out just a bit longer on his own. What could possibly happen to him while he was shut in a hotel room?

At six, Katie arrived at his doorway with a sandwich and paused. Marty's eyes were intent on the screen. Sometimes he yelled if she interrupted him, but Father had asked her to deliver the food, so she stepped forward and plopped the plate and glass of milk on the counter.

Marty jumped, looked at her, and flicked off his monitor. "You weren't looking at that, were you?" he asked.

She climbed up on the stool a couple yards away. "Not really. Why?"

"It's not something you need to see. It's bad." He snatched up the sandwich and checked the time as he bit off a huge hunk of bread and ham. He hadn't realized how much time had passed. It was almost eight.

She sighed. "If it was the preacher that got shot, I already saw him. They showed it to us at school."

That angered him, but didn't surprise him. He took another bite.

"Why did they shoot him? I mean, I know it's because he was hollering about Jesus, but why did they shoot him for it?"

"There's the million dollar question, Katie-girl." He swallowed a mouthful of milk. "Mostly because they don't want people to know about Jesus."

"Why not?"

He took another bite and thought about it while he chewed. He'd never really considered the reason behind their agenda, at least not about their hatred of God. He understood the lust for power, for control, the elitist ideology. But what was the real core of the matter? All the preaching he'd been exposed to in the underground must have taught him *something* that would make sense to Katie. He did the best he could. "Jesus is a threat to them. If the people have Jesus, they don't need the government so much because Jesus offers them more than any government. He is love. He is forgiveness. He is life everlasting." He grinned, proud of himself for producing such a succinct answer.

Katie wasn't as pleased. "It still doesn't make sense. To kill somebody because they're talking about Jesus, I mean."

Marty nodded and stuffed the last bite in his mouth. "I know."

Katie wanted to tell him what was really weighing on her mind but she couldn't tell him or anybody. If they knew she'd made a comment about Jesus in school, they'd be mad at her and give her a lecture that would go on for hours.

Marty held out the plate. "Can you take this back for me? I've got to get back to work."

Katie slipped from the stool and took the plate.

"Wait," Marty said, and fumbled in a cluttered cardboard box until he pulled out the remains of a chocolate bar, unwrapped it, and split it in half. "Here you go, Katie-girl. I forgot to give you some the other day."

She took it and shoved the whole thing in her mouth as she headed out the door wondering what old Miss Heidi would say if she told her.

Marty pushed himself to finish up the newsfeed. He already had the pictures ready with caption, and he'd hacked the system and prepared the altered interview questions. A few more details and he had it all ready to go first thing in the morning.

His phone vibrated. Police alert. Disturbance. At the Midway Inn.

He rushed through the doors and hallways, collected his bicycle from the last room by the exit, and took off.

* * *

Darkness had invaded the house by the time Markus entered and headed toward the living room to shut down the rowdy music. His head throbbed, Joanne had talked continuously about the Dominian all afternoon until Markus became crazy with fear for getting involved and ended up at Happy Zack's again, trying to find some relief.

Silence. He glanced toward the stairs, and in the eerie glow of the computer, he spotted glimmers of shattered glass on the carpet.

"Betty?" he whispered into the stillness. He glanced at the open cabinet, knowing her weakness, and imagined her wasted again, flopped across the bed in disarray. Wearily he pulled himself up the stairs to check on her.

The bubbling water stalled him. He didn't want to talk to her right now. He retreated two steps and paused.

She hadn't screamed when he'd turned off her music.

From the landing, he looked toward the darkness of the bedroom for a full minute.

"Betty?"

No answer.

Sighing, he continued down the hall.

"Betty?" His heart skipped as he felt for the bathroom light switch. His eyes, momentarily blinded by the bright glare of white tile, came to focus on the tub, and the naked figure floating in the bubbles, her golden hair fanned out across the surface of the water like silken seaweed.

* * *

Marty made it to the hotel in seven minutes, slowing only when he was on the path through the park. He left the bicycle in the woods and crept along the tree line to see what was up.

His heart stopped. Blue lights were flashing in the parking lot. How stupid was he to have left him alone?

He stood, concealed by the darkness of the trees, and watched two UO officers interrogating someone. But it wasn't the Dominian.

He circled up by the Anne Frank City School and approached the hotel room from the back side, walking slowly, keeping close to the wall till he reached the room, third from the end. He held his hand on the doorknob for a minute, wondering what had happened while he was gone. Wondering if this was the end. Then pushed the door open just enough to slide through.

As the door shut behind him, he saw David asleep on the bed with Frankie. He sighed with relief—until his peripheral vision kicked in and he saw something in the farthest corner, by a table. A seated man staring a hole through him.

* * *

Trudy reclined the seat of her car and closed her eyes. On her way home from work Jessica Main had stopped at Sears to buy a blouse, and that was it. By ten, her lights were off. She couldn't be expecting company; even the entrance was dark.

The biggest excitement of the night had been listening to the neighbors throw dishes, or furniture, or something loud, at each other, until their fight spilled into the street, inviting other neighbors to scream at them. Finally, they gave it up, one retreating to the apartment, the other going on to a neighbor's. The ensuing silence lasted about ten minutes, until a tenant cranked up some *skred*—a popular mix of thrash metal and rap—and blared it out open windows as three cars full of teenagers arrived. Trudy had pulled her purse into her lap, feeling more secure with the little pistol within grasp.

Despite the noise, the stakeout had left a lot of time for thinking about her baby. As she drifted off to sleep, just a catnap she promised herself, she made one firm decision. If she determined why the Dominian stole Anne's baby, and he wasn't loony, she would seek asylum. She had to. Either that or kill the Better World Bill, which was impossible as long as Axyl Houston breathed.

* * *

Marty stood stock-still until his eyes focused on the man in the corner, until he could make out the shape of his long nose, high forehead, and narrow chin, and then he crossed the room as quietly as possible.

The man drew his face into a frown and whispered under his breath, "I expected you hours ago."

"I know. I *was* here," Marty whispered back, his voice softer than his softest murmur. "But I had to leave. They'd seen him and I had to divert them. How long have you been here?"

"It doesn't matter. He's sleeping now."

"You didn't have to stay. He'd have been okay."

"My maid saw him."

"And?"

"I told her to get on with her work."

Marty appreciated his authority. "Sorry I inconvenienced you."

"My people have been there, too."

"How so?"

"They have them all imprisoned in that reservation just waiting to slaughter them."

"Do you think they'll do that?"

"Why else would they be keeping them in a cage? The time will come."

Marty's heart pounded. Was he expecting a rebellion? "Time for what?"

"One way or the other, the end."

Rebellion, Marty thought as he grinned into the dark and thought of the images he had ready to release on the world.

"I have done what I could to help him—I kept him in hiding. When he wakes, he must go. This isn't an attic or a cellar. My family . . ."

Marty knew that was the deal.

David stirred in his sleep. He could hear voices, he thought, but they seemed far away, dreamlike, and it was so warm and comfortable where he was, that he didn't want to find the voices.

Marty trained his eyes on the sleeping figure, watching his body twitch and settle back into sleep, and then focused on the baby and thought of Katie. He couldn't believe she had the nerve to leave the school grounds to check out a baby.

The man glanced at his cell and stood up. "I must go."

Marty thought about Katie's question and followed him outside. "I know you're Jewish," he said to the man, "but can you explain to me why they see Jesus as such a threat?"

The man locked the door and headed toward the back of the hotel. Then he stopped and looked Marty in the eye. "They think Jesus is the only thing that can defeat their agenda. And maybe they're right."

DAY THREE
JULY 4, 2042

Axyl sat at his desk watching the 7 a.m. news. Anne's screaming baby had ruined the early-morning peace he usually relished, so he had escaped to his office.

Henry Burth was commentating this morning. He hated Henry.

Good-looking man, early thirties. He captured viewers' attention. Sincerity shone from his tranquil face as he spoke directly to his audience. "For years, the public has trusted the government to handle efficient termination of unwanted neonates. Today we go behind the scenes to talk to Miss Kappi Hillis, Chairperson of Development for the Gift of Life Center." He turned toward his guest, a white-haired woman impeccably dressed—hair, makeup, nails, clothes all perfect. "Miss Hillis, you have been chairperson of the Gift of Life Center for ten years, correct?"

The woman stared at the camera instead of him. "Yes, it's a very rewarding position."

"I'm sure. Tell me what you consider to be the goal of the Gift of Life."

"Certainly. Gift of Life is such a fitting name. There are two branches to our work. One, of course, is the gift of organ donations received through Public Medical Services—as you know, our bodily organs become public health property at death. The other branch of our work is the NFCCs, the National Family Counseling Centers. When a parent or a Unified Order official determines that it is in the best interest of the child to be removed from the home environment, for whatever reason, he or she becomes a gift to the whole community. Some children are transferred to UO Institutes and counseled to help them recover from the anguish caused by improper care. Other children become military students, a true gift to our country." She smiled and blinked at him.

Back in his office, Marty was watching, too.

He felt pulled in two directions. He wanted to get back to watch the Dominian, but his priority right now was the newsfeed. Priorities! He'd orchestrated everything perfectly. The Dominian would have to wait.

He held his breath. Burth was reading straight from the teleprompter, exactly what he was counting on. "Just one more question," he murmured to himself.

"Can you tell us about the success rate of the children that enter through the NFCCs?"

The woman smiled. "Oh, gladly. We pride ourselves on our numbers. Ninety-five percent of the children who enter our program through the National Family Counseling Centers become productive citizens. Many become educated in UO Institutes, according to government standards. Of those, 80 percent carry on to military positions, becoming the very men and women who patrol our streets every day, maintaining peace."

At that, Marty tapped his screen and sent an altered question to Burth's prompter. Marty knew he would spout it out without thinking twice. His mind was probably on the afternoon football game.

"And the remaining percentage, they are medically terminated, correct?"

The reporter flinched just slightly after realizing what he said but let it pass. It was a harmless question. Terminations didn't raise alarm with anyone anymore.

Miss Hillis didn't find the question the least bit unnerving. "Some children suffer from irreversible anomalies or illnesses and are mercifully released from life. The parents are made aware of that possibility."

"Just how are these decisions made?"

"Through precise medical testing by qualified staff under the officiating Health Continuity Counsel."

He nodded. Marty doubted he even heard her response. The next question was already on his screen. Marty counted on Burth being clueless or still disconnected. "There is one other station to which some children are 'gifted,' isn't there? The Gift of Life program?"

Her stiff smile remained unchanged. "Yes. Some children fill our Gift of Life commitment, which benefits all of society."

"How so?"

"By bringing improved health to citizens, Henry. They are *quite literally* giving the gift of life by furthering research to cure disease, or by making donations that will increase people's health scores and overall quality of life."

Teleprompted: "Without objection, of course."

She looked confused for a split second. "Objections? Embryonic research began over fifty years ago. The Gift of Life program grew from that. Why would anyone object to something that helps all humankind?"

Axyl stood, shoving his chair back forcefully, as if he anticipated that something huge was about to happen.

It was all set to go. Marty tapped a few keys and suddenly pictures overlaid the newscast and began to roll across the screen—shots of the kids he'd seen strung to tubes in the Counseling Center, of the man being shot and the boy being pulled back inside, and then to pictures of live organ donors and experiments in the Gift of Life Center. Beneath them ran a caption: *Your children are being turned into experiments while they're still alive.*

Axyl grabbed his phone, realized no secretary sat at the other end this early, and glared at the screen. Somehow, Jack Friday was involved, alerting people to what was going on. He was a turncoat, out to ruin him, probably out to steal his position under the Minister of World Peace. He fumed as he selected another number. "I need a name tagged . . . Jack Friday . . . Yes, the senator."

He listened for a full minute to the voice on the other end.

"Find someone to help, someone you trust. It should look like an accident. Make it worth his while to do it right."

Only 25 seconds of film ran before the studio regained control, going full black with *For the Good of the Nation, for the Good of the World* plastered across the screen for another thirty seconds until a government commercial took over.

Marty jumped in the air. "Yes! Perfect! Take that, you scum buckets."

Miles away, Axyl stared at the screen with a thousand epithets rising to his lips. He would have somebody's head before the show was over. If the public got stirred up about deviants now, he would never slip the Better World Bill through. Not with elections in four months.

He picked up his phone and spoke as calmly as possible, "Connect Damius Fise, station manager, WGOV." He would know the informant's name before the hour was up. And that person would die.

* * *

Markus rose from his kitchen table and retrieved the coffee pot. Joanne sat staring into her cup. It was the first time she'd ever been in his house. He poured her more coffee and touched her cheek. Her eyes were much bluer without the heavy black eyeglasses framing them. She appeared even more vulnerable. And lovely. Tears welled in his eyes. "I love you, Joanne."

She patted his arm. "Hush, now. That's emotional distress talking. I can't imagine how upsetting it must have been to find her that way."

He laid his hand over hers. "I'm just so glad you're here with me, Joanne."

* * *

A door banged shut.

Trudy jerked awake and rubbed the sleep from her eyes as Jessica's neighbor strode past her car toward the bus stop as an angry co-hab reopened the door and screamed at his back. With another slam, silence settled again.

It was a rude awakening to a clear-skied day. The rising sun blazed through her car windshield. She unfolded her stiff, knotted limbs, tidied her hair, chewed a teeth cleaner, and applied a touch of makeup to her unwashed face. She didn't feel fresh, but she looked better.

She clicked on her cell, to check out the news headlines—such as they were in public media—while she waited to see something, anything happen, but with nothing new listed about the Dominian, she changed gears. Something had been tugging at her dreams: the book she'd picked up in Jessica's apartment, the words from Cardinal Newman. *Independence will not carry us on safely to the end.* She wanted reassurance that she wouldn't be alone in the bleakness of her future. But she couldn't find the conviction in her heart. Could she find it in the Dome?

Her thoughts were interrupted as Jessica stepped out her front door—a new, improved Jessica with curled hair, lipstick, mascara, a pretty pink blouse, navy skirt, and flat dress shoes.

Trudy sat low in the seat and watched as Jessica walked the quarter mile to the bus stop and sat primly on the bench. When the bus picked her up five minutes later, Trudy followed.

Every bus stop on the route presented a problem for Trudy. Should she pull over or pass the bus? The first two stops were in residential areas, so she sat behind the bus like a courteous driver, waiting for the few passengers to embark. The third stop was downtown, where crowds were assembling for the Unity Day Parade.

Trudy groaned. The parade. She wouldn't be permitted to park. Road blocks were being erected.

She zoomed around the bus, pulled into a parking slot on a side street, and watched out the passenger window. Jessica got out and headed her way. Trudy scrambled out of her car, ran her palm over the parking meter, and scanned the growing crowd again. After a moment of panic, she caught sight of a carefully curled head of hair walking away from her. Yes, that was her.

Staying a pace behind in a crowd was easy. She entered the Shadow Café behind Jessica and five other people.

* * *

"Katie," boomed the teacher's stern voice, "Principal Mannsey is waiting for you."

Katie came to attention in front of her teacher. "Yes, Mr. Fenmore."

She trudged down the hall, stopping to look out the windows three times before reaching the principal's office. Mr. Willis, the guidance counselor, sat opposite Mr. Mannsey.

"Ah, Katie," the principal said in his usual formal address. "Come join us. We were just talking about you."

"I bet," she muttered under her breath. She took a seat and folded her hands quietly in her lap. She refused to speak unless directed to. Jeffrey had taught her that.

"Hello, Katie," said Mr. Willis.

She nodded.

"Principal Mannsey and I were discussing the possibility of you attending one of the art magnet schools."

Katie came to life, her big blue eyes widening, and a smile lighting her face. "Really?"

Mr. Mannsey twirled a pen in his fingers. "Would you be interested in that?"

"Yes! Oh, yes!"

The two conspirators smiled knowingly at each other. "Well, Katie," Mr. Willis said, "we have to fill out this form first."

"Okay."

He spread a paper out on the desk and proceeded to ask her a dozen school-related questions about grades, teachers, and interests.

"To whom do we owe our allegiance, Katie?"

"The UO," she replied. Everyone knew that.

"Why?"

"Because they bring us peace and provide for our general welfare."

"When I say you must be a good steward, what do I mean?"

"We are all stewards of the earth and must take no more than we can give."

"And if we do?"

"Anyone who does not create a balance creates a . . . a . . ." She teared up, unable to think of the word. They would flunk her.

"That's okay. It's a hard word. Deficit."

She repeated the whole thing to get back on track. "Anyone who does not create a balance creates a deficit and must be corrected or removed from the equation." She grinned at remembering the word "equation."

"Very good. Have you learned the motto of the World Church in religion class?"

She nodded. "*Standing united for the good of the world.*" She pulled at her left sock, which was slipping down again.

His voice remained soothing. "Now, here's something you may not have covered in class. Do you believe in God?"

Katie frowned. Daddy had told her to never discuss God in school. Ever. But the teacher had run the video of the man being shot for yelling out about believing in Jesus. Maybe she shouldn't have said anything about it being wrong that they shot him.

"Well, Katie," he urged, "do you?"

Mommy was in Heaven watching, and she had said never to lie, especially not about important stuff. Plus, what if she said she *didn't* believe in God and God thought she meant it and wouldn't let her go to Heaven? She would never get to see Mommy again.

"Katie, answer the question. Do you believe in God?"

Mommy! "Yes."

"Fine," said Mr. Willis as he made a notation on the paper.

Katie was relieved that he didn't get mad or rant and rave like she expected him to.

"Does your father tell you about God?"

"Yes."

"Does he take you to church?"

"Yes."

"Do you like going to church?"

She thought about that a moment. She liked seeing her friends. And she loved Jesus. But sometimes church was boring. "Sometimes I do."

"But not always?"

"No."

"Does your father make you go anyway?"

Katie hesitated. "Yes."

"Even if you say, 'I don't want to go to church today?'"

"Yes. It is a sin not to go to church on Sunday."

Mr. Willis seemed to like that answer. He smiled and wrote a bunch of stuff down.

"That's great, Katie," Mr. Mannsey said. "We're done. In fact, I'm going to take you to that art school this afternoon, at dismissal."

Katie couldn't believe how much she had disliked him just minutes earlier, and now he was granting her wish. "Oh, thank you!" She skipped all the way back to the classroom, not even caring why he suddenly liked her. Maybe he was doing it just to get her out of his school. That was fine with her. Just fine. Wait till she told her daddy the exciting news.

Mr. Willis shook hands with Mr. Mannsey. "That was a piece of cake. That art school idea really did the trick."

"She talks about art all the time. Kids are open books."

Mr. Mannsey escorted the guidance counselor to the door. "Thank you. I appreciate your cooperation in handling this."

"Sure."

Mr. Mannsey finished filling out the form and called his assistant into the office. "Make arrangements for Katie Smith to be relocated to the UO Institute this afternoon."

The woman nodded. "Yes. Right away."

"I should have suspected religious practices. I always knew there was something priggish about that girl."

"How about the parents? Shall I tag them for questioning?"

"No. They'll automatically take care of it on that end when she's processed."

With a press of a button, he filed the paper, and then, guessing that both siblings were being indoctrinated, he buzzed Jeffrey's classroom to have him sent up.

* * *

The air of the Shadow Café hung heavy with tantalizing scent of strawberries and the lighter aroma of cantaloupe, kiwi, and pineapple being served with croissants and fat-free cream cheese bagels.

Jessica stepped up to the hostess.

"Just you, ma'am?"

"No, I'll be meeting someone here."

"Fine. Follow me."

Trudy followed a pace behind without consulting a hostess as Jessica was ushered to one of the last window seats, almost impossible to obtain on parade days. Trudy slipped into a small aisle table within earshot of Jessica's booth and ordered a fruit smoothie.

Jessica pulled up a book on her cell but only read a few sentences before turning to look out the window at the crowd forming and the officers clearing the roadway. People elbowed their way through to opposing destinations.

Neither woman noticed the approach of clean-shaven David.

He slid into the booth across from Jessica with Frankie nestled comfortably asleep in one arm. "Good morning, Jessica."

She looked dazzled, her eyes widening in question. "Good morning."

He touched his finger to his lips, winked and nodded just slightly.

"Looks different. But I like it," she whispered. "Except you look so young now!"

He laughed. "Don't worry. I'm aging fast."

"May I hold him?" Jessica asked, motioning to Frankie.

He laid Frankie in her waiting arms and watched the stress in her face fall away to tenderness and contentment.

The waitress approached. David bit his lip and whispered, "I hate to ask this on a first date, but do you have any money in your account?"

Trudy listened closely. Of course, he couldn't use his UIC. And Jessica, no doubt, was forever broke. If they left, she would never find them in the crowd, especially by the time she paid and got out.

Jessica looked up and grimaced for an instant. "I have five credits. That might be enough for breakfast."

"No problem," David said, and smiled at the waitress approaching the table. "Just coffee for both of us, please."

Trudy sighed. If they weren't eating, they may not linger long, but she ordered breakfast anyway. Her pregnant body was starving.

David dove into small talk about the weather and the parade to make Jessica comfortable, struggling to be heard over the grumblings of a man several seats away. "Did you come to the parade last year?" he asked. She was about to answer when the jerk finally stood up and hollered at the waitress. David looked down the aisle to see why he was so upset, but it wasn't the man that caught his eye. It was the lady from the airport, Trudy. He felt sure she had followed one of them, so he redirected the conversation to mislead her. He had to find a way to get his message across to Jessica without Trudy finding out. He pointed subtly to where Trudy sat and shook his head slightly. Then, staring straight at Jessica, he said, "Please, honey, tell me everything's all right between us now. Can I come back home?"

She almost laughed. She loved the idea of pretending to be his wife again. She ran a finger around Frankie's little face and then concentrated on David. "I don't know. Just whose house have you been staying at?"

"No one's. A hotel."

"Really?"

"Yes, really. The Midway." He realized too late what he'd done. Had Trudy heard him? He couldn't tell.

Jessica smiled into her coffee and then at him. "Sure, you can come home."

Thirty minutes later, after animated meaningless talk about the crowds and the baby, their conversation wound down.

Trudy listened to every word, pushed her plate away, and waved to the waitress. The waitress approached, pulling her order scanner from her apron pocket. "Everything okay?"

"Yes. Delicious." Trudy held out her palm and the young waitress scanned her UIC.

"Thanks. Come again soon."

Trudy hurried out and hid herself behind a drink vendor who had claimed a prime selling spot. Two minutes later, David and Jessica emerged from the restaurant, waded into the growing crowd and down the sidewalk, weaving between people as they worked their way toward the bus stop.

Trudy followed them at a distance until she saw them board the right bus, then walked back to her parked car. She didn't have to hurry. She knew where they were headed.

A discord of sound assaulted them as the bus rounded a corner and passed the parking lot where the marching band was assembled and tuning their instruments. Majorettes twirled their batons. Two color guards leaned on their flags chatting while the other four fiddled with hair and uniforms. Floats of princesses and cartoon characters lined the side street, preparing for the procession. David pointed to the jugglers between the first two floats. "I can juggle."

"I bet you can," Jessica replied, then sat grinning, wanting to poke him, but not quite that at ease with him yet. Instead, she laughed softly. "That was cute, saying you stayed at the Midway."

"But that wasn't a lie. I did!"

"*Heavenly accommodations as cheap as Hell.*"

"What?"

"That is their slogan. Get it? Midway. Not Heaven, not Hell."

"Heavenly, eh?"

"How did you pay for a hotel room?"

"Someone paid for it."

"Really? Who?"

"I can't say." He kept his eyes on the window. A quarter mile later, it came into view, and he thought of the park. They could talk there; Markus taught him that. He stood at the next stop and waved for her to follow.

"What are you doing?"

"We need to talk."

* * *

Back in the car, Trudy debated what to do. She still felt compelled to tell Anne where her real baby was. Maybe because it seemed like the right thing to do. She started the car and took off in the direction of Anne's house.

Less than a mile into the trip, moving slowly through a commercial zone, she spotted Senator Jack Friday standing outside a toy store, bag in hand. That made her laugh. The guy was a total jerk. He came on to her every time they crossed paths. And yet she knew he secretly doted on his son. Big bad Jack Friday buying a toy for his boy. She wondered if he would take him to the parade as well.

Which made Axyl and Anne seem all the more pathetic and made Trudy determined to put Anne's imperfect baby in her arms just to test her, just to see if she might actually be human and not some kind of robot.

Besides, it might put Axyl's attention back on Anne and their baby and off her own pregnancy, at least long enough to make plans, to get away.

She picked up her cell and called Anne.

"Hello."

"Remember the story you told me about your baby being stolen?"

"Trudy . . . ? What about it?"

"You were right. He *was* stolen."

"He's right here, in his crib, finally asleep. And I don't want to wake him up . . ."

"Wait! Don't hang up."

Anne groaned.

"That's *not* your baby. They just gave you that baby to shut you up. Your baby was stolen. If you want to see him, I'll come pick you up. I know where he's being kept. At least I'm 99 percent sure, anyway."

Anne was silent on the other end.

"Look, Anne, I know you had doubts about that baby when they handed him to you. You can't believe they just lost your baby somewhere and suddenly found him in a closet or something, can you?"

"I don't know. I've never worked in a hospital."

"Come on. Do you want to see him or not? If you don't, fine. Go on with your life. I've got other things to take care of."

"Wait. Tell me what you found out. Where is this other baby?"

"Government housing on the south end of town, 120-3 Brown Square."

Anne hesitated. She couldn't drive in that part of town. "Come get me."

"All right. I'll be there in an hour."

* * *

David led the way down the path to the park, one arm bracing Frankie against his shoulder, the other hand gently rubbing his tiny back. Jessica followed a pace behind, toting the baby bag. They stopped at the edge of the park.

"I love this place," Jessica said. "I often come here to watch the children play." She took a seat, opened the bag, and pulled out a baby bottle. "I think he needs this."

"I think you're right." He smiled down at her. "Why don't you feed him?"

She took Frankie into her arms, cooing at him and touching his nose. She kissed his forehead, then placed the nipple in his puckering mouth.

Rays of sun edged across the grass, stretching shadows of playground equipment into long stripes. A warm breeze tickled their hair.

He propped his right foot on the seat beside her and leaned on his raised knee. "Tell me about yourself, Jessica."

"I should be saying that to you, you bad husband that I kicked out and now I'm taking back home again." They chuckled, then she became serious again. "Do you know that woman? Trudy? Axyl Houston's assistant?"

"Axyl's assistant? *Senator's assistant!* Why didn't I connect that before?"

Jessica watched his dismay. "What is it?"

"Axyl and I used to be friends. A lifetime ago."

She tried to comprehend how such a relationship could have been possible. "Are you sure? With Senator Houston?"

"Yes, before . . ." He glanced around to make sure there weren't any cameras, pulled out his phone, and motioned for her to turn hers off.

"I knew him when I was a kid."

"At the institute?"

"Before that."

He leaned forward and wiped bubbles from Frankie's mouth as he formulated what to say next. Everything about her exuded honesty. He had to trust his instincts. He had to trust her.

He sat down beside her and pulled the crucifix from under his shirt. The corpus glinted in the sunlight.

Her attention had been on Frankie, so it took a moment for her to notice, but her eyes suddenly lit up. "You're Christian?"

He nodded and slid the crucifix back into hiding.

She smiled and cast her eyes upward. "Thank you, Jesus."

Relief flooded through him. "You too?"

She nodded. "But I've never seen you . . ." she let the words trail off. It could be a trick. She might give away the whole underground if she wasn't careful.

He threw caution to the wind. God had brought him this far, putting so many people in his path, he had to trust that Jessica was part of his plan too. "My real name is David Rudder, and I'm from the Dome."

David. David Rudder. "The Dome? But what does that have to do with Frankie?"

He gave her a short explanation of what had happened in the delivery room.

She listened intently, only turning away to gaze compassionately into Frankie's sweet drooping eyes. Now she looked at David with new wonder, new admiration for his courage. "So what next? Will he be safe in the Dome?"

"Yes, if we can make it there. But we need help to get there. I was hoping . . ." He hesitated. *She must trust me now.* "If you're part of the Christian underground . . ."

She nodded without missing a beat. "I'm part of it."

"Tell me more."

"There's about a hundred of us in our group, not counting the children. But there are other groups all over the place, some of them a lot bigger. We have Bibles, a safe place to worship, some priests and ministers . . ."

"Can they help? Can they help me get the baby back to safety?"

She nodded.

He wanted more. He sat beside her and placed his hand on her arm. "Tell me about you."

Jessica felt her usual hesitation passing. She knew this man was different. He was compassionate and courageous. For the first time in a long time, her heart pounded with expectation. She had eyes for him, and by some miracle, she could tell by everything about him—the way he leaned toward her, his gentle touch, the look in his eyes—that he felt the same toward her. "I'm single. Two co-habs, both disastrous. I live in government housing. I'm broke."

David nodded for her to continue.

"That's all there is," she said.

"How about family?"

"I was an only child. My parents got divorced when I was 13, and I never saw them again. My mother hated me, always did as far as I remember. She was a skinny sexy thing with dreams of a beautiful daughter. My dad? Well, I did something really bad and he couldn't forgive me. He left me, deserted me when I really, really needed him. I went to live with my aunt, and eventually ended up in foster care until I was 17. So, I guess you could say I don't have a family."

David looked at her hard. He tried to conjure up what bad thing such a kind-hearted girl could do that her father would disown her.

She couldn't meet his eyes. She looked instead at Frankie, though that was almost harder, and she could still feel David's eyes boring through her. "Don't stare at me like that."

"I'm sorry. I didn't mean to."

"Yes, you did. You're trying to think of what I did. Well, it was horrible. As horrible as what you're thinking."

"You set your cat on fire?"

She couldn't even laugh at that.

Silence lay between them. He didn't want to make light of it. Not when he wanted to depend on her to help with Frankie.

"I killed my baby boy."

David held himself in check.

She answered his continued silence. "I was 13 years old and 6 months pregnant, and my mother made me have an abortion."

He pulled her into his arms. "Oh, Jessica. Poor girl."

The words flooded out like water from a pail, filled over a long time by a slow drip, finally knocked over. "But she didn't make me. I mean she wasn't there, didn't take me there. She just said go do it. And I should have said no. I should have run away. But I didn't, and then they kicked me out anyway." Tears choked her, emotions clogged the back of her throat, but she continued. "And my daddy. My daddy. I loved him so much. He always took such good care of me. And he hated me. I'd always been his princess, and when he found out I'd slept with Eddie, he hated me for it. Things were already bad between him and Mama, and that just seemed to be the last straw. He and Mama fought all the time after that, until he finally packed up and left. Then Mama kicked me out. She said it was all my fault and she couldn't stand the sight of me anymore. She sent me to my aunt who had no use for me, either. And it *was* all my fault. *All* of it. All of it."

Her tears fell on Frankie, distracting him, making him lose suction on the nipple. He whimpered.

She sniffled and bounced him, touched his delicate features and helped him find the bottle again. She buried her eyes in David's shoulder, and he held her quietly for a while. When she could speak again, she continued. "And then my aunt kicked me out. I was passed from foster home to foster home. I was so messed up over the experience, I just couldn't get myself together. Finally, I ended up with a wonderful family, for a while anyway. They taught me about Jesus and his forgiveness, but I can't quit reliving it." Her whole body shook with quiet sobs.

Finally when the anguish ebbed away and silence lay over their quiet embrace, he whispered, "My daughter and my wife both died because of my negligence. I shouldn't have left Elizabeth alone. I knew she hadn't been feeling well. The pregnancy was such a drain on her, but I figured that was normal, and she still had a month left to go. I had business to take care of, and I was gone most of the day. When I got back, she was collapsed on the kitchen floor in a puddle of blood. Placental abruption."

David gritted his teeth, reliving the memory. "By the time I got her to the hospital and performed a c-section, she'd lost a ton of blood and went into shock, which led to kidney failure. And Bethany was in distress too long. She survived the c-section but died two days later. Elizabeth never held her. If the conditions weren't so horrible in the Dome, they would have stood a chance, but our equipment and knowledge are all so antiquated . . ."

He swallowed. "It was my fault, pure and simple. I should have been there for her. I shouldn't have left her alone that day."

Jessica had begun to cry again. When she finally pulled away from him, she turned to wipe her red, swollen eyes on her new blouse. She sat up straighter and fixed Frankie better in her arms as he drank himself to sleep. With a deep breath, she took control of her wavering voice. "What are you going to do about Frankie?"

"I'm trying to get him back to the Dome. That's why I need your help."

They sat in the dwindling afternoon, trying to come up with a plan. She had no transportation or money. Neither did he.

Silence hung around them, broken only by birds chirping and squirrels chattering until the shrill clanging of a school bell pierced the quiet, and children spilled out the school doors.

David turned to watch the kids spread across the playground toward the buses.

"School must be dismissing early for the parade."

David searched the faces, hoping he could pick out Katie in the crowd. "I met the cutest little girl yesterday afternoon," he said, and described the conversation to Jessica.

Jessica grinned. "I bet that's our Katie."

"Ours?"

"She's part of the underground church. Her father is a wonderful man, extremely intelligent. We've been trying to convince him to run for office as one of Them, and then vote our way. He's afraid to do it, afraid to jeopardize the safety of his family."

"Then Marty is part of the underground, too, isn't he?"

"Sort of. How do you know Marty?"

"He brought me pizza in the hotel room, then ran off, promising to come back, but I haven't seen him. But I'm assuming this means it's the underground church that provided my accommodations."

Jessica nodded. "It sounds like it. I'll have to check. Maybe they can help get you back to the Dome."

"Aren't there others outside your underground church that don't like what's happened to the country?"

Jessica answered off-handedly, her eyes drawn to the children. "Yes. The Liberty League. I used to go to their meetings. They're more politically oriented than the Christians, and many of them don't have any religious beliefs at all, though in other ways we share a lot of the same goals." Her attention shifted to two officers emerging from a UO car parked in the corner of the lot. "And I think there are other people who don't like what the country has become, but they've just surrendered to the idea of getting what they can from the system." She sat up straighter and pointed to the uniformed men. "I wonder who they're after."

David sucked in a deep breath. "Me."

"No, they're walking toward the school."

They followed the officers' movements as they were greeted by a man, the principal perhaps, and waited as a nearby teacher hollered for a student.

As Katie's name echoed across the parking lot, Jessica shifted Frankie to one arm, pushed herself to her feet, and took two steps forward.

The assassin knew Jack Friday's schedule. He leaned against the building down the road from the school, waiting.

David and Jessica watched as Katie looked toward her teacher, then caught sight of the UO officers and turned away.

Jessica's eyes widened. "She knows what a UO officer means . . . we've told her over and over. They're going to take her away. What did she say? Why do they want her?"

"She knows who I am. She said she saw me on the news."

"Everyone saw you on the news. That's not it . . ." Jessica's voice trailed off as she edged forward. "Where can she run to? We have to go get her."

Jack Friday was already late to pick up his son, and the exclusive academy was still a few miles away. His car's speedometer topped fifty as the buildings and people in the busy commercial zone zipped by.

The assassin touched a remote switch that activated the Safe-Stop circuit in Jack Friday's car—not to activate the brakes but to disable them.

Katie rushed across the sidewalk, saw a green light above, and ran into the road without pausing.

Red light ahead. A little girl rushing heedlessly across the intersection. Jack pressed the useless brake pedal, pressed it harder, cursed, and heaved the steering wheel hard to the left. The driver of a sedan, seeing Jack coming into his lane, swerved to the left, saw Katie and swerved back, and clipped Jack's car at the right rear wheel, sending Jack's car into a 180-degree spin back the way he'd come. Katie crouched down in the road, her scream filling the air as the sedan slid past her, jolted over the curb and plowed into the brick school sign with a sickening squish of metal and the crackle of glass shattering as bricks caved over the car.

Jack's car, already riding on two wheels, hit a pothole and flipped on its side, skidded several yards into the curb, spun into the air and landed right side up twenty feet from Katie. All four wheels popped out from under it and went flying in different directions.

One wheel struck Katie. For a moment her thin body was a tangle of limbs as she was driven backward through the air toward the sidewalk. Then she landed, the back of her head hitting the curb with a thud.

They dashed down the path toward her, David shouldering through the onlookers and Jessica hanging back a ways, holding Frankie close to her chest and stifling sobs. With the help of a bystander David eased Katie onto the sparse grass and examined her sliced forehead, then eased his finger around the back of her head to the depressed skull fracture. One eye had dilated so that the eye was more black pupil than blue iris. Her breathing slowed. She lay there stupefied but not unconscious yet.

The wail of a siren announced the arrival of an ambulance. Paramedics hustled from one vehicle to the other.

"Over here," David yelled.

The older of the two paramedics hurried over.

"Traumatic brain injury," David said. "Blown pupil. Intracranial pressure. She needs mannitol administered immediately."

The shadow of the paramedic's heavyset body engulfed Katie as he took her tiny arm into his large hand and scanned her wrist. "Code nine," he hollered over to his partner. The partner stopped what he was doing, hurried over, scanned her with his scanner, and nodded agreement as he pressed his green button to send the data to some official at some desk at PMS, then rushed back to work on the first victim. A moment later, both scanners flashed red: code nine affirmed.

The paramedic heaved himself to a stand and took a step toward Jack Friday's car before David hollered to him. "What are you doing? Check her vitals."

"She's a code nine."

"And?"

The guy narrowed his eyes at David. "No extreme measures for resuscitation."

"Give me the mannitol." David stood. "I'm a doctor. I'll administer it."

"Sure." The paramedic half-laughed. "Go home." He turned away, continuing toward the vehicles.

David stepped after him and grabbed at his arm. "She needs immediate intervention and neurosurgery."

"What's your problem?" the paramedic said, his annoyance clear in his face. "We'll sustain her when we're done with the other two." He pulled away and rushed toward the cars.

David returned to Katie's side and applied pressure to the wound.

"Poor thing; code nine," one of the bystanders said.

"Probably has leukemia," said another. "My neighbor's kid was tagged for that."

Another person stepped back. "Or AIDS."

"No," said the first one. "They don't tag for STDs. Diabetes, I bet. What a drain on the system that is."

"You'd never think she had anything, she's so pretty," said another. "What a shame."

Katie's body twitched with a seizure. David laid a hand on her chest.

"Hey," someone shouted, "they've got Senator Jack Friday over here."

People moved that direction, Jack Friday's name murmured among them.

Suddenly, tires squealed as a driver looked up from the coffee in his lap and realized too late what was going on at the intersection. The After School Scholars van packed full with 12 kids headed to afternoon tutoring, was being directed through the wreckage by a policeman when the inattentive driver slammed into it and sent them both skidding into the other two disabled cars.

Screams rose as the crowd shifted and moved to get to the children.

From the crowd a woman emerged and went to David's side. "Can you lift her?"

The familiar voice startled him—Markus's friend from Social Services, the woman who'd given him the crucifix. "Joanne? What are you doing here?"

"Pick her up," she urged. "Let's go."

"She's losing consciousness."

"Come on."

"We need mannitol. It's too severe . . ."

She shook her head, tapped him, and waved him toward the park.

"She could have a spinal injury, too."

Joanne pulled at him. "Come on. Now."

With a furtive glance at the paramedics and then at Jessica standing apart from everyone, he supported Katie's head, neck, and spine down one of his arms as best he could and scooped her up.

Across the schoolyard, the two teachers were occupied with detouring their charges around to the opposite side of the building, and the principal and UO officers seemed to be looking for another student. Jessica nodded at David and waved slightly with one hand to indicate he needed to follow Joanne, then set off on her own down the hotel path. Joanne pointed him toward a car in the parking lot by the nature trail.

David slid into the back seat with her. "We have to reduce the pressure. Her brain is swelling inside her skull."

Joanne backed out. "Get down. Don't draw any attention to us."

"Wait! Frankie . . . a woman has him."

"I know. She knows how to get there."

David had no idea where *there* might be, but he relented, leaned over Katie, and whispered soft prayers into her blood-soaked hair.

* * *

Small for a boy of 11, Jeffrey slipped through the crowd of kids unnoticed, joined Marty behind the slide on the school playground, and followed him silently through the treed area where the schoolyard and park met, until they reached a side street. If he had been ten still, he would have reached out and held Marty's hand. "I tried to get to Katie."

Marty nodded. "You did good. You contacted us as soon as you suspected something. That's all you could do." He could see the fear in the boy's face. He tugged on the brim of his ball cap. "It's gonna be all right, kid. Just stick with me." *We couldn't respond fast enough*, Marty thought, but the self-incrimination gave way to the more pressing issue of what lay ahead. They now had two kids, a baby, and a Dominian on the run. The underground stood in jeopardy.

* * *

Joanne passed the largest of the town's many soup lines, continued several miles further, and drew the car to a stop outside an abandoned building.

"If you have a cell phone," she said, "leave it on the seat. Go in the back door, turn left, end of hall, down the flight of steps. At the end of that hall is another door that leads to a tunnel that joins the entire block. Go past five doors, enter the sixth. They're waiting for you."

He clamored out of the car and relinquished all common sense to complete trust. What option did he have?

He followed her instructions without a backward glance.

The building echoed with his heavy footsteps. Not a soul stirred inside the dim walls. Dust danced in the fading sunlight slanting through the random dirt-caked windows. Down the steps to the third door. He had to shift Katie's weight to one arm to open the door. She moaned. He held her against his chest and spoke in her ear as they continued onward, down the next hall, and through the tunnel.

The sixth door. He stood in front of it a moment, held his breath, and prayed.

The door led into an empty room with some old fold-up tables stacked to one side. He turned one direction then the other, uncertain what to do, when a door on the far wall opened and a round face with wizened gray eyes poked around it—the woman who had given him the hotel key.

"In here," she said.

"It's you!"

Her only response was to hold the door open.

David crossed the room, the hair rising on his neck as he passed through the door into another hallway. A young blond woman rushed up to join them, speaking with labored breaths. "They say it's clear."

"By the Lord's mercy," the old woman said, and creaked down the hall with David at her heels to a windowless storage closet turned dormitory room, containing ten small cots. "The fourth bed is hers."

Two more people arrived bearing a plastic crate full of medical supplies.

David laid her down and straightened out her limbs as she twitched and curled into herself, then slipped into unconsciousness. He glanced at the crate with disdain. "I thought I was being led to a hospital. She needs surgery, not a first-aid kit."

The old lady shook her head. "Not possible. Do what you can here."

"There's nothing I can do here!"

"Something."

The blond woman looked over his shoulder.

"Get me clean towels, soap, and water," David demanded. He leaned forward and rubbed his knuckles down her rib cage. Katie winced. David nodded. She'd reacted. She wasn't too far gone yet.

The old woman waved the young woman out. "Get them."

"Where am I?" David asked as he searched through the crate for supplies.

The old woman shuffled back out the door without responding.

Ten minutes later, Marty burst into the room with Jeffrey on his heels. "Is she going to be okay?"

David looked from Marty to the freckle-faced boy in the green ball cap and answered his own question. "That's what I thought. The underground. Literally."

No one paid any mind to his statement.

He knelt at her side and checked her pulse again. Respiration increased, pulse slowed. Not a good sign.

The old woman returned with water. "Did they follow you?"

"I'm not stupid," Jeffrey said. "I knew how to answer their questions."

Marty edged around them to see what David was doing but answered the woman. "They were after several other kids, none of them ours. High test scores," he said. "Taken for intelligence training." He turned to David. "This is her brother Jeffrey."

David cast his eyes in Jeffrey's direction for a mere second. "I'll do everything I can for her, son, but you may not want to be in here."

"I can handle it," he said, and took a seat on the next bed.

David turned his attention to the supplies. There was nothing there, nothing at all, to help her.

An hour later, her life had all but ebbed away. Jeffrey sat in a silent heap staring at his sister, his face unreadable.

"Talk to her," David said. "She needs to know you're here."

He moved to her bed, sat on the foot of it, and told her about how stupid their school was, but she jerked and it scared him.

"Something happy," David urged. "About your mother."

Jeffrey nodded, understanding far too well for a boy of 11 what he was being told, and murmured soft words about their mother and some kitten they used to have.

David moved away to give him space. He had asked again about getting her into a clinic somewhere, but he knew as well as they did, perhaps better than they did, that nothing would be done.

Her father, George Smith, arrived with a flustered face. The small gathering parted for him, and he eased into the vacated chair at her side. Tears welled in his eyes as he swept the hair from the pale pearl oval of her face and kissed her sallow cheek. Jeffrey slid from the bed and stood beside him.

David sat across from them. "I wish I could do more for her. She needs surgery."

The man looked up at him. "Not with her code." He caressed her hand. "Can she hear me?"

David nodded. "She's unconscious, but yes, I believe she can hear you."

He swept her curls back. "My princess. I know the Angels are calling to you, but don't leave me yet." He kissed her forehead and the palm of her tiny hand so limp and fragile in his.

Father Simeon appeared with his stole around his shoulders and oil for the Last Rites in his hands.

David stepped aside. He couldn't do anything else for her but pray. And cry. He saw in Katie a five-year-old version of what Bethany could have been, full of life and laughter. Her eyes, as she spoke to him in the park, so full of determination, contrasting with the innocence of her soft baby face and head full of angelic curls. And he saw his failure doubled: the absurdity of having the knowledge, the ability to save both of them, and yet failing because of timing, because of lack of equipment that should be at his fingertips.

Dizziness nearly overcame him. He leaned on the back of the chair and breathed deeply, trying to regain his bearings, when he realized he had been so absorbed in dealing with Katie that he had no idea what had become of Jessica and Frankie.

Joanne saw the panicked look on his face and touched his elbow. "Follow me." She led him down the hall to a sitting room in the bowels of the basement. "Jess . . ."

Jessica swiveled in her seat and sprang to her feet. "How is she?"

David shook his head. He was no stranger to death, but today it had been too much, impossible to watch, especially in a child who was so vibrantly full of life just hours earlier. He met Jessica halfway across the room, took Frankie into his arms, and breathed in the smell of his newborn skin. They stood that way for a while, embracing each other and the moment, measuring time with the beats of their hearts until Joanne dashed into the room. "Hurry!"

David arrived in time to see her draw her last breath. He stepped forward to resuscitate her, but her father stayed his hand. "There's no need. We can't do anything to help her, can we? It would only mean another hour of pain."

David jerked his hand away and set to work on the tiny body. "We never give up. That's the oath, at least the old one. We don't just shrug and say it's not worth it . . . until there is no hope." He worked on her for five minutes, the hands of the old windup clock on the wall ticking loudly, mocking his efforts. When ten minutes had passed, he succumbed, his head resting on her chest as he cried a moment. "It's not right . . . It's not right . . ." He rose to his feet, fists clenched, tears flooding his eyes. "What's wrong with this world?"

Katie's father pulled her into his arms and swallowed the sobs caught in his throat. "Father Simeon?"

Father Simeon nodded.

They carried Katie into the main room and laid her on a table. The room began to fill with people, and it took a moment for David to realize it was for her funeral.

"So soon?" David asked. "There's not even a casket for her."

Jessica shook her head. "The body becomes government property at death." She clutched Frankie to her chest as Father Simeon began the funeral rite.

* * *

The gathering stood in heavy silence, punctuated with quiet sobs as the funeral service concluded and Father Simeon stepped up to the table to cover Katie with a white sheet. He paused at her chin. Tears streamed down his cheeks as he placed one hand on her disarray of blond curls and kissed her forehead, then laid the sheet over her face. He remained there, staring at her shrouded form, shaking his head. "Such a futile death."

Marty moved to the front of the crowd. "This has got to stop. It's their fault. She could have been saved if it weren't for that stupid code. What's wrong with you people? You old folks tell us stories of how things used to be, of how we had the best of everything in this country. Why don't we do something about it?"

George pulled his attention from Katie and turned to speak to the gathering, his voice soft at first but gaining volume with every word. "It's a tyranny under the guise of equality. That's why we're here in a basement. A basement! My daughter's funeral in a basement, and I can't even go bury her properly in a graveyard."

"We all live like beggars now," the old woman said, "living in public hovels, hiding in basements just to pray. Rags to riches used to be the American dream. Now we're all in rags except *them.*"

Marty was fired up. "We need to do something about it!"

"Yeah!" hollered someone in the back.

George spoke earnestly. "I won't stand by any longer and let this government, these people who are no better than you or I, tell me that America was ever meant to be like this— innocent children dying because the bureaucracy says her life is less valuable than somebody else's."

Jessica, standing beside David, held Frankie aloft. "They wanted to destroy this baby, too, just because he has Down syndrome, and David has been criminalized for trying to *save* him." She shifted Frankie to her shoulder and continued. "We've become a nation of droids that walk, eat, and speak as instructed. People turn a blind eye out of fear, or they just take what they can get for themselves. The system is a prison and we're all trapped in it."

David put his arm around her and squeezed her shoulder.

George spoke again. "You're right. American pioneers founded this country on ingenuity, hard work, and Christianity. I don't know how they managed to erase those values from this nation. But we've got to put them back!"

Marty pulled a chair to the front and stood on it. "Not just us! There are others, like the Liberty League, who are serious about taking the country back. They're not believers, but that doesn't mean they can't be allies."

David stepped between people to reach the front of the room.

Marty jumped down and waved him toward the chair, sure that the Dominian had a plot ready. It was really going to happen—a revolution! And he would be one of the leaders of the pack.

David stepped onto the chair and drew the attention of the crowd. "I'm sure most of you know by now that I'm not from around here." He paused. If he was going forward with this, he had to trust these people because the entire project would be built on trust. It had to begin with him. "I am a Dominian." A murmur arose among startled faces. He quieted them with a wave of one hand.

"I didn't come here to start a revolution," he continued in a firm, controlled voice. "I'm not a prophet. I'm not even a leader. I'm merely a man caught in these hard times like you, in this culture of death. But I know this: I can't bear the tragedy of what is happening to us. Of what has happened to Katie." He closed his eyes a moment to collect the words he needed to say. "I lost my wife and daughter for the same reason. That's why I had to save this baby. And that's why I want to fight back, against the death panels and World Church and Unified Order." His words settled on them. "*But* we're not going to win our nation back overnight. We have to be patient. We have to be crafty."

A steely-eyed man with gray hair and broad shoulders turned to face the crowd. "Yes, sir. That's how *they* did it, slowly infiltrating every facet of society with their propaganda. We have to do the same thing."

"Exactly," David continued. "We failed before because too many people relied on someone else to react, to protest, to stand up. This time we must get it right. We must step forward, every one of us, and urge others to do the same. A united front with everyone involved at every possible level. No voice is too small or too insignificant to make a difference."

Marty shook his head. "I say we stand up for our rights and start a real rebellion! Storm the streets and make our voices heard!"

David stepped down and laid a hand on Marty's shoulder. "No. I would love to say we could march on the capital tomorrow and drive them out, but we can't. We're not going to win back our nation by force. We don't have the numbers, and we know that they control the courts and the media. It would end before it started. No, we need a long-term plan . . ."

"They'll still catch us, and eliminate us," interrupted a voice from the back.

David closed his eyes. He, himself, was a coward; who was he to demand that anyone risk life or limb?

"I'm not worried for me," said a woman midway to the door. "I'm worried for my children. They will be dragged off to those institutes or end up dead like poor Katie."

"And the institutes are full of mind-bent kids that lick at their feet like dogs," said another.

"Not all of them," Marty interjected. "I talk to some of them still. Some are lost for sure, but many hide their beliefs like we do. And the Liberty League is already working at this. They've been placing people into positions of power for some time, people pretending to agree with the agenda until there are enough of them in place to turn the tide."

David stepped up on the chair again. "That is what we need—to connect, to plan, to infiltrate and coordinate. We should unite our efforts. There must be enough desire for freedom that the Liberty League and Christians can find joint issues to promote. It's time."

Heads nodded. A couple of people hollered, "Yes!"

George, wiping the tears from his eyes, seconded the idea. "He's right. It's time. I've lost my wife and my daughter. Enough is enough."

A middle-aged man who looked like he'd once been in the military stepped up. "Let's get started. Come on." He strode into the next room, and the group, called to action, followed him out, away from Katie's still body.

Marty frowned. *Wait and see,* he thought to himself. *Not a fight, but there will be a rebellion. Word will spread about what I exposed on the news and people will react. The silence ends today.*

He glanced at his cell, expecting an alert to come in any time saying people were gathering at the Counseling Center, rallying and rebelling, demanding that their children be returned.

I will join them when the time is right.

* * *

It was evening when David accompanied Jessica back to her apartment. The Christian underground had agreed to help David escape with Frankie, but Jessica asked him to go home with her first to rest and eat—and for something else. She wanted to give him something to remember her, and after much thought she decided one of her books would be most appropriate since the Dome was so limited in resources. A book he could read time and again.

They were famished by the time they reached the government housing block.

"I've got a few things left in the pantry. Let me see what I can fix that won't take too awfully long. But first, I'm going to lay Frankie on my bed. Make yourself at home."

David followed sheepishly behind her. They had bared their souls to each other in the open park, yet here he felt he was invading her space. She glided to the back room and out again, her thoughts on Katie as she passed him.

He looked around the room, taking no notice of the cheapness of the furniture or lack of luxuries; those things, material measurements, only spoke of money or lack of it, and there had been no luxuries in his life since his distant childhood. In comparison to the squalor of the Cloistered Dominion, Jessica appeared rich.

What he noticed were the personal items: tiny china puppy dogs and a plastic prancing stallion arranged on a shelf, an old rag doll and teddy bear sitting in a corner basket. Stacks of old-fashioned paper books and magazines in an eclectic variety: fiction and philosophy, science and politics and art. Beside it, a plain brown spine stood out, not shoved in level with the rest. He pulled it out and ran his hand over the hard brown fabric cover. No title, or any other indication of what it was. He flipped through pages, nodding at quotes by Cardinal Newman, then slid it back into place and ran his finger down the leather spine of a Bible—a *real* Bible. He eased it out intending to sit on the sofa to read it but instead carried it to the far end of the main room to inspect a sketch of a mother, father, and infant huddled beneath a bridge in rags—a homeless family of the twentieth century before the government solved their problems by imprisoning them in work houses. He deciphered the initials "JM" scrawled in the corner of the sketch.

Her voice crept up behind him. "A modern depiction of the Holy Family. The original setting gets a person into trouble, so I created my own."

He turned to her, his blue eyes shining.

She read his thoughts. "It's like one in a million chances that we met, isn't it?"

He set the Bible on a small table by the bedroom door and embraced her. He kissed her hair and she looked up. Buried emotions rushed to the surface. Not flirtatious love, spontaneous and light-hearted, carefree and youthful, which had bound him to Elizabeth, but wholesome and comfortable, aware of good and evil and imperfections and each other's humanness.

He bent and kissed her tenderly, and she responded by wrapping her arms around him, melting into him.

A sharp knock at the door surprised them both.

* * *

Marty cornered Father Simeon when things had quieted down. "Father, I want to be baptized and confess my sins."

"You do?" Father Simeon regretted the note of incredulity in his voice. Everyone knew Marty was a skeptic—always prodding, always questioning, never accepting.

"Yes. I . . . I know I've been resisting it a long time. But I understand everything, and I'm ready now."

Father Simeon nodded. "We'll do it this Sunday during Mass."

"Now, please."

"Right now?"

"Yes, sir."

"Marty, this is an event the entire community needs to celebrate."

"How about if we celebrate it on Sunday but we do it now?"

Father Simeon raised an eyebrow. "Is there something going on that we need to talk about?"

Marty thought about what to say. If he was going to do this for real, he'd have to be honest, but he didn't have to tell the priest everything. "You know. I could have died today. Scary times."

Father Simeon couldn't argue against that. Marty took a lot of risks. He walked to the closet and got out his stole again.

* * *

It was midafternoon before Axyl stormed into the news station to address the station manager. He screamed into his face. "What was the purpose of that story and who gave you the authority to run it?"

"The content was approved."

"*Those* questions were approved?"

The man shifted back and forth from one foot to the other. "The original content was approved."

"What are you saying? It was changed, or that Henry Burth improvised?"

"We think the teleprompter was hacked."

"Hacked?"

"While the show was running. We couldn't break the connection."

"The footage of the Counseling Center as well?"

"Bled in by someone outside the station."

As the man droned on with some stupid excuse, Axyl wondered if there could possibly be someone standing against

him and the Better World Bill, or if the timing were just coin-
cidental. As the past couple days played out in his mind, he
first thought it might have been connected to Jack Friday and
the bill. But then the truth flared in front of him—Anne's
news interview at PMS. She'd told him that night about the
dumping bin and donor center. Everything clicked together.
Anne. Anne had somehow raised alarm to the media, probably
off camera in some casual conversation with a reporter disloyal
to the UO. She'd told someone about her fears, and they'd
jumped at the opportunity to investigate.

Anne. How could she be so naive? Stupid, stupid, stupid
Anne.

First things first. He had to turn this event around somehow. "Put a camera on me," he said. "I'm going to make a
statement about Jack Friday's sudden death."

The station manager raised his head. "Senator Friday is
dead?"

"Yes, in a car accident by his kid's school. Don't you have
someone over there covering it?"

The manager snapped his fingers at someone behind him
and got a camera set up.

A bulb atop the camera lit green, and Axyl began coolly
and levelly to relate his sorrow over his friend and colleague
Jack Friday's untimely death. Jack was more than a great public
servant—he was a visionary. "And now is the time," he added
with a rising tone, "to honor Senator Friday's vision by passing
the Better World Bill, for which he worked so tirelessly. Jack
often shared with me his dream of a world without disease,
without suffering." Now he clasped his hands together, and

when he spoke his voice nearly broke. "Help us to make his dream a reality!"

The camera light went off. Axyl's face snapped back to a scowl. He walked quickly from the building to his waiting car and placed another call, his anger now growing in waves. He could imagine people standing that very moment outside the Counseling Centers demanding to examine procedures. Sure, it was all perfectly legal but better off ignored, kept out of public sight. People would begin to wonder about the practices. Not just guilt-ridden parents but interfering do-gooder groups. New lobbyist groups would form. The whole thing could become some New World save-the-children movement, just in time to derail all his plans—and his career.

He was only doing what was best for society and the world! Ordinary people were too ignorant to comprehend the benefit of a genetically controlled nation, too irresponsible and emotional to make rational life decisions. He could save them from the trials they now endured, save them from being exposed to procedures better left unexplained. Now they were doomed to wrestling with misguided inner fears of moral obligations.

He knew what was best for them.

He wouldn't allow ignorant citizens, least of all that airheaded twit, to ruin his plans—to subvert the great destiny that was his to claim!

Uncontrollable rage filled him.

At that moment, his phone alerted him to an incoming text: *Axyl, remember I told you I thought our baby had been stolen? I was right. I know where he is, I'm going to get him. Please meet me here and see your true son. It's 120-3 Brown Square.*

He looked at her image on the screen and detested it. He wanted to break her perfect upturned nose and yank out handfuls of her blond hair by the roots.

He calmed himself enough to think clearly. It wasn't enough anymore to punish Anne for her stupidity. Now he had to make sure that she and that deformed baby went away for good.

Getting rid of her would be a problem. He had made her into a public figure, so he couldn't just eliminate her. Too many questions. Another accident? No, something more subtle. He had to discredit her, before she discredited him. Ahhh. Mentally incompetent? A breakdown!

Axyl tapped another number. "Yes. This is Senator Axyl Houston. My co-hab seems to have had a mental breakdown. She is delusional. She has our new baby at home, yet she thinks someone has stolen him. She's quite out of control . . . Thank you. It *is* very disturbing. Can you send someone out to my condo to pick her up? . . . Yes. It may take me a while to find her. Say in about two hours . . . Good-bye."

He made a mental note: Better World eliminations— start with Sunshine Center Mental Health Unit. "That gives you about one month, Anne."

* * *

Nerves raw, Marty crouched with his camera by the bushes that edged the National Family Counseling Center parking lot. Those in the crowd gathering around the entrance were strangely silent, shuffling with their heads down in shared guilt for what they had done to their children. For some the guilt was newly awakened. Others had felt it from the moment the custody termination was completed.

Inside, employees huddled around the director. "If anyone asks, their kids were sent to the Army Institute. We're sending a news team there today to verify it for the six o'clock news." They only half-listened to the pep talk. They'd kept the doors locked all day. They were afraid to face the people.

A few people outside muttered epithets. Anger began to spill into short sentences, and strangers turned to respond to one another's comments . . .

"I just brought him yesterday. Do you think he's still here?"

"I brought my son two weeks ago. Two weeks ago."

A woman, softly sobbing, collapsed into a moaning heap. A man bent to help her. "Ma'am. Ma'am, come on. Stand up before you get trampled over in this crowd. What's your name?"

"Sarah. Sarah Chance," she said blubbering. She took his hand and he helped her up. "I didn't want to give her up, but they kept telling me I couldn't take care of her. That she would be better off. My baby . . . my baby."

Another man, nearby, stood stiffly staring at her. As he nodded empathetically, tears streamed silently down his face. A woman, a stranger, moved to his side, wrapped her arms around him and wept loudly with him.

Recrimination and guilt lit in one and spread like a flame through the growing mob.

A huge woman forced her heavy body through the mass of bodies, creating a path where none existed. "My Shanna. Oh, Shanna. Girl, your mama's here. I didn't mean to leave you here, Shanna. I cried all night at what I done to you." She reached the front window and began pounding on the glass. "Y'all better let me in. You better get my Shanna for me! You hear? You open this here door right now. I ain't leaving till you get Shanna for me!"

Sirens blared.

* * *

Allison Gatryl intercepted Markus in the hallway and waved him toward her doorway. "In my office. Now."

Markus knew what was coming.

"When your shift ends today you will be on probationary leave, pending the outcome of my investigation. You will be held accountable for whatever happened in that delivery room. You made a fool out of me, and if I can prove that you were involved in any manner, I will make sure you never practice medicine anywhere in the system again. You can kiss away your special rights, your cushy salary, your car, everything in your world. Do you understand me?"

Markus kept his face emotionless. "Yes, ma'am."

She glared at him, then finally waved him off. "Get out of here."

He trudged down the hall, his mind far from the work at hand, when a nurse ushered him into room 203.

He stood at the foot of the patient's bed, looking at a baby's head that had crowned. But the woman couldn't push the head out.

"You're almost there," said Markus, "Just one really good push. Concentrate."

But the woman only whimpered and looked around her fretfully.

Then the nurse's eyebrows raised as Markus leaned over and grasped the woman's hand, urging her in a soft, almost intimate whisper, "Come on, now. Push! Really hard! Push and you'll have your baby."

The woman bore down, focusing on the baby, pushing with all her might, until she felt a sharp pain, then the relief of the head passing through the cervix.

"Great! Just the shoulders . . ."

She pushed again.

Markus maneuvered the shoulders through, pulling the infant into the grasp of his large hands. "There's your girl!" He cut the umbilical cord, wrapped the baby in a blanket, and laid her in the mother's arms.

She arched her neck to look at the newness of the infant and smiled a sweet, exhausted smile. "Her name is Andora."

Markus paused and looked intently at the newborn, so alive. Such a sign of hope. He leaned in and gently placed a hand on her tiny head and whispered, "Thank you." Then he turned, and set about his postnatal tasks.

He had to see Joanne. *Only three more hours.*

* * *

Jessica opened the front door of her apartment, alarmed by who was standing on her doorstep. "Anne Shelton! What are you doing here? And with—with *her?*"

Trudy looked from Jessica to Anne with eyebrows raised, wondering how they knew each other.

Anne looked equally surprised. "Jessica?"

Trudy stepped forward. "May we come in?"

"What do you want?"

Trudy pushed her way in, closed the door, and addressed Jessica. "I'm Trudy Bullock. We met before, you remember, and I . . ."

"She works for Axyl," Anne interjected in a terse tone, "and she says that you stole my baby." Anne glanced around the room, her wrinkled nose expressing everything her words left out. Poverty, lack of taste. Jessica's home was as lower class as . . . her eyes returned to Jessica . . . her clothing. Lower class, but not criminal. "The idea of Jess stealing my baby is ridiculous! In fact, impossible, Trudy. I've known her most of my life. She's not the criminal type."

"Not her," Trudy said. "Him."

"This is the baby's legal mother?" David asked.

"Yes," Trudy said. "Anne Shelton, Axyl's co-hab."

"You mean Frankie is *Axyl's* son?"

Trudy's brow furrowed. "You mean you didn't know it was the senator's baby you stole?"

"He didn't steal him," Jessica whispered fiercely.

"You mean it's true? This guy really stole my baby?"

"No, he didn't," Jessica said. "He saved him, you idiot."

Anne gasped and started to protest.

Trudy interceded. "What do you mean, saved him?"

David's voice boomed over them, excited with the possibilities. "Don't you see what this means? You can put me in touch with Axyl. He can stop this madness."

Trudy didn't know what he was talking about. She had her own puzzle to solve. "But if you didn't know it was Axyl's baby, and this isn't some Dominion plot, why did you steal a deviant?"

Jessica fumed. "He didn't *steal* Frankie."

Anne was spinning with confusion. "But Jess, you must have known he was mine. You're even calling him by his name!"

"I didn't know his name. I named him Frankie because it suits him," David said, his mind still spinning. "And there was no plot."

"Then why did you steal him?"

"I told you, he *saved* him," yelled Jessica, exasperated.

Frankie whimpered in the bedroom. Sudden silence.

"I'll get him," said David.

Jessica sighed. "Look, sit down." Trudy joined Jessica on the couch. Anne, shaking, stood beside the rocker.

"Frankie has Down syndrome," explained Jessica. "He was going to be eliminated, and David . . ." she paused on the word, the knowing of his real name, the stories binding them, the taste of him on her lips, "David saved him. He couldn't bear to put him in the box, the gas chamber thing, so he walked out with him. That's it." She looked from one woman to the other. "That's it. Just walked out the door with him."

David entered on cue with Frankie and stood before Anne until she sat in the rocker and held out her arms for her son. She squirmed slightly. "What is Down syndrome? It's not contagious, is it?"

David spoke sternly. "No. It's caused by a genetic mutation. He may be mentally deficient to some degree. Heart defects, intestinal problems, visual and hearing impairments, but he should live a long life."

Anne relaxed and cuddled him, rocking slowly as if his condition made him more breakable. "He looks like Axyl, doesn't he? I knew he would. It's really him, isn't it? I mean the other baby, the one at home with the nurse, he's not Axyl's son?"

"No, not Axyl's."

She stiffened. The only reason she wanted a baby was to hold a part of Axyl—a part that wouldn't pull away, or shut her out, or go out of town to other women. But a child with an abnormality? She caressed his fuzzy head, trying to release herself with some dignity. "He's sweet, isn't he?"

Jessica nodded but said nothing. Already she felt possessive of him. She wanted to snatch him from Anne, but she knew Anne well enough that she could guess at the thoughts developing in her shallow little mind; Anne wouldn't want a retarded child. She preferred perfection, whatever society deemed that was.

Anne rubbed his forehead. "His eyes look Asian."

"That's from the Down's."

She rubbed his fist, opening his hand. "He certainly has stubby fingers. My Frank has long ones."

Trudy groaned. "He *is* your Frank."

"I mean the Frank I have at home." She would have to change Frank's name. She didn't want to think of this Frankie every time she called his name out. What would she do with a child that wasn't Axyl's? Wasn't hers? Wasn't really anybody's? All these months she had formed an image of who he was, who he would be, and now he wasn't anyone. Not the Frank who would grow up to be like his father. It would take a while to think of this new boy with past generations she would never know.

Anne squirmed as Frankie began to fuss. "Oh, is he hurting or something?"

Jessica couldn't stand it. She got up and took Frankie. "He's just like any other baby. When he wakes up, he's hungry."

"Where's his bag, Jessica?" David asked.

"Over on the desk, but I don't know if there's any formula left in it."

"So," Trudy said, "you see this baby, determine he has Down syndrome, and decide to steal him?"

"No." David slammed the bag down, angry that it was empty, and madder at this woman plaguing him. "I know it's hard to believe, but they expected me to kill him. I wouldn't do it. So," he thought momentarily of Markus but decided to leave him out, "I walked out with him. I thought I could find someone else to keep him. But I can't. I know it sounds impossible and horrible, but that's how it is."

Trudy grabbed the pacifier off the scarred chest. "Here, this might help." She put the pacifier in his mouth and touched his red cheek. She imagined she could feel the stirrings of the child growing within her, even though she knew it was too soon. She grew somber, thinking of the terminations and the Better World Bill. "Not hard to believe at all. It's going to get so much worse."

Anne touched his tiny hand again. "He would have ended up in that dumping bin, wouldn't he?"

David was still trying to redefine his boyhood friend. "You mean Axyl knows his son would have been killed off just because of Down's and did nothing to prevent it?"

Trudy rolled her eyes. "Axyl Houston had his own father locked up. He helped convict him of crimes against the state for being Christian."

Anne stared at her in disbelief.

"You remember the Conformity Clause way back when?" Trudy continued. "Thousands of Christians put in work camps. It was the final scare tactic to liberate the states from evangelists who wouldn't conform to the wonders of the World

Church. His father was one of them. He is not someone you want to cross. Believe me."

"You know nothing about Axyl," Anne insisted. "If he knew what went on at the medical center, he would change it. He's going to stop them from hurting those children. I told him all about it."

Trudy laughed. "Eliminating deformity and unproductive citizens is his number one priority. He wants to create a genetically perfect society as an evolutionary prize for all humanity—and as a legacy for himself."

"You make him sound like a monster."

Jessica, bouncing Frankie in her arms, hissed out a response so she wouldn't wake him. "He *is* a monster."

"How can you say these things to me?" Anne asked.

"A lot of people out there know what's going on, but they are afraid to speak out for fear they'll be the next one killed off."

David spoke up quietly. "Axyl's behind it all?"

"Yes, David. He and others like him."

He began pacing. "Someone must get him to understand the gravity of his sins. Get him back to God. It's not too late. He has the power to affect the whole nation. There must be a way I can reach him, to return him to his Christian upbringing."

Trudy snickered. "Not Axyl. He hates Christians."

Anne looked at them strangely. "Everyone hates Christians. What's wrong with that? They're backward, intolerant people from another time. They never valued the unity of the world. They couldn't understand that the melding of all the world's religions was the only way to achieve total peace. They're dangerous, and the UO had to remove them for the good of the nation. Now everyone is happy." The propaganda gave her strength. "And I think Axyl is right about the deviants. We can't let disease or deformity get in the way of perfection."

David stared at her in disbelief. "You can't mean that!"

"Yes, she does," mumbled Jessica.

"You're a hypocrite, Anne," Trudy said, "You just said you were glad that David saved Frankie."

Anne stared her down. "I did not. I implied that I wouldn't have wanted him to end up in the dumping bin."

Jessica stepped forward with Frankie. "Look at him Anne. He is alive. He is a person, the same as you and me. He deserves to live."

She evaded the baby. "Why?" she asked. "Why should he live when he will never be able to provide for himself? Who would *want* to live like that?"

"Because God made him, the same as he made you. God didn't make this planet just for perfect people."

"I don't believe in some all-powerful, judgmental God. And I couldn't take care of a deformed child. I wouldn't know how. So, he'd be better off dead."

"There is a God, Anne, and He said *Thou shalt not kill*, not *Thou shalt not kill unless it will make your life easier*," David said. "Life on Earth is not meant to be easy. It's meant for serving God through one another."

Tears trickled down Trudy's cheeks. She stared silently at Frankie, blinking her watery eyes. "But how do I know He's really there?"

David whispered. "Open your heart to him, Trudy. Ask, and you will receive."

"You don't know what you're talking about," said Anne shrilly. "Axyl thinks only of the world. Of creating a better world. He talks about it all the time."

Trudy said, "His Better World is killing off anyone who isn't perfect. You, me, Frankie, my baby. My baby. Just wait till his new bill goes through. You'll be afraid to catch a cold."

"Just wait until he gets here," Anne yelled. "You'll see. You'll see I'm right. He'll explain it. He can explain it better than me."

Trudy's head snapped to attention as if she'd been slapped. "What do you mean, 'when he gets here'?"

* * *

Jeffrey stood in Marty's control room and stared at the screen as the camera swept across a mob in a parking lot. He whistled like Marty would have. It was different from the usual news. The camera flashed around from place to place, and no one was standing in front of it talking like they did on a normal broadcast. No one was telling viewers what to think about it.

Which made him think about it even harder. *What were these people screaming and crying about?*

Some big fat lady was pounding on the window, then leaned on it, her hand and faced pressed up to the glass, crying, "Shanna! Shanna!"

Other people stood huddled together, some arm-in-arm swaying back and forth. A couple of men hollered cuss words.

Jeffrey was about to turn away when sirens obliterated the voices and twenty-some faces turned toward the camera, toward the approaching sirens. Angry faces. Scared faces. Shocked faces.

The camera twisted around, swinging past people, past a few parked cars, to the road, to officers climbing from patrol cars, running across the pavement. Bunches of officers. Ten? Twelve? The camera flipped back and forth too fast to count. Black uniforms.

People moving forward. Camera swinging back to building. Doors to building opening. People rushing forward. Officers yelling. A voice booming out. "Stay where you are with your hands up."

Camera turns again. Guns aimed. Bodies falling to the ground. Dead bodies like in a movie. But not a movie.

It didn't bother him. Movies showed dead people. The news showed dead people. Every day.

But not really like this.

They were screaming and yelling up close.

The camera swung around.

Nice lady crying, then crumpling. Man trying to hold her up, then falling on top of her.

Faces.

A scream, louder, in the camera.

Camera twisting sharply.

Going down.

Spinning in circles: people, building, bush, cars, people, building, bush, cars, people, building, face.

Still shot. Face.

Marty.

Jeffrey dropped Marty's bowl of homemade chips.

Black screen.

For the Good of the Nation, for the Good of the World.

The bowl shattered.

* * *

Blood pooled under Marty's chest. His body jerked uncontrollably as he strained to pull air into his lungs. The screams and gunfire swirled together with the blueness of the sky. Something pulled at him, and he floated into the blueness with a deep, cleansing breath, swirled in the clouds and in the noise and in the chaos, hanging above himself for a moment. He saw that his camera had skidded to a stop under a bush fifty feet from his broken body, and then he felt and saw nothing but a flood of intense, warm light unlike anything he'd ever known.

* * *

Everyone was staring at Anne as she sobbed. "Yes, I told Axyl where I was going. So he could see his baby." She dropped back into the rocker.

Trudy waved her hands "We've got to get out of here. He'll kill us all!"

Outside, a car screeched to a halt. They looked at each other in panic. David pushed Jessica and the baby toward the bedroom as a car door slammed and three quick footsteps smacked the sidewalk. The front door flew open.

"Axyl!" exclaimed Anne.

Axyl strode across the room and snatched her by the collar of her silk blouse, pulled her to a stand in front of him. Letting go of her shirt, he slapped her across the face with the back of his hand, sending her sprawling sideways across the couch. "You stupid . . ." He yanked her up by her arm and slapped her again.

Anne's screams pierced their ears.

David, coming from behind the couch, sidled past the bookshelves to push Trudy toward the kitchen alcove. "That's enough, Axyl."

Axyl's focused rage heard nothing, saw nothing. "I can't believe you. You've ruined my bill." He kicked her. "You don't know anything about politics."

Trudy stepped out of the kitchen. "Stop!"

Her voice didn't register.

David stepped into Axyl's range of vision and stood rigid. "Let go of her, Axyl."

Axyl faltered as memories stirred. He stared into David's eyes, recognition slowly creeping into his mind as he connected the name. "David Rudder." It escaped his lips as a hoarse, throaty curse.

David paled at the words. This twisted man could not be his old schoolmate.

He half-circled David. His eyes focused on him, burrowing into his soul. "Why do you fight me?"

"Me? You're the one blasting in here, beating up Anne."

"I represent peace, and yet you do not follow me. I am the light!"

"The light? Christ is the light."

"Christ is a lie. The true light unifies the world. You fight the ways of peace and unity."

"I'm not fighting anyone."

"Do you not want peace?"

Confusion blurred David's mind. "Of course I want peace."

"You are dividing a world that wants to be unified by forcing your beliefs on others. I lead them to peace."

The baby cried, touching David's mind, giving him momentary clarity. "You promote killing. You destroy peace and hope."

"No, I give hope to all, and blissful death over the pain of life. You bring chaos—men fighting wars in the name of God. Think back on history—centuries of fighting all in the name of religion."

Suddenly David's became almost hypnotized with visions of war, genocide, and suffering. He nodded numbly. "Yes, we need peace."

Jessica slid along the wall by the bedroom doorway to pull her Bible from the small table. With the baby clasped in her left arm, she held the Bible high in the air and screamed, "We believe in one God, the Father Almighty, Creator of Heaven and Earth. You only offer *false* peace. You are the death and destruction. God is true peace!"

Axyl spun around to face her. His eyes gleamed. "The deviant. Give it to me." He pulled a small, curved dagger from a sheath in his breast pocket and stepped toward Jessica.

With Axyl's back to her, Trudy eyed her purse.

Axyl reached for Frankie.

David lunged at him, and Axyl swiped him with the dagger, leaving a bloody slice across the front of his shirt. David fell in front of the couch, clutching his chest.

Jessica backed up one, two, three steps. "God, help us!"

Axyl's fingertips brushed Frankie's blanket as Jessica turned and ran for the bedroom.

From the floor, David crawled forward and grabbed at Axyl's feet, trying to trip him, but steel muscles jerked from David's feeble grasp. With exaggerated potency, Axyl's foot collided with David's head. A second kick slammed his stomach, doubling him into a fetal knot. With another step, Axyl was beyond the couch and headed toward the bedroom. David struggled to his feet in pursuit, climbed over the couch, and leapt onto Axyl's back. In one swift movement, Axyl knocked David off, grabbed one wrist, twisted it behind his back, then held the dagger to David's neck.

Anne screamed.

Pain shot through David's shoulder. The blade nicked the skin of his throat, but he didn't surrender. He swung his free arm up, striking Axyl across the chin. As he twisted around, Axyl kicked him in the groin and let him buckle to the ground before kicking him in the chest.

Having edged across the room without drawing attention, Trudy plucked her purse from the couch and pulled out her pistol.

She dropped the purse to the floor and cocked the gun. "Stop it, Axyl! Freeze!"

Axyl looked at her as if seeing her in the room for the first time, his own voice breaking through for an instant. "Trudy?"

"Get out of here, Axyl."

"We will not give up our faith or this baby," said David, raising himself off the carpet.

Trudy aimed her gun at Axyl, waiting for a clear shot.

Axyl turned and strode toward Jessica.

Jessica screamed.

Pain wracking his body, David gathered himself and made a final desperate spring, driving Axyl into the wall and knocking the wind out of him. They grappled over the knife. Axyl bent back David's wrist, got hold of the knife, and stabbed it into David's leg. David fell forward, and Axyl twisted around, preparing to drive the knife through his back.

Trudy had a clear shot at Axyl, but Anne sprang up and crashed into her as she pulled the trigger, sending the shot wild. Anne snatched the gun, swinging it around uselessly. "Stop it!"

David pulled himself up, flinging his arms against the onslaught of the knife, and threw his weight against Axyl as Jessica sidestepped them and stumbled against the wall with Frankie.

Anne screamed and fired at David just as Axyl pushed back, knocking David to the floor.

The blast ripped through the air, and Axyl's body went limp, a stream of blood trickling from a hole in his temple. David looked at him, stunned, as the dead weight of Axyl's body slipped to the floor.

"What have we done? Axyl! Axyl!" Anne backed away from the blood seeping into the carpet and crouched shell-shocked against the wall.

Jessica clasped Frankie to her chest and soothed him.

Trudy picked the pacifier off the floor, wiped it off, and held it out to her, then gave them a nudge toward the door. "Hurry. We've got to get out of here."

Jessica pressed the pacifier to Frankie's quivering lips. "It's my apartment. They'll track me."

"We'll figure something out," Trudy replied, as she bent to help David to his feet.

"You'll never get out of here with me like this."

"Yes, we will. Come on. Up with you. Can you walk?"

He gritted his teeth and leaned on her.

Anne looked up at them with desperate eyes. "What about me?"

"What about you? Take Axyl's car and go home. You have a son waiting for you," said Trudy.

"But Axyl's dead."

"Get a grip, Anne. He was going to kill all of us, including you."

"But what do I *do* now?"

"I don't really care," Trudy replied from the doorway, "Just remember that if you say anything about us, you'll be implicated too."

"But I didn't mean to kill him. I loved him!"

"Try staying here and explaining that to the officers. We're leaving."

They scrambled out the door to the car.

* * *

Anne quaked from head to foot all the way home. She could barely drive. She hated driving anyway, and with her nerves on edge she crawled along far too slowly to suit the rest of the traffic. Horns blared at her every few minutes as cars whizzed by.

She parked under her condominium and pulled down the visor to touch up her make-up. She didn't want Vicky looking at her suspiciously.

She stared out at the lake rippling slightly in the afternoon summer breeze and a sailboat gliding by on its waters. So free. So unfettered. She walked around to the front entrance, as she always did when Vicky was on duty, vaguely noticing the delivery van parked out front, mentally wondering for a fraction of an instant what the neighbors had purchased. She unlocked the front door and stepped inside. Coming in through the foyer made her feel more like the lady of the house.

"Vicky, I'm back," she called out. "I'll have coffee in the living room please."

She dropped the car keys on the foyer table and passed into the living room, stopping at the sight of Vicky sitting on her sofa with two white-coated medics opposite her.

"Ms. Shelton," one said, standing up and extending his hand.

"Vicky is something wrong with Fr—with the baby? Who are these men?"

The other man stood. "We're from Sunshine Center, ma'am. The senator asked us to pick you up. We just need to run a few tests on you. To see what's bothering you."

Anne backed away. "There's nothing wrong with me. Get out of here."

"Well, now, that's not how the senator sees it. He thinks we may be able to help restore you."

"Vicky, tell them I'm fine."

Vicky smirked. "Sure. She's fine as they come. A real lady."

"You have to understand," Anne said, her feet slipping from living room carpet to the hardwood of the foyer, "my baby was stolen and I found the man that did it."

The men nodded. "The senator told us all about that. Now come along, Ms. Shelton."

Together they grabbed her arms. The taller of the two quickly injected her with a sedative, and they escorted her out to their van.

Vicky went to the nursery and stared at the baby in the crib, wondering what to do with him. She knew for certain Axyl wouldn't take care of him.

* * *

David slumped in the back seat, nursing his wounds and working through in his mind the plan for reentering the Dome unmarked. Jessica and the baby sat in front with Trudy to give him room in back.

"What about you, Trudy?" he asked. "You didn't change UICs."

"Don't have to. I have a second chip. Real one in my right wrist. Fake one in my left. When my brother Jimmy died, my father finagled a way to have his UIC installed in me, and created a new child's record. So on my right, I'm Trudy. On my left, I'm Tabitha."

"New meaning to split personality," David said wryly.

"Your father expected you to get into some future trouble?" Jessica asked.

"No. He expected the future to get into trouble. He was right. He warned me never to use it unless it became a life or death emergency. I think this warrants it."

"So, where are you taking us?" asked David.

"Long range, the Dome of course. Short range, I could use an idea."

Jessica swiveled to face David, resting her chin on the back of the seat, and smiled. "I think I know a place."

David looked into her twinkling eyes for a moment, then smiled back. "Perfect."

"Where?"

"The Midway Park."

Trudy nodded. "Sure. Great. You two hide out there while I get rid of this car and get another rental and become the very sweet, unassuming Tabitha Bullock."

David leaned forward. "Are you planning to stay in the Dome? To become a Dominian?"

Trudy nodded. "I hope I can. Do you think I can?"

"We welcome anyone who wants to live as God set forth. The Christian God, I mean."

Trudy nodded again. "I understand that. But I have to be honest. I have another motive."

Jessica, with womanly insight, smiled. "You mentioned a baby, your baby that Axyl wanted to terminate."

Trudy laid her left hand over her stomach. "The meds say he has a genetic anomaly they can't fix with gene therapy. I don't even know what the problem is. They couldn't tell me." She delved awkwardly into her pocket as she drove and retrieved the wadded copy of her baby's genome map. "This is what they gave me. Nothing. Nothing I can define."

David took the paper, unfolded, smoothed it out, and studied it in silence. Jessica stared at him over the seat. "Well? What does it say?"

David sighed. "I'm not a DNA specialist. I really don't know. But really, Trudy, does it matter? Will it make any difference? He's your son no matter what that paper says. And you're both welcome in the Dome."

"Son? It's a boy?"

"But the Dome is dirt poor. I don't know that you can stand it."

"Poor or dead. Simple choice."

"I feel like I'm putting you both in jeopardy. It was my apartment. They'll be searching for me."

"No more than they're searching for Rex Montane," David said. "But I have an idea. The council created a false

ID for me. We'll create one for you with Elizabeth's ID. We're pretty slack about reporting things to the Feds, so she's not legally dead."

"You don't report when people die?"

"They don't check much."

"But her chip . . ."

Trudy broke in. "A replacement card, like David has."

"Exactly," David said. "The only issue is getting you in, but if we get close enough, we'll work that out. There are ways in and out that only we know about."

Trudy laughed. "I don't doubt that."

As they entered the downtown area, they were met by crowds of people. The parade was over, but flags, balloons, clowns, and food booths still attracted people from one end of Main Street to the other.

"Terrific!" exclaimed Trudy. "I forgot about it being Unity Day. No one will notice you in this crowd, so get out here. It can't be more than two blocks."

Jessica smiled. "Yes. We'll watch for you on that side street.

"Okay. See you in an hour."

As they walked off, Trudy put her cell to her ear. "Norman, this is Trudy. Axyl left a number on his desk for an officer . . . Yes, that's the man. Get a message to him. I have no idea what Axyl meant by this, but he said *Drop the matter because he took care of it himself.* Does that make sense to you? . . . It does? . . . Okay . . . What's that about Anne? He had her committed? Wow . . . That explains it . . . Well, he told me he was on his way to, uh, what was her name? Jane? No, Jessica. Jessica Main? To celebrate something big. I didn't realize he had a new girl right now. Ever met her? . . . Me neither. Wonder how long this one will last, eh? Well that's it. I won't be in next week. Axyl gave me an ultimatum—the baby or the job—and I need some time to sort things out. So, I'll see you in a week. Hold down the fort."

She hung up and dialed again. "Hello, Mother. It's Trudy. Remember that trip Dad always said we would need to take someday? . . . Well, today is the day. Pack up. I'll be there in a few hours. Love you."

Grinning, she rolled down the window and tossed the phone into the bed of a pickup truck as it passed by.

* * *

Jeffrey was out of breath by the time he reached the Counseling Center. Ambulances lined the road. A dozen cop cars were pulled at odd angles, their lights flashing. Officers stood overseeing the removal of people, dead and alive.

Jeffrey kept to the walls of the building till he reached the cover of the bushes and shimmied around till he stood within a yard of Marty. His eyes were open, staring toward the bushes. Jeffrey knew he was dead, knew he wasn't looking at anything specifically, but he turned to follow his dead gaze anyway and saw Marty's camera far under the bush. He crawled under the branches, grabbed it, and panned it across the scene, bringing it to a stop on Marty. Bile rose in his throat. He shoved the camera into his pocket and turned, planning to scramble away, but heard a whimper behind him. There under the dense branches of the next bush he saw a small pair of bare feet.

"Hey, kid," he whispered.

The whimpering stopped then burst for a second, then stopped again.

Jeffrey crept to the backside of the bushes and whispered. "Come on, kid. I'll help you. Come on." He could hear someone approaching. "Hurry," he hissed, "before they catch us."

The kid crawled out, a tiny blond boy, his face dirty and tear-stained and pale with shock. Jeffrey grabbed his hand. "Where's your mama?" The boy shook his head. "Your dad?" His face crumpled and tears poured again. "Okay, okay. Come on. Stay beside me. Don't say a word." He stepped around a lifeless little girl, her braids and ribbons stained red, and pulled the boy away, between the buildings, to the back alleys that had led him there. "What's your name, kid?"

"J-Johnny."

Jeffrey looked at him gravely for a moment, then smiled. He pulled off his green ball cap, tightened the strap, and fitted it on the little boy's head.

Johnny looked up at him, tears pouring down his face.

Jeffrey winked. "It's gonna be all right, kid. Just stick with me." He took hold of his hand again and led him down the alley.

* * *

At the PMS center, Allison Gatryl was pacing in her office with a blond newborn in her arms when Kim Lui arrived.

"Here," she said, almost throwing the baby at her. "Get rid of it."

"Where did it come from?"

"After all that crap we went through with Anne Shelton, her nursemaid showed up here ten minutes ago to tell me that the senator had his wife committed to a mental institute and that we should take the baby back to whoever it came from."

Kim rolled her eyes and left, carrying the baby down the hall. Rounding the corner of the obstetrics unit, she saw Markus Holmes in the hall.

"Markus, take care of this," she said, holding out the baby.

"Do what with it?"

"Dump it, of course."

Markus stared at her, his mouth puckered in anger. "What's wrong with it?"

"Let's just say it's extraneous."

"Why don't you do it?"

She put on her sweetest smile. "Because it's your fault."

"How so?"

"Anne Shelton decided she didn't want it."

He looked at the little fellow. It wasn't Frankie. Which left one conclusion—it was the baby they'd shown Anne Shelton holding on the news.

"What about his real mother?"

"That's not happening. The record's sealed. There's no way I'll let you complicate this further. She thinks he's retarded. She thinks he died at birth, and she's glad of it. She's smart enough not to want a deviant."

He didn't doubt Kim Lui had destroyed the records. They wouldn't leave evidence hanging out there. And the nurses wouldn't have paid any attention. Even if they had noticed what was going on, they wouldn't say. They were afraid to get involved.

He felt sorry for the parents, who were certainly grieving, but he couldn't help them. However, he knew what he could do. He knew what he *would* do.

He reached out, took the infant into his arms, and caressed him gently before turning determined eyes on the Head Med. "No, I won't dump him. Not this time, or ever again."

"You will, or you'll have the state after you."

"Fine," said Markus, not sure where the courage was coming from. "How about I tell them the story of where this child came from? About the mother who was told her baby died so you could give this one to the senator? No one is killing this baby."

Kim hesitated just a moment. "There will be a warrant on your head. Healthcare is a UO jurisdiction now. If you remove a child without authorization . . ."

Markus wasn't listening. Joanne had been right. God really did have a plan, even when he hadn't been willing to admit it. As Markus glanced at the baby boy, as he felt the tiny heart beat against his own, he felt more alive than he'd felt in twenty years. He clasped the infant to his chest, turned his back on the head med, and walked straight down the hall and out the door.

Kim Lui rushed to Allison Gatryl's office and told her Markus had walked out with the baby. Allison growled and reached for the alarm, but Kim grabbed her wrist. "Wait. Think about it a minute."

"I don't have anything to hide," Allison replied defiantly.

Kim raised her eyebrows. "Maybe not. But there'll be a full investigation about this, and then there'll be nothing you *can* hide. Do you want that? Look, the real kid, the one with Down's—has already been taken out of the system. He's dead. And Markus is done. Just let him go."

Allison cursed and jerked her arm away.

* * *

Joanne had been waiting all day for Markus to call. She'd told him she would walk home with him. The day was sunny and dry and it would give them a chance to talk before reaching the house and having to deal with the reality of Betty's death, of the house being empty and his life being at a crossroads.

She snapped up the phone as soon as it rang.

"I'm on my way," he said, "and I have a surprise."

"What?"

"Wait and see."

"Tell me."

"Our son. He's beautiful. We're going to raise him together and take him to your church and he's going to be surrounded by all the love we can give him."

Joanne felt tears begin to well in her eyes. He was a fool. He'd walked out with another baby after everything that had happened around Frankie. He knew they couldn't keep it. They would be found out. That's why they'd never done it before. But she wouldn't say that just yet. She was stunned by the love he was expressing—for her, for this child he didn't even know, and even for God. "Oh, Markus, I love you so much. I'm heading your way. I'll meet you halfway, at the first intersection."

She rushed out of the Social Services building, down the granite steps and across the road like it was the first day of her real life. Her feet carried her as if on wings, she felt so light and free.

As she rounded the corner, everything moved in slow motion: the blissful expression on Markus's face aimed first at the baby and then at her. He was still a hundred yards from her, but he held the baby out like an offering, his smile pushing his fat, round cheeks up into his eyes.

"You sweet fool," she said when she reached him. "They'll come for him. They'll come for you. Especially after everything . . ."

"Do you like the dark?"

"What? Markus, you're not making sense."

"It's done. I'm done. I don't think they'll come after me, but I can't go back. We said there needs to be a safe house. Guess what? We're doing it. You and I. We'll live like moles. We'll keep low and take every baby that my friend Luke can sneak out to us—he hates dumping them as much as I did. He'll bring them to us."

"Are you sure?"

Markus nodded.

Joanne peered into his eyes, trying to read his inner thoughts, but all she saw was happiness and levity, new emotions for her solemn friend. She took his hand and they walked down the path. She already knew where they would go—a group of apartments in a different segment of tunnels. They wouldn't need much. And no one would think it odd to see Markus move after the sudden death of his wife. It really might work.

There was time for planning later. They both gazed at the baby. Joanne sighed. "He needs a name . . ."

* * *

David and Jessica settled in a wooded area of the park to examine David's wounds. Jessica whispered in the silence as if the crowds in the street beyond might possibly hear them. "You gave me her name."

"Partly her name. The Rudder part is mine and I was thinking of giving it to you anyway."

She looked up at him. "Really?" All her fears and misgivings about men had vanished. He was different. Everything was different. Love and faith melded together through the miracle of Frankie.

"Yes, really. Crazy considering we've known each other for less than 72 hours. Would you like to marry a crazy man?"

"Well," she smiled, "as long as I've got to have your name, I may as well get a diamond ring for it."

He laughed. "You haven't seen my account. It may be a very small diamond."

He kissed her, then looked at her seriously. "Elizabeth Laura Rudder. You know I can't call you Elizabeth, though."

"You won't believe this, but my middle name is Laura. Jessica Laura Main."

"Laura. Laura Rudder."

"Do you think Trudy is coming back for us?"

"Yes, I do. There's more at work here than us, you know. Her father didn't come up with that idea of two UICs out of the blue without something helping him with the idea. It's just that some people follow 'hunches' and other people ignore them."

"And what hunch did you follow?"

He cocked his head to one side. "Lots. But one hunch told me this mission was going to heal my heart. And that was right."

* * *

As the sun set behind the downtown buildings, people began approaching the NFCC from all sides in total silence, their solemn faces lit in the round bouncing light of the candles held before them. They filed into place, forming row after row, covering the center's grounds from the front door to the road, their silence broken by the sirens that wailed into the scene for the second time that day and against the pounding footsteps of armed officers who took up positions to surround them.

As the officers drew their weapons and waited for permission to sweep the crowd, the officer in charge stepped in to full view and raised his hand. Everyone expected the national hail, but instead he spoke three words: "Hold your fire." Every officer looked at him in dismay. "They aren't doing anything wrong."

A whisper started on the front row and spread quietly throughout the crowd. *"Though I walk in the shadow of death, I fear no evil, for thou art with me. Thy rod and thy staff, they have comforted me . . . "*

The nearest officer scowled. "That sounds like the Bible. That's infringement."

The murmur grew. *"Thou hast prepared a table before me against them that afflict me."*

"They aren't saying it to you," the chief officer replied. "Ignore it or listen. Your choice."

"Thou hast anointed my head with oil; and my chalice which inebriateth me, how goodly is it!"

"Freedom from religion," insisted the other officer, aiming his gun.

"Thy mercy will follow me all the days of my life."

"Put your weapon down. If you fire, I'll have your badge for instigating a violent situation. There's been enough bloodshed today. No more."

"*I will dwell in the house of the Lord forever.*"

The officer eyed the crowd, carefully choosing his victim: the heavyset woman on the front row who was swaying and weeping; from the size of her, she obviously disobeyed more than the Tolerance rules. She would have to break every diet rule set forth to get to that size. She was probably slotted as a code nine anyway. And her fervor! Clutching something to her chest. Probably a cross. A believer. One of the rumored underground. He took aim.

His commander saw what was in his mind and stepped in front of his weapon. "I said stand down, and I meant it. You are relieved of duty."

* * *

Darkness hovered over the Midway Inn parking lot by the time Trudy returned, this time in an old gas-powered sedan. She pulled around to the far side, where the path led to a playground, guessing correctly that the threesome would take refuge on the park benches. They emerged at the sound of the car, first just Jessica and Frankie, but with a wave behind her, David limped out. Trudy's mother sat buckled into the front seat humming to herself, so they climbed into the back, buckled Frankie into the infant seat Trudy had secured for him, and in minutes they were on the road.

"All's clear," Trudy said. "You're off the news, replaced by a story about people being gunned down at the National Family Counseling Center for rebelling against the treatment of their children. Angry protests all over the country, in fact. They're calling for congressional hearings on the counseling centers." She twisted half-way around to glance at him. "Did you have something to do with that?"

"The Counseling Center? No. I've never even been there. Is that the place Marty was telling me about? Where they transfer kids to UO Institutes and donor centers?"

"Marty? Wow. I bet it was him." She paused, thinking. "He didn't answer his phone earlier . . ." She thought of what that meant but didn't say it aloud. Instead, she told them what she knew. "Someone—probably Marty—aired pictures of kids in the donor center and institutes, and it set off a powder keg. Between that and Axyl's death, the Better World Bill is as good as dead."

"But what about the police chase? They may still be on my trail, especially now that Axyl's dead. If they've figured out I'm from the Dome . . ."

"I have to confess something. I am a member of the Liberty League."

"What's that?" David asked.

"A nationwide grassroots society devoted to bringing freedom back to our country. We watch each other's backs. More importantly, the agent in charge of your search is on our side."

"What?"

She laughed. "Tracy Studler. One of our best. He and his partner are the only two who know who you are now that Axyl's dead. He was worried for a bit as to how he was going to get you off, but with Axyl gone, he's fixed the file. I already fed him a story on Axyl's murder about Anne being jealous over his new lover. If no one else pokes around—which they won't because those people at the med center have their own tails to cover—the file will stagnate."

"Are you sure?"

"Yes. In fact, once it becomes clear what's going on in the Counseling Centers, people may begin to see you as the hero you really are."

David settled back in his seat. "I'm not a hero. Don't ever call me that. I'm just a guy putting one foot in front of the other."

She smiled into the rearview mirror. "Keep on stepping, then, David Rudder. Keep on stepping." Then she laughed. "Do you want to hear something funny?"

Jessica leaned forward. "That would be a nice change."

"Axyl went on the news saying how sad he was that Senator Jack Friday died in a car wreck, and how he intended to pass the bill in his memory, but an hour later the news station learned Jack hadn't died. He was actually at the hospital being treated and released."

"Wow," Jessica said.

Trudy paused to make a turn, then continued. "It gets better. Jack countered Axyl's comments with his announcement that if the bill ever gets to the floor, he's voting against it." She peered up the road. "We're about to pass the Counseling Center up around this corner, but I'm sure everything from the police shootout will have been cleared away by now."

As the Counseling Center came into view, Trudy slowed and they simultaneously gasped. A sea of candles swayed in the summer night. She realized what her friend had started. "Oh, Marty . . ."

Jessica crossed herself.

David twisted in his seat to watch till they were out of view. "It has begun."

ONE YEAR LATER

"Laura, someone is at the door," hollered David's mother as she spooned green baby food into Frankie's mouth.

Jessica touched her hair, knowing it looked good: softly curled, not too fixed but no longer frizzy and unkempt. Sometimes she could imagine that she had always been Laura; that Jessica's existence had only been a bad dream. Smiling, she went to the door. Today they were celebrating Frankie's first birthday, and all the family had been invited. David's family. Now *her* family.

There was nothing pretty about their home—a plain brown brick square box sitting on dry, barren ground—but Jessica loved it anyway. The property's saving grace was one beautiful elm that towered fifty feet above the front of the house and two old cottonwood trees, their branches reaching out at odd angles, that shaded the side yard where children would play some day. Their house was small but always filled with babies routed to them through Joanne and Markus, on their way to new loving homes. In the years to come, some children would stay and become theirs.

Jessica smiled as she reached the door and saw Trudy with three-month-old Andrew, as perfect a baby as a mother could want. "Hello, Tabitha," Jessica said. "Come in." She hugged her and swept her back through the house to the kitchen. "Look. Our first guests."

David's mother stood up. "It's good to see you. And Andrew! How he's grown this month."

"Where's David?" asked Trudy.

Jessica, wetting Frankie's washcloth and attacking the mess on his face, grinned. "Where else? Hopefully finishing up a council meeting. They meet practically every day lately. Today he was talking to new recruits."

Trudy took a familiar seat at the kitchen table. "I should have gone. He asked me to, but I've been too busy with my district and the Liberty League. In fact, I have three new recruits to pass on to him. They're going to infiltrate primary schools."

"You do enough without showing up at his every invitation. Now bring Andrew back to the nursery and help me dress this birthday boy."

ABOUT THE AUTHOR

Michelle Buckman loves writing fiction that rethinks life. She lives with her husband and five children near the Carolina coast, where she enjoys spending her free time walking the long stretches of sandy beaches. She shares news and welcomes comments from readers through her website at www.MichelleBuckman.com. *Death Panels* is her fifth novel.